Ram Van Bamf and the Doomsday Conspiracy

JOHN FRISCIA

DEDICATIONS

For my family, all of whom foolishly continue to support me in spite of the complete lack of reciprocation on my part, especially my four favorite nephews, Ryan, Joseph, Nicholas, and Anthony.

For all of my close friends, who appreciated my friendship before I was rich and famous.

For Sylvester Stallone, who has never heard of me and would probably prefer I did not mention him.

1

If hostility were a sport, Ram Van Bamf was the mascot, the MVP, the all-star team, and the riot that breaks out in the stands and kills twelve people. With a neck like an erupting volcano and arms so beefy that Sherpas tried to mount flags on them, Ram could lift cars with his face and suplex them into a pit of acid, which he did on a regular basis. When he walked down the right side of the street, cars drove on the left side of the road. When he walked down the left side of the street, drivers gave up completely and jumped out of their still-moving vehicles in the hopes that concrete was a less painful death.

Nothing could be done about Ram. Firstly, a tactical nuclear strike was the least expensive plausible method of stopping him, which had been out of the question ever since the city budget had been spent constructing pits of acid. Secondly, Ram had never committed a crime in his life. As it so happened, Ram suffered from Ram Van Bamf Syndrome, named for Ram Van Bamf, its sole sufferer. This condition demanded that Ram do things to demonstrate his masculinity at erratic intervals, regardless of the risk to himself and others, including eating raw steak, chugging viper poison, scaring ghosts, pushing mountains back into the Earth, inhaling tornadoes, drowning sharks, punching fire, and chucking skyscrapers at the moon.

The great burg of Ultratropolis had no interest in arresting Ram for having a physical disorder, especially since his very presence was a boon to the city. Ram Van Bamf, when not in the throes of illness, was an exemplary citizen, and he would go out of his way to prevent crimes if he saw them being committed. As a result, most crime ceased to exist, and the police were free to pursue their dream of becoming a successful thrash metal band. Their first single, "You Fought the Law (And We Kicked Your Ass!)," had received airplay on local radio stations to much acclaim.

"That Lieutenant Murdock can really shred," said Ram, nodding his head to the beat.

"I agree. Are you the man who suplexes cars with his face?"

As it just so happened, Ram had his head through the window of this particular person's rusted car at the intersection, hoping to hear a bit of the song on the radio before the light turned green.

"Well, maybe. There's no guarantee I'm the only guy in town who does that."

"Could you not do that to mine?"

"You got it."

And the driver would have gone on his way in peace as the light turned green, except that his engine began to choke and stutter like a first-time comedian.

"Ah shucks, not again," said the driver as he fiddled with every knob and button. The people behind him began to honk, so he started to sweat. He had never been good under pressure, and he envied people who lived on mountains or rocket ships.

"What's the problem, pal?" asked Ram with sincerity.

"The car's stalling. I was supposed to be on my way to the company picnic, but I guess I can forget about it now. That's just the way it goes."

Ram gave this man the once over. Sporting a white short-sleeve shirt and a lime green tie, he seemed better prepared for a company meeting than a picnic. Browline glasses hunched over his broad nose, muting the luster of his hazel eyes. And although he was encroaching upon middle age, his slight frame and bowl haircut rendered him indistinguishable from the kindergarteners across the street who were pointing and laughing at him. It was his naturally droopy shoulders that interested Ram the most though, since they would make him more aerodynamic if Ram suddenly needed to throw him like a missile.

"I can help you," said Ram. By now, the honking had ceased because everyone had realized this man was talking to Ram Van

Bamf, and the drivers presumed that honking in the general direction of Ram Van Bamf was akin to yelling in the face of a sleeping grizzly.

"Oh, no, I couldn't ask that of you," the man said with a bashful smile and fingers interlocked. "I just need to get to the side of the road and call a tow truck."

"Where's your company's picnic?"

"The outside benches at Nice to Meat You, the burger restaurant. You know, the place with the motto, 'Gobble it all up! Because it's poisonous after the first thirty minutes.' "

"Hey, I like that place. You don't even need to kill the animals before you eat them. It's a real convenience," said Ram with dreamy wonder. "Sure, I can get you there."

"Really? Is your car parked nearby?"

"What does that have to do with anything?"

Before the man could contemplate what was about to happen, Ram lifted the old sedan with his face and started jogging. To onlookers, a vertically-inclined motor vehicle flying down the street at speeds penetrating the sound barrier was no cause for concern. If anything, it was a relief, as it was one of the less outlandishly fatal objects Ram could have been carrying at any given moment.

"Just a free metro," shrugged one bystander.

As the man in his car watched the world degenerate into a blur of confused shapes and colors, his first response was to scream, but he could not scream because he was too busy vomiting. Instead, he started to think about what he would like engraved on his tombstone. "Loved by few" and "Equally forgettable in life" were the first to come to mind, allowing him to realize for the first time just how little he thought of himself.

Ram, for his part, had always enjoyed an easy stroll through the city that he was pleased to call home. Snuggled between Mount Slipendie in the west and Duround Beach in the east, Ultratropolis had been an idyllic locale long before towers and apartment complexes supplanted the massif in the skyline. Even with the most violent penitentiary in the world located at the northern city limit, citizens felt safe and happy at all times, except of course when Ram was crossing the street. From video arcades to music venues, the city provided entertainment for all ages, and if not for the problem of the slums, Ultratropolis would be an undisputed paradise.

"Here we are," said Ram, the taste of rims on his lips.

The trip had ended just as abruptly as it had begun. The car rested safely again on the Earth, except that the tires had fallen off and there was an unconscious war veteran hanging out of the trunk. The driver took a few hesitant steps out of the vehicle, worried the planet might race away from under him. Once he was convinced that he would not be hurtled into the vacuum of space, he collapsed into the grass in such a stupor that he did not mind when ants mistook his tie for leaves and hauled it back to the nest.

"Where are we?" he asked eventually, his eyes glazed over like there was an accident at an extreme cake competition.

"The company picnic, I hope," Ram said. "I kind of forgot what I was doing for a while there."

The man nodded in a manner that suggested he might be able to remember the company for which he worked if given a couple minutes to really think about it. But then he received a strong hint that thrust him back into his senses.

"Jerry! You made it."

There was a distinct melody in the voice that somehow ensured it could only belong to a beautiful woman, but there was no adequate ritual by which to prepare the eyes for the severity of the beauty at work. With natural curves in all the right places and gams that went on forever, she was the constant cover model to whatever happened to exist behind her. Obsidian hair fell over marble skin to produce a starlet of black and white cinema in the modern day. Polka dots spilled across her sundress in wild blotches as a matter of necessity, as they offered the only respite from what was otherwise the most flawless woman anyone had ever seen or even dared to imagine.

Men just noticed the breasts.

"Hey, have you seen Leonora today?" asked one picnic-goer.

"Who's that?" responded another.

"The pair of hooters holding up the sundress."

"Is that what you call them? I call them Laverne and Shirley."

The dazed beneficiary of this woman's attention, evidently named Jerry, overcame his nausea just long enough to regain his footing on the Earth. He instinctively moved to fix his tie that he was no longer wearing, and he suddenly cursed the industriousness of the insect kingdom.

"Oh, um, hi, Leonora," he stumbled. "Yeah, I thought I wasn't going to be able to make it. But then I, I guess I made a new friend."

4

"Sure," said Ram, and he gave Jerry a gentle pat on the back that nearly severed his spine.

"You made friends with Ram Van Bamf?" she asked, her eyes reflecting light like diamonds as they grew big with surprise.

"He's really a very thoughtful person," said Jerry after a moment of reflection.

"Well, that's wonderful," said Leonora, having recovered her composure. "I am sure he is safer company than the media would lead us to believe."

"Well, I wouldn't go that far," said Ram in all honesty.

"It's just like you to make friends with a person like him, isn't it?" she asked.

"Yep, sure is!" said Jerry, though he actually did not understand the question at all.

"While I tend not to eat much meat, this is a picnic," and Leonora nudged her head in the direction of a pyramid of hamburgers on a table, "so I think I'll try to fill up without making a hog of myself."

"Oh, no, you could never resemble livestock if you tried," said Jerry, which, in the case of Leonora, was the truth.

"If only we could fill the world with people like you, Jerry," she sighed, and she wandered off in the direction of food.

"She seems nice," said Ram.

"She's the most pleasant and engaging woman I've ever had the privilege of conversation with," offered Jerry. "It's not fair that nobody seems to notice."

"What do you mean? Seems to me there's plenty on her to notice."

"That's the problem. She's stunning. Women have a difficult time talking to her because they can't help getting jealous, even if they're otherwise nice people. I get the feeling she's pretty lonely."

"But that's just women. What about the guys?"

"Well, see for yourself."

Leonora grinned at a man who was in the precarious position of keeping fat drops of sauce and burger grease from migrating to his shirt from his chin.

"I'm not really sure how to keep clean either," she said.

"Sure, I'll take you out to dinner," he responded.

"Excuse me?"

"Take my money and my watch. The watch is a fake, but the seven dollars are real."

"I don't understand."

"Does your body come with an instruction manual, or do I need some hands-on training?"

"Neither. And why are you taking your pants off?"

"I don't know. Is it a problem?"

Leonora fled without another word to a more secluded corner of the picnic area. She found solace underneath a tree that overlooked a pit of acid the size and depth of a baseball stadium.

"You see, Ram? Men lose all sense of reason around her," said Jerry.

"Yeah, guess you're right. What makes you different?"

Jerry lowered his head. Ram could not tell if he was smirking or grimacing as he spoke.

"Leonora is like an angel. If you spent any time with her, you would understand that she's as beautiful on the inside as she is on the outside. And me? I'm just a man, and not much of one. I guess the difference between me and other men is that I just can't imagine a world where I could ever have a chance with a woman that terrific."

"Yeah, I can't imagine that either," Ram agreed. "But don't let that stop you. You just need to work on your pecs a little. And your triceps. And your delts. And your trapezius. And your calves. And your abs, I would assume. And your lats. And your forearms."

"What about my biceps?"

"Well, I wasn't gonna say anything…"

Jerry nodded and tilted his neck to one side, intent on moping, until he suddenly noticed Leonora standing at the edge of the pit of acid.

"Leonora!" he cried, running toward her.

She had actually been in no danger at all, but the unexpected yelling of her name jolted her into a fright that sent her teetering off the side.

"Leonora!" Jerry screamed again.

"Even I think it's weird that this city just has pits of acid lying around," conceded Ram.

He and Jerry rushed to the edge of the pit, finding Leonora had not been engulfed but was clinging to a side of the cliff that was not as steep as other sections. Rather than shout for help, she only gazed upon the bubbling acid beneath her, seemingly entranced with the thought of her own demise.

"She's alive. She's alive," said Jerry with trembling clenched fists. "Ram, please save her. Do whatever it takes!"

"You got it," Ram said. He put a hand on his chin. "Anybody got a car?"

In what was apparently a terrific coincidence, nobody present at the picnic had ever owned a motor vehicle at any point in life, especially not one that Ram could demolish. Jerry had volunteered his car immediately, but Ram needed a vehicle that still had tires. He finally resolved to commandeer a vehicle, which turned out to be more challenging than he had expected when he stepped out in the street and found all of the vehicles swerving and diving off of bridges to evade him. But luck prevailed when a bus continued undeterred toward its stop, located in front of Nice to Meat You.

"Thanks. You've got a big heart," said Ram, having believed the bus stopped specifically for him. He proceeded to lift the bus with the driver and passengers still inside, carrying it to the edge of the cliff from which Leonora hung. Then he simply dropped it, allowing the bus to make a very quick and sharp descent down the side of the cliff.

"How is this helping, Ram?" yelled Jerry.

In a burst of agility, Ram leapt from the edge of the pit to land at the point where the roof of the bus met the backside. As the hapless vehicle passed Leonora, Ram grabbed her with a swift hand, leaving not a single perfect hair out of place on her exquisite head.

"Catch!" said Ram, hurling Leonora into the air directly toward Jerry. While Jerry did not catch Leonora so much as he intercepted her flight with his face, the fact remained that her life had been saved. Meanwhile, Ram allowed himself to roll off the side of the bus, and just as the sea of acid came into arm's reach, Ram took the bus back in his jaws so that only he found himself colliding with the bath of boiling green broth.

"Okay, that dude's impressive," said a picnic-goer as Ram swam through the acid with a bus in his teeth.

While nobody was surprised that Ram Van Bamf could brave a pit of acid with no adverse effects, it was more remarkable that his clothes remained untouched as well. He wore a white wife beater, blue jeans, and black combat boots every day, all of which seemed as durable as himself, and it was hypothesized that Ram was just too much of a man for his clothes to embarrass him by tearing or disintegrating. Regardless of how it was possible, Ram soon emerged from the pit fully clothed, tossing the bus aside, forgetting about it completely.

"Thank you so much for saving me," said Leonora, too refined in manner to even hug him out of turn, but her sentiment was genuine. "I suppose I'm lucky the media hasn't exaggerated after all."

"No big deal," shrugged Ram.

"Yes, Ram, thank you," said Jerry, rubbing his newly bruised eye. "But Leonora, what were you doing so close to the edge in the first place?"

Her expression was empty then.

"I was just trying to see to the bottom," she said.

Not wanting to overstay his welcome, Ram opted to excuse himself.

"Hey, glad I could help you out, Jerry, but I need to get running."

"Oh, really? The picnic is technically just for employees, but the least I could do is get you lunch after everything you've done for us. You said yourself how much you like this place."

"That's nice of you, pal, but I've got bigger fish to fry. There's been a tiger shark in my freezer for weeks."

"Alright then. I hope we run into each other like this again someday."

Jerry stole a look at his broken down car, which had recently burst into flames.

"Actually, I hope we don't ever meet like this again."

"I don't blame you," said Ram with a sympathetic shake of the head.

And so Ram Van Bamf departed the picnic, unaware that the proceedings of this exceptionally mundane day would serve as a prologue to a series of events so spectacular that the world itself would never be the same. There was one thing that suddenly occurred to Ram, though.

He was late for his execution.

2

Only the most dangerous and morally bankrupt prisoners found themselves at Ultratropolis Penitentiary, so it was really prestigious and difficult to receive admittance. Entry requirements were unyielding and had aspiring criminals squirming in their bunks at night at all of the lesser prisons across the country. A minimum of fifteen grisly murders and three coded messages to the police mocking their inability to stop the murders were the first step in getting the penitentiary's interest. Beyond that, it was the extracurriculars that pushed someone over the top. Embezzling millions from a corporation and using the stolen funds to finance a white slavery ring was impressive, but being the owner of a corporation that specialized in white slavery in the first place was the sort of deviance that really turned heads. One notable prisoner received admission by building an abortion clinic just so he could blow it up. Then there was the woman who got expelled from the penitentiary for faking the drowning and dismemberment of her children; as it turned out, the bodies recovered were merely the bodies of someone else's children.

Fraud had been on the rise for the past decade amongst those seeking admittance. It became such a problem that several earnest prisoners requested new trials following their convictions just so that they could say they had been found double-guilty of the horrific crimes committed. Eventually, the penitentiary had to accept that some errors in the admission process were inevitable, but that did not mean they would become lax in their obligation to discerning the truth.

To that end, they had hired Ram Van Bamf to interact with prisoners on a regular basis. The theory was that prisoners would rather confess to not being the criminals they claimed to be than tell a lie and be ripped in half and shaken like maracas by Ram Van Bamf. Although Ram would never actually do such a thing to these prisoners, the penitentiary officials would go into excruciating detail about the ways Ram would massacre the prisoners if they did not tell the truth.

"Ram will literally punch you out of existence!" had been graffitied on the walls by the officials themselves.

Today was business as usual. Louis Goodie, better known by his media name of the "Grandma Grinder," was scheduled for execution at an hour past noon, but the penitentiary officials wanted to know for sure that his crimes were legitimate and genuinely attributable to him. Enter Ram Van Bamf.

"Van Bamf, finally!" exclaimed Warden Warmaker, a man with refrigerators for hands. His pectorals pressed like a stampeding bull against his uniform at all times, and his graying flattop hair signified years of untiring service to his country. Warmaker would not survive for one second in a fight with Ram Van Bamf, but he was a force to be reckoned with under any other circumstance.

"Hey there, warden. Sorry I'm late," said Ram as he swallowed a piece of fin.

They stood just outside the execution chamber, separated only by a large piece of glass. Strapped on a table inside the chamber, Louis gave a toothy smile and a big thumbs-up, eager to get the show on the road.

"I don't know about this Goodie. He seems like too much of a, uh, goodie," said Warmaker.

"Leave it to me, warden," said Ram.

A new guard who had stumbled into the job of watching over the execution interjected into the conversation, curiosity getting the best of him.

"Excuse me, warden," he said, rubbing his neck to acknowledge his interruption, "but Mr. Van Bamf's specialty is making people believe he will kill them viciously, right?"

"You know it!" said Ram, and he and Warmaker shared a high-five.

"Okay, well, how does that apply here? Mr. Goodie is already scheduled to die today. How does Mr. Van Bamf threatening to kill Mr. Goodie make him confess to being undeserving of execution by us?"

Ram and Warmaker turned to look at each other. What began as restrained mirth quickly evolved into hysteria as the two of them laughed and laughed. Warmaker's lush handlebar 'stache danced with hypnotic rhythm.

"These kids today," remarked Warmaker, shaking his head and wiping a tear from his eye with his knuckle. "Getting executed is nothing like getting killed by this animal! Getting executed at Ultratropolis Penitentiary means getting all the pride and the glory that goes with it. Being killed by Ram Van Bamf is like getting a hundred thousand hydrogen bombs punched down your throat while jackals play keep-away with your intestines and scorpions use your genitals to teach acupuncture."

"Well, as long as it's for education," reflected Ram, holding his crotch with distress.

"But warden," it turned out this new guard was persistent, "this prison is full of nothing but brutes and psychos. Some of these guys can barely tell the difference between 'asleep' and 'a corpse.' How can you threaten them with death if they don't even really understand what it is?"

"Oh, come on. We don't have time for that hippy crap around here," Warmaker said, losing patience. "Look, man. The point is, Ram Van Bamf is a man's man. He can unexpectedly dish out the kind of violence that would make the Taiping Rebellion look like a dull church potluck. Ram Van Bamf doesn't just kill you. He *destroys* you. He takes the whole concept of you and runs it over with a steamroller until your children have a blank spot in their memories about who gave them that black eye for their birthday. He convinces you that you were never born but that you will somehow still die in ways too brutal to comprehend. He will grab your soul as you reach for Heaven and say, *No.*"

By now, the guard's nose had started to bleed for seemingly no reason at all, and he shook as if he were learning the cha-cha.

"For what it's worth, I've never killed anybody on purpose before," said Ram, hoping to alleviate fears. Then he added with reluctance, "But yeah, everything he said is true."

While the other guards arranged for a stretcher to pick up the shaking bleeding husk of a human being on the ground, Ram entered the execution chamber and sat down on an industrial-strength stool developed by the military specifically to sustain the impossible density of muscle that existed in every cubic millimeter of his body. He examined Louis Goodie with a keen eye, and in spite of the circumstances, Louis still appeared pretty good-spirited about everything.

"Hello there, sir," he said. "Will you be the one to stick it in me?"

"Well, I'm not a prejudiced guy or anything, but I don't stick anything in dudes."

"I meant the needle."

"Call it whatever you want. You can't have it."

"I'm talking about the lethal injection."

"I see you've been talking to some girls I know."

Frustrated, Louis decided to start the conversation over again.

"Why are you here?" he asked.

"Oh, that, yeah," said Ram. "Are you really the Grandma Grinder?"

"Yes."

"Really?"

"Yep."

"Are you sure?"

"Totally."

Ram stared dumbfounded through the glass at the warden. They took turns shrugging at each other.

"Has anybody told you who I am?" Ram asked.

"Of course not. I thought you were here to kill me," said Louis.

"So then you do know who I am!"

"Oh, so then you *are* the man with the needle?"

"It's a lot bigger than a needle! Why are you trying to hurt my feelings?"

This line of conversation persisted for half an hour before Warden Warmaker finally decided to investigate. It turned out the convulsing fool who had been removed on the stretcher was the same person who was supposed to brief Louis Goodie on the existence of Ram Van Bamf, and so Louis was not experiencing the proper amount of terror in his interrogation. This had never

12

happened before, and Warmaker was at a loss for what should happen next.

"You're awfully giddy, Goodie," said Ram as their circular dialogue continued.

"No, I'm exhausted. I wish someone would just kill me already."

"We'll kill you if you grinded all those grandmas."

"I did!"

"Oh yeah? Well, I'll kill you if you didn't!"

"Good!"

"Why is that good?"

"Because that's what is supposed to happen!"

"It is?"

"Of course it is."

"That doesn't make any sense at all."

"You're telling me!"

This went on for so long that most of the people involved finally just went home. The actual person meant to dispense with the injection was hopefully in the bathroom, but Warmaker did not much care anymore. His mind began to drift back to his time in Vietnam, when the solution to everything was just to light another tree on fire. Now Warmaker lived in a more complicated world, where threatening to murder a man in order to stop his execution was not as cut and dry as it sounded. He wished he could just beat the truth out of Louis, but he knew violence was not the answer.

"He confessed. He didn't grind any grandmas."

A drowsy Ram stood at the door that led into the execution chamber.

"You did it!" said Warmaker. "But how?"

"Well, one way or another, we got to talking about grandmas, and he said how his grandma was always nagging him to make something of himself. I told him that his grandma should lay off, and he remarked that his grandma must really be stinging now that he was the Grandma Grinder. So I told him that I actually met his grandma once, and that she was really proud of him for getting into the newspapers—that's a true story, by the way. Anyway, that got him real steamed, because I guess he became the Grandma Grinder in order to, well, grind her gears. So he confessed to me that the entire thing is just a big hoax."

"Nice work, Van Bamf! But then where did all the missing grandmas go? And whose remains did we recover?"

"The missing grandmas are all living comfortably and apparently never even left their houses, but since they're all senile and nobody likes to visit old people anyway, nobody ever noticed that they weren't dead. And all the recovered body parts were actually just expired meals from Nice to Meat You."

"Of course!" said Warmaker, and he tapped himself on the forehead. "You've really earned your fee this week, Van Bamf."

Warmaker handed Ram a sack of money with a dollar bill symbol on it, which was Ram's preferred method of payment. Louis Goodie was charged with several new crimes afterward, but none of them were worthy of his continuing to stay at Ultratropolis Penitentiary. Louis would have to leave this finest of institutions in shame, but at least that would really stick it to his grandma. Still, it would take time before the proper paperwork was filled out, so Louis would remain at the penitentiary at least a few days longer. But with this case solved, there was already another brewing.

"Van Bamf, there has been a matter troubling me for some time now," Warmaker said at a later location, an out of the way place in the penitentiary where he could sit and collect his thoughts. He drank whatever hard liquor was on hand, whereas Ram drank faucet water. A man as deep in the Y-chromosome as Ram Van Bamf metabolized alcohol and cyanide alike into something as harmless as water anyway, so there was no good reason to drink anything else. Ram had drunk the entire contents of volcanoes without consequence.

"What's the beef, warden?"

"I listen to the murmuring of the inmates. Something bad is brewing. Brewing in a pot of evil and deceit."

"Well, there's your problem. You don't wanna brew in a pot like that."

"Uh, yeah," and Warmaker shot an exasperated glance sideways, "but look. I don't know where, I don't know when, but I believe there is a plot in the works to bring a reign of terror down on Ultratropolis. And you are the only man who can save this city."

"Okay."

Ram got up and left the room. Warmaker continued to sit in silence for a while.

"That's what I like about the man," he decided. "He takes direction."

And so Warmaker finished his drink alone.

3

There was more than one way to investigate an impending city-wide apocalypse, and Ram Van Bamf's strategy was to explore none of those possibilities. He figured that if the truth of this conspiracy was not immediately apparent, it meant that somebody did not want him to know about it, which was all the reason Ram needed not to bother trying. Rather than waste time failing to unravel the mystery, Ram thought it made a lot more sense to just let the bad guys do whatever they wanted. Eventually, one of them would have to show their face, perhaps when the leader appeared on TV to receive his crown and scepter and declare himself Super Führer. Then Ram would be there to punch him, saving the city and allowing the cable stations to go back to their regularly scheduled programming. The guys at the barbershop told Ram this was a foolproof plan, which was nice to hear, because Ram had heard on good authority that fools provided the best proof.

"So what can I do you for today, Ram?" asked Elmo, the spry, ancient owner of the barbershop. He emigrated from the old country nearly a century ago, and he had the leathery complexion to prove it, a new layer of wrinkles forming in his skin annually like rings in a tree trunk. Although Elmo maintained a slight accent even now, no barriers lingual or cultural had ever hindered him from making intimate acquaintances; more women had found their way into his bed than the majority of men would even meet in their lifetimes. Elmo had more illegitimate children than the NBA fall roster.

"Just the monthly shave, Elmo," said Ram, rubbing his cheek.

Ram Van Bamf could grow a beard thick enough to suffocate a mastodon if he so desired, but through sheer force of will, he maintained nothing more than a perpetual five o'clock shadow. To let it grow any further would have been grounds for a catastrophe, as even his facial stubble was harder than diamonds. Ram's face was so sharp that he had used it to carve his own likeness into Mt. Rushmore, and although art snobs found his work to be derivative, the general public embraced it as a welcome and necessary addition.

"Oh, is it that time of the month already? This old, forgetful mind of mine. It is going on me, just like the setting sun on the horizon."

"Aww, come on, pops. You still got it," said Little Jimmy, a neighborhood boy who liked to hang around the shop. He was not related to Elmo by blood, but there was a time when Elmo accidentally cut himself with the scissors and bled on Little Jimmy, which was almost the same thing. Little Jimmy wore the same olive newsboy cap everywhere he went, so he himself seldom required a barber.

"Yes, yes, I have still got my hands. That is all I require." Then Elmo shot the rest of the room a hesitant look. "I am a barber, right?"

The rest of the patrons nodded and mumbled their agreement, much to Elmo's relief.

"I sure hope you are. Otherwise, I let a masseuse give me highlights!" said Fuzzy, sitting in the corner. "Because, you know, masseuse is another job that involves hands." Fuzzy considered himself to be the comic relief of the shop, which is why he adopted the name Fuzzy and wore garish sweaters, but he tended to try too hard with his jokes. Fuzzy had been incarcerated more than once for telling jokes that would cause any normal self-respecting person to die of shame.

"Strangler is also a job that involves hands," said Ruttiger, giving Fuzzy the evil eye. Ruttiger was Fuzzy's foil, a burly no-nonsense type with a healthy adoration for flannel. They both worked at the local car manufacturing plant, which stayed in business thanks to Ram personally taking so many old cars off the road each month.

Together, Fuzzy and Ruttiger were a more depressing take on classic comedy duos.

"Go on, Rut! Where would you be without me?" said Fuzzy, and he smacked himself in the face with a lemon meringue pie.

Elmo pulled a special silver case out from a drawer under the cash register. The warning "DO NOT OPEN EXCEPT IN CASE OF NUCLEAR WAR OR FEMALE PRESIDENT" had long since warn off the case, so he popped it open without a second thought. Inside was a razor blade originally forged out of radioactive meteor rock more than two centuries ago. Several legends surrounded the blade, though few had ever actually heard of it, as it seldom exchanged hands. The most accepted story was that an unearthly red lightning had struck it immediately after its forging, lending it a supernatural power that seemed descended from the heavens themselves. Regardless of origin, it was the only object on Earth capable of penetrating a part of Ram's body.

"Alright, Ram, no shaving cream for you. Let us just get down to it," said Elmo brandishing the king of razors. He had a brief flashback to the first time he had tried to shave Ram. As he applied the shaving cream to Ram's face, Elmo discovered pulsating lacerations all over his hands from where they had made contact with Ram's stubble. The doctors said Elmo would never use his hands again, which was when Elmo sold his barbershop to become a kickboxer. It was at this point in the flashback that Elmo began to suspect that his recollection of events was not entirely accurate.

"Looking forward to it, Elmo," said Ram. He sat down in his special chair, which had received military-grade modification like the prison stool.

As the razor made contact with Ram's skin, sparks of electricity spewed and erupted in all directions like Chinese New Year had gotten into a turf war with the Fourth of July. The fluorescent lights in the ceiling began to flicker in spasms, as if the razor itself was cannibalizing their energy in a mad bid for power.

"Hey now, I thought I came here for a *shave*, not a *rave*!" said Fuzzy. He looked around at the room, motioning with his hands for some laughs. After a lack of response, he honked on a bicycle horn.

"Look, Fuzz, you keep this up and I can't promise that everyone in this room won't just treat your head like a batting cage," said Ruttiger. As these words were being uttered, Little Jimmy realized he had been about to heave a fastball at Fuzzy's cranium.

"Wow, Ruttiger! You're right!" exclaimed Little Jimmy as he held the ball up for all to see.

"Alright now," interrupted Elmo, finishing the last razor swipe. "This just about does it."

The lights show ended in an instant, but the smoke lingered, the silhouette of a juggernaut on his throne the only intelligible image through the haze. Everyone braved the danger of the mist for the sake of being able to admire the clean-shaven face of Ram Van Bamf. His skin was flawless, the consequence of impenetrability. The line that traced his jaw was so angular that it could have been mistaken for the blueprint to the Pentagon. His hard sloped brow and pouty lips were ferocious in a manner that could only be compared to a rhinoceros drunk on its own desire to kill. The nose stood like a monument to manhood itself, an imposing granite monolith erected unapologetically on a glorious foundation. Then there were the eyes.

"Have you ever seen lovelier eyes?" said Elmo. "You want to just scoop him up in your arms like a kitten. Hello, kitty! Hello!"

Everyone nodded and smiled in thoughtful silence.

"So, what do I owe you?" asked Ram as he got up from his seat.

"Please, Ram," and Elmo shook his head and waved his hand, "the privilege of working with your head is payment enough. You know this."

As Elmo went to return the razor to its case, he stopped suddenly. At his age, any abrupt stops were cause for concern. Stopping in mid-step, stopping in mid-sentence, stopping at a stop sign—all were very alarming. Time froze in moments like these, as deep thought and brain death had an awful habit of looking alike at a glance.

"Say, have I ever told you boys the story of how I got this razor?" he asked at last, having beaten the reaper once again.

"Aww, don't worry about no stories, pops," said Little Jimmy. "We heard enough tall tales for one day."

"No, no, this story involves a dame," Elmo said. "And I never forget my dames."

"I dunno, Elmo. Those stories are seldom for impressionable ears," said Ruttiger.

"Hey! I'm plenty experienced already. My gal Sally and I have been holdin' hands now for three weeks," boasted Little Jimmy. "In fact, I kind of wish she would let go."

Sally, who had been in the room the entire time holding Little Jimmy's hand, started to blush.

"No, I was talking about Fuzzy. The guy may be thirty-five years old, but he has the maturity level of a Girl Scout bake sale."

"Very funny, Rut, but why don't you just leave the wise guy stuff to me?" said Fuzzy with a chuckle. He did not mind a good-natured jab at himself, since they hurt a lot less than the physical jabs to the face.

"Am I to be telling a story or not?" asked Elmo, and the shop hushed. "Alright then. I purchased this razor at a garage sale many years ago from a grieving mother. Her boy had recently discovered the razor, though I do not recall where. He was all excited to use it to shave for the first time, to kiss his face with metal and present his manhood to the world. But this boy was not very bright—he did not recognize how this razor is like the lion's jaws. His head exploded into a hundred smoking chunks, which, as you might have suspected, was the source of this mother's grief. It wounded me in the soul to see a dame so deflated! I had no choice but to console her, so I threw her down on the dusty mattress with the nine-dollar price tag and did what I could to help her replace what she had lost. The garage sale largely ended about then, though a few lucky voyeurs remained. Her caress lives on in my memory with every wobbled step I take. She could do things with her feet!"

An assortment of disturbed glances met Elmo when he looked up from his recollections.

"But maybe my audience is uninterested in that aspect of the story," he recovered. "At any rate, once it was over and the last of the spectators put away their home movie cameras, the mother found herself in higher spirits. It was then that she confessed to me a secret that I have held close to my heart for all my days since then."

A significantly more engaged set of eyes fell upon Elmo when he spied the crowd this time.

"She is probably dead now, and I do not think her spirit will nag me as all the living women I have blatantly betrayed do. So, this secret, I share now with all of you. Immediately after her son died— this was nearly sixty years ago—a few shady characters appeared around her home inquiring about the razor. They offered her a large sum of money for the trinket, but sensing with canine-like instincts that they would use it for nothing good, she refused to sell.

"For a long time afterward, she could swear people were watching her. They disguised themselves in all manner of ways to blend in. They were baggers at the grocery store, waiters at the restaurants. One of them went to medical school so that he could become her doctor. Finally, she just decided to get rid of the razor altogether."

"By selling it?" butted in Ruttiger. "She didn't want to sell it to the bad guys so she decided to dump it on anyone else at a garage sale? What if one of the bad guys had shown up in another disguise and bought it before you did? What sense does that make at all?"

"Well, allow me to use my words like this," said Elmo. "She was a mental deficient, her skull filled with cobwebs and unfinished games of checkers. Fortunately, the rest of her body was filled with depravity and alcohol addiction."

Still running through the story in his head, Ruttiger rubbed his forearms, which were furry enough for onlookers to mistake him for a clothed bear on more than one occasion.

"So that's it then, huh?" he asked. "The secret was she was being followed by some creeps?"

"Well, in part, yes, but I have not yet introduced the element of this secret that causes it to sparkle as it does. You see, the men who originally appeared at her doorstep never hid their occupation."

"Gee, pops, were they barbers like you?"

"Not at all, Little Jimmy. They were candy men! They worked at that shop on the other side of town, the Tooth Decay Hooray. I can only imagine these men never knew I specifically acquired the razor. Otherwise, I see no reason why they would not have hounded me as they did her."

"Wow, pops, that is a secret!" exclaimed Little Jimmy. "Who woulda thought my favorite place that ain't your shop would turn out to be a lair of evil and decadence? Let's tell the cops!"

"The cops are still practicing for Battle of the Bands," said Fuzzy. "They're probably too busy for anything like an evil lair."

"Well, then, you go bust them, Ram!" said Little Jimmy, poking Ram in the ribs. "You're better than a million police anyway."

"Me? I dunno. I'm kind of tired from threatening that prisoner's life all day," said Ram. "Besides, all those evil candy men probably died twenty years ago. Elmo is really old."

"Aww, phooey. You old-timers really cramp my style sometimes," said Little Jimmy as he adjusted his cap. "Let's get outta here, doll."

Sally collected her purse and sauntered out of the shop hand-in-hand with Little Jimmy, a cozy sunset inviting them on.

"Say, Elmo, you don't really think there is anything evil going on at the Tooth Decay Hooray anymore, do you?" asked Ram, stroking his newly smooth chin.

"Nah."

"Okay."

At least the Tooth Decay Hooray was one business Ram could cross off the list of groups bent on destroying the city, though according to Ram's current victory strategy, it did not matter in the first place. In fact, his strategy seemed to be working so well so far that Ram's mind could afford to drift off. He started to think about Jerry and if he would ever see him again. He wondered whether Jerry would ever wind up with Leonora. He even wondered if that war veteran had gotten out of Jerry's car before the fire got him. It was times like these when Ram noticed that life seemed to ask a lot of questions without providing a lot of answers. He thought that finding the answers was what made life worthwhile, but, as Ram already knew very well, he was not very good at finding things that were not already looking for him.

"Say, has anybody seen that banana I had?" asked Fuzzy. He took one perilous step forward, slipping on a banana peel on the floor and landing squarely on his rear. "Boy, next time I should really keep my eyes *peeled*!"

Elmo promptly called the police, who were never too busy to drag Fuzzy away in cuffs.

4

"Oh, God! What have you done?"

The Hottie Body clothing store on Delilah Street had once been home to all of the cutest tops, skirts, dresses, pants, and accessories for the fashionable girl on the go. Now it was home to a Tyrannosaurus rex skeleton on top of several hundred tons of mountain. It was a recent change in inventory that had not been approved beforehand by the owner, owing to her current outrage.

"You know, I'm not a glory hog, but I start to get tired of God getting all the credit for the things I do."

Ram Van Bamf lifted a hefty chunk of potassium feldspar out of the way of the woman. By all accounts, at the ripe age of 24, she was a looker. Her shoulder-length sienna brown hair fell in wavy layers intended to accentuate the lips and cheekbones, and she wore a plum corduroy blazer with a charcoal turtleneck and skinny jeans for an attractive business casual look. All of this was lost on Ram.

"The name is, uh, Ram Van Bamf," he said with a raised eyebrow and a crooked smile. He tried to project pride, but his embarrassment at having caused a localized disaster for this specific woman was palpable. He motioned to shake her hand, already knowing her name was Fran; everyone knew the name of the most successful woman in Ultratropolis.

"Oh, trust me, I definitely blame *you* for this," she said, ignoring his hand and dusting herself off in hard, quick strokes. "But I've been in worse scraps than this."

The world of business was a man's world, and to make it in a man's world, a woman had to be strong. This was not just some old adage; Fran was attacked all the time. Executives representing several of the world's largest firms regularly sprang out of the bushes with chains and PVC pipes to bludgeon Fran, because successful men knew the most convenient way to stop a growing threat was to send it to the hospital for brain hemorrhaging. Unfortunately for them, Fran was not the type to take a life-threatening beating lying down. She had extensive training in boxing, capoeira, and knitting, all of which translated into deadly fighting technique.

"I would have had her if it wasn't for the knitting," read a quote from a recovering would-be assailant in the newspaper.

Fran only owned one store, but the Hottie Body had risen to prominence faster than Will Smith in a space ship. In the beginning, several firms had offered to purchase her business and provide Fran with a lofty position within their companies. One firm offered her a vice presidency and stock options. Another firm promised a private jet and travel to exotic locales. Then there was the firm that wanted to worship her as a fertility goddess and impregnate her with the Destined Seed to begin Operation Lilith, but since the president of that firm was the same man who took pictures of Fran through her bedroom and bathroom windows, she worried the personal nature of their relationship would interfere with any potential business ventures. In the end, Fran declined all offers, and always for the same reason.

She was incapable of settling. In elementary school, Fran received an A- on a diorama through a technicality in the grading process, and the teacher incurred a string of bizarre, near fatal accidents until the grade was finally rectified. Although Mrs. Smiley retired from teaching forever afterward, she would wake up screaming "A! You deserve an A!" in the middle of the night for the rest of her life, and Mr. Smiley would cite this during the divorce proceedings. Since those days, Fran had matured in her methodologies, but her drive for power and independence had only increased. Selling her business would have been unacceptable for the simple fact that she would rather die than serve someone she knew was intellectually inferior. In a society of sycophants who worshipped and bathed in the fecal matter rained down by their superiors, Fran alone had the audacity to retain her self-respect at any cost.

And it was precisely that kind of attitude that had so many people trying to write her a coroner's report in the first place. Even other female executives had arranged unsuccessfully for Fran to meet the business end of a sledgehammer, though the novelty of such encounters had worn off long ago for her. Fran had simply come to understand the loosely guarded truth that all world industry revolved around extravagant acts of violence. The success of every national economy since the Peace of Westphalia in 1648 could at some point be traced back directly to a man swinging a rake. Fran herself had once crashed a school bus packed with bundles of TNT disguised as children into some of the competition next door. The owner of the competing business was understanding about the situation, and he and Fran had a good laugh about it once it was all over.

"Tell me who sent you," Fran demanded with arms akimbo, somehow staring Ram down even though she had to look up to see him. "Was it Hector? Because Hector said we were cool now. He said putting hats and backpacks on the explosives was clever and inventive."

"Uh, I wouldn't know anything about that," said Ram. "But nobody sent me, honest. I never meant to throw a mountain at your store in the first place."

"Or destroy my livelihood?"

"That either."

"Well, that makes me feel a lot better."

"Oh, good. I guess I'll be going then."

"I was being sarcastic!"

"Well, I was being Ram Van Bamf, but next time I'll pretend to be someone else too."

"Look—just tell me the truth. Why is my entire store underneath Mount Slipendie? And why do I see what looks to be a dinosaur skeleton sliding down the side of the mountain toward us?"

"I'm actually still getting to the bottom of all that myself, but if you want to come with me, that's okay."

Fran took a despairing look around. In any other city on the planet, the odds of her store having been displaced by a mountain on any given day would have been appreciably low. But, as Fran had learned, Ram toppled logic and probability with the same effortless gusto with which he toppled mountains. She finally just sighed and rolled her eyes, both of which would become a part of her daily routine now that Ram Van Bamf had entered her life.

"Sure, might as well come with you. It's not like I have a business to run anymore."

"You're really good at adjusting to change in your life."

"Uh, thanks."

And just like that, a dynamic duo of brains and brawn had been assembled, which was fortunate, because this was a mystery that would require both. As Ram would explain to Fran, the day had begun normally enough. He woke up, ate a cow, bench pressed the Philippines, and ate another cow. Then things took a turn for the unusual.

"We need to go to the post office," said Ram as he and Fran walked down the street. Cars zigzagged in every direction desperately attempting to escape his trajectory, causing more than one vehicle to crash into the same unlucky woman's living room.

"Why is that?" asked Fran, watching the woman pull one of the injured drivers out of his car so that she could more easily shoot him in the head.

"Because I'm beginning to suspect the guy I met this morning wasn't a mailman," said Ram as the injured man pleaded for his life.

"Yeah? Well, did he try to deliver anything to you?" asked Fran as the man and the woman started wrestling over the luger.

"Sure did. He showed up with a letter from a local television station saying to meet their filming crew at Mount Slipendie. I was promised five hundred dollars and a pet monkey," Ram said as the luger fell out of the woman's hands.

"Did it pan out?" asked Fran with feigned curiosity, and the man grabbed the woman by the wrist before she could lunge for her lost weapon.

"Do you see a monkey?" responded Ram with a tinge of sadness, and the man and the woman began to suck face like two colliding vacuum cleaners.

"Sometimes things just don't turn out the way you expect," concluded Fran, and the man's pants came off.

In short order, Ram and Fran arrived at the post office, an unremarkable building filled with unremarkable people. So many hideous and inept yokels worked there at any given time that it was as if mailing envelopes had undergone a process of spontaneous generation to produce them all. Ram was not one to judge, though. As a gag, he had on occasion contemplated having himself put in a big box and mailed to a friend's home. Once he arrived, Ram would spring out of the box and surprise his friend by revealing there was not a package inside the box but in fact a human being. Ram was proud of how wacky and original an idea it was and thought for sure he should make it happen someday.

"We need to find the postmaster," said Fran, scanning the swarm of lifeless faces in the room.

"It's usually the person with the biggest hat," said Ram.

"That would be me then," said a man of queasy complexion with bags under his eyes. He was a tall, lanky man in the first place, so the vintage top hat he wore only increased his resemblance to a jaundiced nutcracker. "I'm Postmaster Phil. What's up?"

"Do postmasters usually wear hats?" asked Fran.

"Probably not," shrugged Phil.

"Phil, I got an important question for you," said Ram.

"Alright."

"Where can I get a hat like that?"

"That's not the question he meant to ask," said Fran.

"Sure it was," said Ram.

Fran just glared at him.

"Alright, maybe it wasn't," corrected Ram, a little concerned about the look in her eyes. "Okay, I have another question."

"Let's hear it."

"Do you know if a mailman got sent out to deliver a letter to my house this morning?"

Phil cackled like a lunatic at this query, sounding like picture frames force-fed down a garbage disposal. Spit shot out of his mouth in a hail of artillery blasts that Fran had to dive to avoid.

"Mister, I don't know you, but I would bet my mother's life insurance policy that nobody delivered any mail to you this morning," he said once he had gotten control of himself. "I mean, there isn't a single person in this post office who even wakes up before noon."

A bunch of toothless grins and chuckling from various workers accompanied Phil's statement.

"So, then who was it that pretended to be a mailman?" asked Fran.

"Couldn't tell you," said Phil.

"No, I was asking Ram."

"Are you sure?" said Ram. "Because I don't know either, so I was hoping you were asking Phil."

27

"Yeah, I thought you were asking me."

"I was asking Ram."

"Okay, but I don't know," said Ram.

"Me neither," said Phil.

Fran had to take a deep breath then to stop herself from breaking multiple laws.

"Anyway, thanks for the help there, Phil," said Ram, and he shook Phil's hand, though Phil's hand could fit several times in the palm of Ram's hand.

"Don't mention it. This is the most excitement I've had in months."

"I don't doubt it. This place looks kind of, uh, rundown," said Ram as a fluorescent light fell out of the ceiling and hit a yokel in the neck. Fortunately, the yokel was used to it and continued sleeping.

"See, the way I figure, there're two kinds of post office," said Phil. "There's the kind with the imbalanced wackos who just might cut your head off and keep your teeth as hard candy if you stub their toe. And then there's the kind that's just full of lazy, incompetent goons that nobody but the government would employ."

"So you guys just decided to go the second route," estimated Fran.

"Uh, yeah," responded Phil, eyes darting side to side. "Say, either of you ever try German rock candy? A fellow named Hans came in the other day, and I guess you could say he helped us with our sweet tooth."

Ram and Fran hurried out of the post office, hopefully never to return in their lifetimes.

"So, this letter you received," said Fran as they both power walked out of sight of the building, "it was supposed to be from the local television station. When you got to Mount Slipendie, did you ever find a filming crew? Was there any shoot?"

"Kind of. I mean, lots of men shot at me with guns."

Fran stopped.

"Look, before we go any further, you need to tell me everything you know," she said. "No more of this in medias res stuff."

"Medea's having another race? I thought the police shut her down."

"Just tell me what happened!" Fran yelled. She would have hit him, but that would have shattered every bone in her body. It was humbling for Fran to meet someone whom she could not kill at the drop of a hat if the right motivation presented itself.

"Okay, I'll tell you on the way to our next stop," said Ram.

"But what is our next stop?"

"Beats me."

Fran shook her head, more from anguish than frustration.

"Tell me what happened. Start from the very beginning."

Ram pursed his lips and nodded.

"Well, my birth was a difficult one. Pumping a three hundred pound bundle of muscles out of a birth canal isn't as easy as it sounds, or so I'm told."

"Never mind. Start from this morning."

"You got it. So, I get this ring at the door. The guy claims to be a mailman, and it seems legit because the words 'MAIL MAN' are written pretty legibly on his blood-stained t-shirt. He just hands me the letter and leaves, so I read the thing. It says what I told you it says. A TV crew wants to meet me on Mount Slipendie at the outskirts of town, and they'll give me five hundred dollars and a pet monkey for my appearance. I assume they want to film me hunting Bigfoot, because his family lives in that direction and I like to play basketball with them. Bigfoot has a mean skyhook.

"Anyway, I jog up to the base of Mount Slipendie in no time at all. The letter says to meet them at the summit, so I take a good leap and there I am at the top. As soon as my feet hit the ground, roughly fifty guys in winter coats jump out and start shooting me with every gun you can think of. Rifles, shotguns, handguns, machine guns, flare guns, ear piercing guns—they have it all. It's no wonder that guns kill so many people each year. I lost count of how many of those poor guys got their faces blasted off each time their own bullets came back at them when they bounced off of me; it got hard to watch after a while. So, I guess the moral of the story is—if you really need to kill a man, just buy him a gun.

"Also, while all of this is going down, there's a helicopter that keeps circling around. A guy inside the copter promises that he isn't filming me, but he does ask that I stop ruining his camera angles and just stand in one spot. But anyway, after a lot of shooting and a lot of people dead from involuntary suicides, a Tyrannosaurus rex attacks. That's when I—"

"Freeze!" said Fran, her head reclining so far backward with incredulity that it was as if the stupidity of the story itself had manifested and struck her in the face.

"What?"

"A Tyrannosaurus rex attacks."

"Well, I'm no dinosaur expert, but it's hard to mistake one when you see it."

"A *Tyrannosaurus rex* attacked you on Mount Slipendie?"

"I guess they're not all extinct. Or, at least they weren't until maybe forty-five minutes ago."

"Fine, if you say so. Just keep going."

"Right. So, a Tyrannosaurus rex attacks. It starts breathing fire all over me, which I have to say is—"

"Freeze."

"What now?"

"The Tyrannosaurus rex breathed fire on you?"

"Yeah. I was impressed. Evolution really kicked it up a notch."

"A helicopter may or may not have filmed you getting shot at by a small army on a mountaintop, and then a dinosaur breathed fire on you? This is what really happened?"

"Sure. But you know, I could finish the story a lot faster if you would stop interrupting."

"Oh. Sorry."

"No problem. Anyway, it's right around then that all the gunmen who still have legs decide to flee, so it's just me and the dinosaur. The first thing I learn is that this dino is the real deal. His lungs don't collapse when I give him a jab to the ribs, which is more than I can say for anyone from my short-lived career as a Krav Maga instructor. He's none too pleased from getting hit either, so he snaps me up in his jaws like I'm the first meal he's had in sixty-five million years. Get it? That was a joke. Anyway, I never thought a T-rex could get so big that it could fit a guy like me comfortably inside its mouth, but there I am, rocking and rolling all over its tongue while it vomits a volcano on me. The whole thing kind of feels like a ride at an amusement park, except without the joy or the possibility of survival. I guess that's why my idea for a children's hayride through a minefield never got past the design stage.

"Anyhow, all good rides come to an end, this one included. It turns out not even a dinosaur can breathe fire all day, and I can tell he's running out of juice when my eyeballs stop smoldering from the heat. Now, I think I'm a pretty practical guy, so I knew in the first place this dino didn't stand the best chance. But boy, what a great fight he's put up. I figure he's earned a warrior's death for giving it his all, so I punch through the roof of his mouth and rip his brains out. Then I eat him. Because, you know, why not? Hence the skeleton."

"I guess that solves one piece of the mystery," said Fran. "In a really, really stupid way."

"Yeah. So, after that, the guy in the helicopter thanks me for all the great footage and tells me it is conclusive evidence of something. I figure conclusive is the best kind of evidence, so I guess I'm feeling pretty proud of myself for helping the guy do whatever he needed. Then the mountain bursts into flames, so I—"

"Freeze!" yelled Fran as she threw her hands up in exasperation.

"What now?" asked Ram with similar irritation.

"The mountain was on fire?"

"Yeah."

"How much of it was on fire?"

"All of it. Big towering inferno. Ask anybody. Whole city saw it."

Fran, determined to do exactly as Ram said, pulled the first person she could find off the sidewalk.

"You there, help me with something."

"Anything for you, pretty lady," said the pleasantly surprised man. His cheap shades and sloppy goatee indicated the rarity with which he talked to women who were not swinging from a pole.

"Was Mount Slipendie on fire a little while ago?"

"Of course it was, but Ram grabbed the bull by the horns and taught that baby how to fly! It made CG effects look like crap! Never seen anything like it. Gotta love Ram, man. Gotta love him."

"Oh," said Fran, her face scrunched up as if there were a glare. She then let the man go, much to his disappointment.

"See? Everybody saw it. You must be a real workaholic to not have noticed the black sky or the people running and screaming or the crazy old preacher that kept grinning and yelling, 'I had to be right eventually!' "

"Yeah, workaholic, that's me," said Fran, and she bit gently on her lower lip. "But come on, this whole story is completely preposterous. Why did the mountain burst into flames?"

31

"Well, the helicopter guy mentioned something about the fire being great for ratings, but that's all I know about that. Anyway, I figured the quickest way to put out the fire was with a big gust of wind. That's when I just decided to pick up the whole mountain and throw it. I figured there would be enough wind resistance to put out the fire, and I was right. I guess maybe I should have aimed it in a different direction though. It's just plain bad luck that your store was at the edge of town and was the only building in the entire city affected by my blatant disregard for human life or good sense. Ram Van Bamf Syndrome, you know? Anyway, sorry for ruining your life."

"Ratings?" said Fran, having blocked out everything Ram had said afterward. "So then a local television station really was involved! We need to get down to the DOA-Thirteen station building and demand some answers. I've dealt with them before."

"Hey, good thinking," applauded Ram. "We're a great team. I'm really happy you somehow avoided being crushed by the mountain whereas your entire store was completely flattened beyond all hope of recovery."

"Uh huh."

The DOA-13 television station out of Ultratropolis was known for its sensational news reports and ultra-violent selection of syndicated programming. The station had been established in 1949 as a locally-owned affiliate of one of the Big Three television networks by a visionary named Moose Tantrum. Rationally predicting that the world would soon be invaded by godless child-eating Martians following the Roswell incident, Moose developed DOA-13 as a station dedicated only to running the most brutally terrifying programming imaginable. His reasoning for this decision was largely immortalized in the station slogan, "Murder is the best deterrent," which had to be uttered with a shaking fist at the end of every news day. Ideally, if the Martians happened to tune into DOA-13, they would see the literal rivers of blood and decide that Earth was not a planet anybody wanted to try to conquer.

Since no Martian attacks happened on his watch, Moose Tantrum was celebrated as a hero in his time. When he passed away, his body was launched into outer space just in case he decided to reanimate and take his fight directly to the Martians themselves. Meanwhile, the DOA-13 station passed into the hands of Moose's only daughter, Bolivia Tantrum. Under her guidance, the station maintained its hard edge while steering its content in a direction more digestible for the masses. Programming such as the reality show *Hunted by a Serial Killer* and the crime drama *Cadaver's Revenge* captured evening ratings, whereas the children's lineup consisted entirely of shows imported from Japan and adapted or reshot for an American audience, such as the live action show *Mega Warriors Infinity* and the animated series *Volatile Mecha-Kaiser Commands the Heavens and Vanquishes the Black of the Heart*. Since so much Japanese children's programming consisted of giant robots in desperate life and death struggles, Bolivia was able to introduce American children to intense violence without having to worry over angry letters from parents about there being too many dismemberments or exploded genitals.

Ram and Fran had thought the station building security might pose a problem when they arrived, and Ram agreed to let Fran do the talking when they reached the entrance gate.

"Is that a Greek God with you?" inquired the gate guard before Fran had even begun to speak.

"That's Ram Van Bamf," she responded.

"Is he here to kill us?"

"Not if you let him inside."

"But if we let him inside, doesn't that increase his ability to kill us exponentially?"

"Not at all."

"Oh."

So the gate opened, and Ram and Fran were free to explore the building. From the outside, it appeared as normal as any other television station, so they just proceeded through the front doors. Fran found a sophisticated layout of the building on the wall beside the courtesy desk. While she studied it for emergency exits in the case that their mystery newsman decided to flee, Ram attempted the direct approach.

"Hey there, ma'am," said Ram to the neatly dressed receptionist at the desk.

"What can I do for you today?" she asked, her voice unwavering and her gaze locked upon him through her crimson cat eye glasses. The slight wrinkles around her lips suggested she was roughly a decade and a half older than Fran, but she displayed the poise of an elder lioness.

"Would you know if anybody in the building filmed a story today about me getting shot hundreds of times or being set on fire by a dinosaur?"

"I can look," she said as her hands became a flurry of fast, efficient movements on a computer. "No. There is nothing to that effect on record."

"Are there any stories at all about me today? My name's Ram Van Bamf."

"Certainly. In the past two hours there have been hundreds of news stories across the world involving your actions today regarding Mount Slipendie. And if I am not mistaken, the Republic of the Philippines runs a daily segment about the crippling physical and emotional damage you cause their economy and infrastructure."

"Oh, yeah? And none of those Mount Slipendie stories mention a dinosaur?"

"I can only speak for this station, and this station has no record of live dinosaurs in current events."

"Huh. Well, has anyone flown a helicopter out of the station today?"

The receptionist made another series of graceful clicks.

"Yes, though I am not of the authority to discuss the nature of the flight."

"Could you just tell me who flew the copter?"

"Sir, to be frank, I do not even know how you got past security. The fact that I have indulged your curiosity at all is a testament to my professional courtesy and the lack of excitement in my private life. I am not at liberty to discuss the activities of this station in any manner with you."

"Please?"

The lady shook her head.

Fran, having sufficiently absorbed the layout on the wall, turned to Ram and the receptionist. She took a deep breath before she began.

"It's nice to see you again, Dot," Fran said, leaning over and putting her hand over the receptionist's hand. "I'm so glad you never got that new pair of glasses like you said you were going to."

"Yes, well, after a woman such as yourself pays my fashion a compliment, I have no choice but to take notice," said Dot, pulling her hand back to adjust her frames.

"You'll have to excuse Ram. He's, you know, stupid."

"We all have our deficiencies," agreed Dot with considerable tact.

"I like the way Dot puts it better," sulked Ram.

"Well, it's funny that you say that, because my deficiencies are all I ever think about anymore," said Fran, and her shoulders dropped as she continued. "Dot, you're like me, a career woman, a single lady. Are you as desperately lonely as me?"

Dot was taken aback, literally, as she almost fell out of her chair. Ram was so befuddled by the sudden shift in conversation that he convinced himself he must have forgotten how to speak and comprehend the English language. He started to bark, then cough, then meow a little, but none of those sounds seemed to make any sense either, so he decided to go on pretending he could speak English.

"Excuse me?" Dot said, inspired to fiddle with her glasses some more.

"It was that sensation of a gaping, festering hole inside of me that saved my life today, or it almost got me killed, depending on how you look at it," said Fran with arms crossed, her fingers digging into her sides. "I wasn't in the store today when Mount Slipendie crushed it. I mean, sure, my employees and several customers are now an indistinguishable paste in the ground, but that's beside the point. What I'm getting at is—I've had a lonely life. I've always wanted to be a successful businesswoman. When other girls were drawing ponies and sneaking into their mothers' makeup, I was reading about monopolistic competition."

Fran stopped for a moment, wondering if her abrupt trip into monologue was as awkward as she imagined it to be, but Dot's hanging lower lip seemed to resonate her continued interest. Ram was busy making clicking sounds out of the side of his mouth, checking to see if he could speak any of the native African languages; he could not.

"It's not like I really enjoyed that sort of thing," Fran elaborated, "but it was like building an arsenal. The more I knew, the more weapons I had at my disposal. The idea of competing with the most powerful people in the world and beating them at their own game... Well, I guess it was an odd obsession for a little girl to have. I can't really say if there was a specific event in my childhood to cause it, though my dad used to sing me a lullaby about a girl named

"That's alright."

"Is your hat hissing?"

"No."

"My mistaken then."

It was at this point that Fran finally squeezed past Ram in the hallway to get at Manuel in his office. Her hands were readied like meat hammers and her eyes had literally turned into balls of fire, which was a surprise even to her.

"Cut the crap, Salas," she said, "because you're about to have a two-part interview with Alice and Wilma."

Before Manuel could even say, "Please, not the face," Fran had thrown a haymaker that struck Manuel in the temple with enough velocity to launch the boa constrictor out the window. She immediately followed up with an uppercut so sharp that manufacturers started selling scissors in the shape of her fist. Manuel collapsed into a pink heap on the ground as his suitcases burst open, their frivolous contents spilling out all over the room. One suitcase was just filled with rocks.

"I'd hate to see what Alice and Wilma would do to the paparazzi," observed Ram.

Despite being in a daze of unnatural agony, Manuel could tell that his face was still in pretty good shape all things considered, so the situation was not all bad. His jaw might even be put back together if he got to the hospital in time.

"Start talking, or I take your head off," said Fran, using a nail file to sharpen the tip of her boot.

"I would be happy to talk to Ram," said Manuel pointing at a vacant wall nowhere near where Ram was actually standing.

"You talk to me," she whispered through her teeth.

"That's okay too."

"I don't mind talking," said Ram.

"Shut up, Ram."

"I'd do what she says if I were you," said Manuel between bouts of sneezing blood and crying.

"You went up in a helicopter today, didn't you?" asked Fran, and she grabbed Manuel by his furry collar.

"You bet."

"Did you take that helicopter to Mount Slipendie?"

"Yes."

"Why?"

"Well, in a couple hours, you'll see I got great exclusive on-the-scene footage of Ram throwing the mountain when it caught fire."

"No!" exclaimed Ram, and he tipped forward with mouth agape. "You said you weren't filming me! I feel so betrayed right now."

"I'm sorry."

"Aww, that's okay. People make mistakes."

"But Mr. Salas, why would you have gone to Mount Slipendie if you could not have known the mountain was going to burn?" Fran asked with as much insincerity as she could muster.

"I swear, I didn't even know that was going to happen!"

"Oh? Then why were you there?"

"Well, it's because… It's because…"

And then the conversation came to a halt, not because Manuel was uncooperative but because he could not talk and have a concussion at the same time. Ram wondered if they should call a doctor when Manuel began banging his head on the floor and rolling around in glass, but Fran was pretty sure he would snap out of it. Eventually, he did, and Fran uncrossed her fingers.

"Excuse me for that," said Manuel, pulling a sharp piece of something out of his neck. "I was at Mount Slipendie because somebody had called in a favor."

"Now we're getting somewhere," said Fran with a slow nod. "Who is this 'somebody,' and what was the favor?"

"I'll tell you, but you have to believe me—I don't know much."

"*That's* not hard to believe at all. Just start talking."

Fran and Ram leaned in extra close for this, as if they were at a good part in a movie but the remote was too far away to raise the volume.

"I only know him by an assumed name. He calls himself 'Gyakusatsu.' He wears a mask and a trench coat so I don't know what he really looks like."

"Gyakusatsu? That has to be another language," said Fran. "Sounds Japanese."

"Well, being a reporter and all, I looked it up. It is Japanese. It means, 'Massacre.' But in spite of that, he was a really nice guy. He took me to the carnival when he was still convincing me to join his evil empire. He even snapped my picture for me on the carousel. He must have had good parents."

"Oh, I remember that carnival," said Ram. "That was the one with the runaway Ferris wheel that divided the shopping mall into east and west wings."

"Yeah! That must've been a heck of a ride."

"You know it!"

And Manuel and Ram high-fived.

"Yeah, great," muttered Fran. "So what was the favor he needed called in? And why did you agree to it?"

"Well, that's kind of complicated," said Manuel, who was finally able to sit up for the first time in several minutes. "Gyakusatsu explained to me that if I just helped him out a little bit here and there, he would reward me with fabulous wealth and fame. And as it so happened, I became a pretty popular character around these parts when I agreed to his terms. Oh, and he promised to give me control of the Andromeda galaxy once he had conquered the universe. So, that sounds like a sweet deal too."

It was upon hearing this that Ram had one of his rare original thoughts, which always signified a serious turn of events.

"Say, Manuel, do you think a guy who wants to conquer the universe might also want to bring a 'reign of terror' down on Ultratropolis?"

"Sure, I guess."

"What's the matter, Ram?" asked Fran.

"I'm not sure yet," said Ram in a slow, pensive voice, "but when I do, you'll be the first to know."

"Anyway," Manuel continued, "Gyakusatsu told me I just had to record Ram Van Bamf on Mount Slipendie today, especially if he were suddenly attacked by gunmen or dinosaurs, and to get conclusive evidence that none of these aggressors could stand up to Ram in a fight."

"So Gyakusatsu is behind the attack on you, Ram!" said Fran.

"Yeah, I guess, but why would he send anybody after me if he was expecting them to lose?"

Fran turned to Manuel with fists clenched, expecting him to answer.

"I have no idea! Honest! Please hit me anywhere but the face. My crotch is wide open!"

By now, Manuel had lost enough blood for various reasons that Fran finally called for an ambulance. But before he was taken away, Fran made it perfectly clear to Manuel that he worked for her from now on. Whenever Gyakusatsu came calling for him, Fran had better hear about it. Since Manuel Salas was prone to instantaneous cowardice in the face of any danger, as had been established by his failed escape attempt and his subsequent beating, he readily agreed to the terms. After all, maybe Gyakusatsu was one of those omniscient mastermind villains who had expected Manuel to be discovered by Ram Van Bamf, and this was all part of his grand design. For all Manuel knew, he was being even more loyal to his dark master by betraying everything he knew about him at the first opportunity.

It was this comforting thought that allowed Manuel to drift off into a well-earned sleep in his ambulance stretcher, just before the ambulance exploded.

6

Officially, organized crime did not exist in Ultratropolis, and both the police and the criminals were much happier that way. It was just less work for everyone involved. In a city where a paragon of justice like Ram Van Bamf could unexpectedly appear at any moment, perhaps brandishing a tree or the George Washington Bridge, the risk of committing a crime outweighed the benefits for the individual. The time that Ram intercepted the four year-old girl who stole a candy bar from the local supermarket was well-documented twice in the newspaper, once on the front page and again in the obituaries. Only an organized crime syndicate had any hope of prospering in Ultratropolis, which is specifically why the city declared they did not exist. It guaranteed that no crimes were ever happening anywhere, even if crimes were happening everywhere. Mayor Dingus considered it his greatest victory as an elected official.

Dingus was a man of convictions, especially of the convictions that were convenient for him from moment to moment. When civil servants went on strike demanding additional benefits, Dingus took a stand against insubordination by firing them all and replacing them with fleeing Colombian drug lords, all of whom Dingus promised would enrich society with their cultural heritage. And when those drug lords started demanding the same benefits that their predecessors never received, Dingus asked the public whatever happened to good old-fashioned insubordination, inspiring the masses to ban together and purge the city of those society-wrecking drug lords forever. The abundance of new jobs created by their abdication was yet another victory for Dingus, and he won his bid for reelection by such a landslide that his opponent apologized for wasting his time.

When the ambulance carrying a hemorrhaging Manuel Salas decided to combust in spectacular fashion, Dingus assured the public there was no foul play, since foul play was technically an impossible occurrence in Ultratropolis. But behind the scenes, Dingus was concerned, so he summoned both the police and Ram Van Bamf to his office.

"This better be worth our time, Mr. Mayor," said Captain Carl, who headed the police. He always spoke with a steady and deliberate inflection. "Battle of the Bands is just around the corner, and we need to get in every second of practice we can."

Carl was the frontman for Lethal Enforcer, the thrash metal band the police had formed when it became apparent their jobs had been rendered obsolete by Ram Van Bamf. Lieutenant Murdock played lead guitar, though he and Carl frequently harmonized during solos, which was the trademark of the band. Sergeant Wilson was the bass player, so he always wore shades and leaned against the nearest wall in a really cool manner. If he was outside, he would lean on himself, and he would just look even cooler. Finally, Detective Fury played drums, and he fulfilled the role of wisecracking realist for when situations got too wacky. They all stood before Dingus now, with Ram just behind them.

Ram and Fran had since parted ways, as Fran wanted to continue investigating on her own for a while. They would meet up again when one of them learned something important, though neither one of them expected Ram to be the person who learned something.

"Carl, Carl, this is a potential murder we have on our hands here. Ambulances don't just explode on their own," said Dingus, his hands extended in a pleading manner. "Well, at least not since we stopped having our ambulances built in the Sudan."

"We never even recovered the man's body, Mr. Mayor. How can we be sure this was a murder?" said Murdock, arms crossed to resemble a very muscular pretzel. He was a bodybuilder as well as a lawman, and his biceps were used as a unit of measurement in Singapore.

"We enjoy a delicious meal," said Fury.

"Oh, I can do that."

"No, no," said Carl, waving his hand, "this is where the investigation begins. You guys keep your eyes open for anything unusual while Murdock and I go have a chat with the manager."

"You don't seriously expect us to find anything here, do you?" asked Murdock.

"No, not at all. But like I said, this is all we've got."

"We could be practicing for Battle right now," mused Murdock.

"Yeah," said Carl with a slight smile.

The two of them made a mad dash for the backroom, having to fight off swarms of invaders along the way. According to their media personas, Carl and Murdock were a world-class tag team in mayhem, a couple of master chefs dishing out a steaming hot bowl of police brutality everywhere they went. Murdock was a veritable wall of deltoids and energy bars, while Carl had a spinning fist that filled up an ER faster than a roof collapse. And although this was neither the time nor the place for such severity, Carl and Murdock took solace in the number of ways they could have killed these poorly paid teenagers if necessary.

"I never realized there was such a large minority of Japanese in Ultratropolis," said Carl as he flicked one of the invaders between the eyes.

"That just means they must not commit any crimes," said Murdock, casually throwing an entire person over his shoulder with one hand. "At least none that we know about."

Their efforts to minimize the violence belied the reality that every member of Lethal Enforcer was actually upstanding and dedicated to the law, but nobody wanted to listen to a thrash metal band that sang about the fairness of the justice system; people only wanted to hear about tracheas getting stomped. And as luck would have it, Murdock was a choice poster boy for brutality with his physique and a stare that could petrify a blind man. Carl, on the other hand, inspired order everywhere he went with his barren scalp and a groomed moustache that wrested control of his upper lip. While it was this harmony of brutality and order that defined Lethal Enforcer, the camaraderie between Carl and Murdock ran deeper than any contrived press release explanation.

It was a mom and pop store several years ago, before Carl was a captain and Murdock was a lieutenant, where a casual interception of thugs in a protection racket devolved into a life and death fire fight. Carl and Murdock faced down seven armed men while defending civilians and the owners, and nineteen tense minutes later, the shootout had ended with seven corpses, none of them police or civilian. That visceral experience, where two men had to work in perfect tandem to survive, connected them in a way that could not be articulated in print or film, but the silly media portrayals would have to suffice.

After enough strong-arming, they finally made their way into the back of the restaurant, and they stopped to take stock of their surroundings.

"You take the rice, I'll tackle the noodles," said Murdock as he filled his arms with boxes.

"No, I don't think we are going to find anything suspicious in their stock room. Too obvious. Let's check out the kitchen," said Carl.

Murdock shrugged and dropped the boxes.

Meanwhile, Ram threatened the integrity of his booth chair as he waited with Fury and Wilson for his meal.

"So, now what?" Ram asked again.

"Wish I could tell you," said Fury with a shake of the head, practicing his drum work with a fork and spoon on the table. He was a shorter man than his bandmates, but no less capable at apprehending villains, having honed his skill with blunt objects into an art form.

"What do you think, Wilson?" asked Ram.

Wilson shot a steady finger in the direction of a particularly attractive concubine. She wore a royal blue kimono with long, hanging sleeves and a design of flowers and lily pads across the lower half.

"You think she's suspicious, huh? Okay, I'll go beat her up."

As Ram got up, Fury too jerked to his feet and grabbed Ram by the arm.

"No, Ram! Wilson just means that she's a hottie."

Then a Beretta fell out of her kimono.

"On the other hand, maybe you should go beat her up."

Ram marched straight toward her as she hurried to retrieve the weapon from the floor, and invaders made no effort to harass him. As he got closer, he started to wonder why she looked familiar. It was slow to come to him, but by the time the woman said, "Ram, it's me, Fran. Stop looking at me like that. I'm Fran. Hey, idiot, it's Fran," Ram decided he had never met this woman before in his life.

"You're not Japanese at all, are you?" asked Ram with a squinty eye.

"No, Ram," she said, followed by a heavy sigh. "It's me, *Fran*. I put on a furisode kimono I had sitting in my closet so that I could sneak around the place and look for anything fishy. What are you doing here?"

"Oh, hey," said Ram with a wave. "The mayor wants me and the police to look into Manuel's death, so I told them about Gyakusatsu. That wasn't much of a lead, so Captain Carl thought the best we could do was at least go some place Japanese."

"I thought the same thing," said Fran. "It's really nothing to go on. I wish Manuel would have had something in his office we could use, but it looks like he destroyed anything that could have been a clue. The idiot couldn't even help us get justice for his murder."

"So, you said this getup you're wearing was just sitting in your closet?"

"It's a big closet, and I'm a fashionable lady."

"It looks nice on you."

Fran had been plotting her next insult; she was not prepared for a compliment.

"Well, thank you," she said with a blush.

"So, now what?" asked Ram to a new audience.

"I've been here for a good while. The front seems squeaky clean. I've investigated the ownership too. They seem like honest, hardworking people. I think we're just wasting our time."

Then the gunshots started, followed by people running and screaming. The guests with a high tolerance for anachronisms in their historical reenactments thought it was all part of the atmosphere, but the guests who were not morons fled for their lives. Ram and Fran headed toward the source of the danger instinctively, though Fran stayed behind Ram as they moved. Fury and Wilson too followed the direction of the shots, which led them all to the backroom area. It was coming from the kitchen. Wilson immediately took cover on the wall, and everyone thought he looked so cool with his gun out. Ram pushed the door to the kitchen open, with Fran and Fury just behind him.

"Ram! A little help here?" said Carl as he fired from his cover behind a kitchen island.

"What happened here?" asked Ram as a few stray bullets bounced off his face.

"A John Woo movie!" yelled Murdock in response as he ducked behind some cabinets.

They were apparently engaged in a firefight with the chefs themselves, who were all armed with Uzis and an endless supply of meat cleavers. Several of them did backflips and rolls while shooting, ostensibly to disorient their opponents, but more than a few of them were most likely showboating.

"What's going on up there?" asked Fran as she rested sideways on Ram's back.

"I think they're filming a movie."

"Please, everyone, stop!" cried a voice from behind Fran and Fury. "Just stop!"

Fran recognized the man as Hiroshi Iwadare, the owner of Hidetora's Castle. As a small, middle-aged gentleman dressed in a fine suit, he was unremarkable in stature, but his hair was so legendary that references to it had been retroactively inserted into the Japanese national anthem. Hiroshi's thriving black pompadour was thick enough to eclipse a football field at noon time, and he mailed so many mocking photos of himself to hair styling magazines that the magazines finally just changed their addresses.

The gunfire stopped immediately as the chefs obeyed Hiroshi's request. Carl and Murdock held their fire as well, since taking a potshot at the owner would have only led to the chefs doing even faster, angrier backflips. Ram let Hiroshi into the kitchen, and his pompadour cast the room in so much darkness that a family of bats decided to roost there for the winter.

"What have you done to my restaurant? Why do my customers flee before the invading warlord can even accost them?"

"Iwadare-san, the police started it!" said one chef. "They opened fire on us while we were cooking."

"Is that true?" asked Fury.

"I was just walking along when all of a sudden there was an octopus flung in front of my face. I thought I was under attack, so I opened fire on the thing," said Murdock. "How was I supposed to know it just slipped out of a chef's hands?"

"Look, even if Murdock did misfire his gun," said Carl, always the voice of reason, "that does not explain why these chefs are all equipped with Uzis. Something suspicious is going on here, and we're not leaving until we get answers."

"What, that?" scoffed Hiroshi. "My restaurant needs to be protected from fools like you, so I allow all my backroom employees to be armed in the case of robbers."

"But Uzis aren't exactly street legal," said Fury.

"Legal? What of it? I give the mayor a paltry sum each month, and he looks the other way. In fact, I just got back from paying him."

Fury rolled his eyes and nodded, as if he had somehow already known Dingus was involved.

"Should we arrest the mayor?" asked Ram after a period of dismayed silence.

"We would if we could," said Carl, "but the mayor has his hands in so many different pockets across the city that our whole economy would collapse if something were to happen to him. I'm still trying to figure out why the city funded pits of acid."

"Or why city money was used to launch a satellite last month, even though we have no space program and no launch pads," said Fury.

"Wait a minute," started Fran.

"What is it?" asked Carl.

"The mayor is getting bribes from *everybody*?"

"More or less," said Murdock, and the other cops nodded.

"Then maybe the mayor is already working with Gyakusatsu and he doesn't even know it," said Fran. "Dingus might be the key to all of this."

The others shot a glance at Carl.

"We need to get back to the mayor's office," he declared, hands together.

"Please! Leave," said Hiroshi. He began to point at all the bullet holes in his walls. "And you can tell the mayor to expect a visit from the invading warlord!"

"Sorry," mumbled Murdock with a furrowed brow.

Ram and the police returned to the mayor's office, this time accompanied by Fran. Dingus was excited to see them all return so soon, as he hoped it meant they had found a lead, but he was even more excited to see Fran, because he thought she was from the illegal massage parlor he frequented.

"We need to talk, Mr. Mayor," said Carl, who stood at the front.

"Sure, wonderful. Everyone take a seat," said Dingus. "The lady will sit on my lap."

"No, she will not," Fran said.

"Alright. She can lie across my desk."

She shook her head.

"Fine! Everybody just stand up then!"

Dingus proceeded to lift every maple chair in the room and heave it as hard as he could, smashing the wood to pieces and breaking another window. His own leather chair proved to be difficult to toss, so he took a hunting knife out of his desk and began hacking chunks of cushioning out of it. By the time Dingus began dumping kerosene all over the floor, Ram decided to intervene.

"I think you might have a problem, pal," Ram said as he took Dingus's gas can away from him.

"I know," said Dingus in a low voice.

"Can we finally get down to business?" said Fran as she stepped around the kerosene.

"Yes, please. Tell me you found something of interest," said Dingus.

"We did. We found out you're a bribe-taking pig," said Fran.

"You just now found that out?" said Dingus, looking at them all with disgust. "You're even more incompetent than I thought."

"Sorry, let me rephrase. *I* found out. My name is Fran. I was the owner of the Hottie Body."

"Lovely, dear. Just lovely."

"Right. But anyway, we realized that with you taking so many bribes from so many people, it is possible that you are already in regular contact with Gyakusatsu yourself."

"Ah ha!" declared Dingus, and he brought a fist down on his palm. "So I'm even more brilliant than I thought I was."

Dingus would not remember being roundhouse kicked in the head immediately following that brazen assertion, though he lay strewn out on the floor for long enough that one of his windows had already been remodeled by the time his heart started back up.

"Did I go all the way with her? Is that why I'm down here?" asked Dingus, on his back, pointing at Fran.

She grabbed him by his tie and yanked him up on his knees.

"We need a list of every person who has ever given you a bribe. Now."

Dingus, who could only ever present the illusion of being a powerful man when dealing with inanimate objects or people who had their backs turned, chose to oblige. He pressed a hidden button underneath his desk, and a secret drawer inside it popped open. Murdock examined its contents, finding a small black book labeled "SECRET ILLEGAL DOINGS." He flipped through the pages, looked up, and grimaced.

"There are a couple thousand names in this book."

"It's a start," said Carl. He put out his hand to Murdock. "Let's do what we do best."

Murdock slapped him five, and then they and the other cops headed for the door. As they were leaving, Ram noticed something odd.

"Hey, Carl, what's that in your butt?" he asked.

Carl felt around, eventually pulling out a large white sheet of paper that had been sticking rather obviously out of his back pocket.

"I have no idea," said Carl as he began to analyze it. "When did that get there?"

Everybody shrugged, not wanting to confess that his ample buttocks were worth the occasional glance. As Carl read the handwritten letter, his eyes grew wider and wider.

"It's from Manuel," he said. "He wants us to meet him at the video arcade."

7

Only children carrying mouthguards were admitted to the Rumble Til Ya Crumble Arcade, because so much blood had soaked into the carpet from disputes between kids following lost games that nobody knew the carpet was supposed to be white anymore. Beating a human opponent at a competitive arcade game was a matter of personal pride, and the only way to uphold one's honor following a defeat was to have it out with fists flying. While brass knuckles brought in from outside were prohibited on the premises, tickets accumulated from game machines could coincidentally be traded for brass knuckles at the prize desk. As such, the best of the best at the arcade came to be known as prize fighters. The physical bouts that took place between any two boys after a round of an arcade game had in themselves become a sport, and bookies took down bets on the backs of bubble gum wrappers with their dinosaur pencils.

"Who's lookin' good in the thoid?" asked one shifty youth, munching on a lollipop.

"Well, Joey Split-Lip's been on a mean streak all week, but I heard his girl just left him for someone with a bigger backpack. Johnny Punchout's a little over the hill, don't have the eye of the tiger no more, but you'll never see a head screwed on any straighter. For my money, I'm bettin' on Punchout," explained a heavier youth with a lazy eye and disheveled dirty blonde hair.

"Yeah? Gettin' that choked up over a goil? Some guys," remarked the first with a head shake.

Ram Van Bamf and the police caught no sight of Manuel as they arrived. Even though Fran had badly wished to go with them, she would be caught up in insurance meetings for the rest of the day that could not be postponed.

"Boy, been a while since I've been to an arcade," said Fury, beaming with nostalgia. "I used to be lightning back in the day. Couldn't stop my haymakers! Bap, bap, bap! They called me Kid Furious."

"And now we are the ones tasked with stopping these kids from beating each other's heads in," said Carl. "I guess it's funny how life works out."

"Where could Manuel be?" asked Ram, lifting a game cabinet to check for Manuel-sized trapdoors.

"There's no guarantee the person who wrote that letter is Manuel, even if we didn't recover his body," said Murdock. "But whoever wanted us here will reveal themselves in time."

"Right, and until then, video games!" said Fury.

For the sake of Ultratropolis, the police proceeded to play every game in sight. Wilson exhibited supernatural technique as he sashayed from machine to machine, racking up high scores everywhere he went with apparently no effort, a parade of youngsters cheering him on all the while. Fury returned to his bread and butter, *Red Star Detonator*, an old outer space shooter where hundreds of enemy energy bullets littered the screen at any given moment. Meanwhile, Carl and Murdock put their skills to the test playing cooperatively in *Crime Crisis Cops IV*, a game where plastic weapons were pointed and fired at the screen to terminate criminals.

"Carl, ten o'clock!" warned Murdock, and he unloaded a whole clip into the unexpected perp.

"Thanks, pal. You really saved my hide on that one," said Carl, and they exchanged a masculine hand grip, their thick forearms flexed.

"It's what we do," said Murdock as he reloaded.

"No way! The sergeant's about to take down King Dedd with the Ultrasoldier!" exclaimed a tall boy with a hanging jaw.

An even larger procession generated around Wilson as he went about defeating the final boss of the *Mega Warriors Lux* arcade game, itself based on a television series that served as a precursor to the *Mega Warriors Infinity* series currently playing on DOA-13. All incarnations of the series involved humans being selected to receive special powers to combat evil as the Mega Warriors, and in *Lux*, the Mega Warriors could summon and pilot a giant robot known as the Ultrasoldier to confront the most dangerous threats.

"Oh, so *that's* how you dodge Dedd's lightning bolts!" said another boy. "Go, sarge, go!"

Ram did not have any such aptitude for video games himself, particularly because the controllers always got demolished in his hands the instant the action heated up. Instead, he was content to wander and observe, and he won fifty cents when he placed a smart bid on Johnny Punchout in the third. But when Ram saw the card for the next fight, he thought he must have been confused.

"Am I reading this right?" he asked to the same heavy youth with the lazy eye.

"Probably, big fella. It's a recent addition, and when I say recent, I mean as of twenty-five seconds ago. It's a fast-paced sport, ya see."

"Aww, don't he know I got Rocky Marciano blood runnin' through these veins? I'm gonna lay him out is what I'm gonna do!" declared Little Jimmy, swinging his free fist with reckless abandon while he still held Sally's hand with the other.

"It'll be an interesting bout, for sure," continued the heavy youth to Ram. "On the one hand, bein' practically handcuffed to his girl is quite the handicap. On the other hand, Little Jimmy's a southpaw in the first place, and that's the hand he's still got to work with. The odds are six to one against him, so there's quite a payday to be had if he wins."

"Put me down on him for a dollar!" said Ram, and the room gasped at his big money gamble.

"Whoa, there, fella. You know I ain't the bookie, and besides, what ya tryin' to do, break the bank?" said the heavy youth.

A little embarrassed, Ram retreated from the limelight, but by then, Little Jimmy and Sally had taken notice of him.

"Ram! Nice of you to come out and support me here," said Little Jimmy, and Sally nodded with enthusiasm. But Sally was clearly excited to see Ram for a different reason, as indicated by her disconcerting pout and the splash of anxiety that had welled up in her bright blue eyes. Nonetheless, even with her long, dark curls tousled and her pink dress crinkly at the bottom, she could not help looking utterly adorable.

"Yeah, about that, Little Jimmy," said Ram as he massaged his knuckles, "how'd you get yourself all tied up in something like this? Prize fighting's a rough game."

"Aww, you shoulda heard him, Ram! Talkin' to my girl, actin' like he could make her happy better than me! And that was after he beat me in a racing game on a technicality. I had a flat tire! What was I supposed to do?"

"So you're gonna fight him now, huh?" asked Ram.

"Nah, I'm gonna tenderize him! I'm gonna give the papers a headline! I'm gonna give him an all expenses paid trip to the bottom of a bottle of painkillers!"

Sally shook her head as much as her neck would allow, tugging on Little Jimmy's sleeve.

"Now, now, Sally, I gotta do it. For my honor and yours both," he said as he fixed his newsboy cap. Sally's shoulders sunk.

"Well, if that's how you feel, good luck to you then," conceded Ram, and he patted Little Jimmy on the head.

"You'se gonna need more 'an luck to win, buddy," said Little Jimmy's opponent, munching on a new lollipop. "And once you on the floor, countin' stars and wonderin' where the moon is in all of it, I'll be steppin' out with your goil!"

Little Jimmy just about took a swing at him then, but Sally refused to budge from where she stood.

"Better watch it there, champ," advised the heavy youth, coming up on Little Jimmy. "You got hunger on your side, but Sonny the Sandman Norton is an established vet. Catch him after his third lollipop and ya might as well play dead."

"For his sake, he better hope he's only *playin'* dead when I'm done with him," said Little Jimmy with teeth showing.

The heavy youth left Little Jimmy to his own devices then, and the match was soon underway. The referee, a retired fighter who had gone by the name Jesse Jawbreaker, presided over the proceedings, and he inspected both fighters' hands before the bout began.

"Alright now, this is a clean match," he said, and he commanded authority from the faint hints of facial hair around his lip. "No weapons, no punching below the belt, and no telling on the other guy to your mom or the principal when this is all over. When you fall down, you have to the count of ten to get up. If you look like a mess, if you look like you can't take another hit, I'm stopping the fight. I am the final word here. Okay, let's have a good fight."

Little Jimmy and Sonny Norton touched knuckles according to tradition, their hands having been bandaged in advance. Sally still held Little Jimmy's hand, but she stood off to the side, hoping not to get punched in the ovaries. A perimeter of boys formed around the three of them, creating a square that simulated a ring. Candi the ring girl strolled across the perimeter, carrying a "ROUND 1" sign, blowing a kiss to the audience as she went.

"Prize fighters, first round, have at it!" instructed the ref.

Little Jimmy came out like a typhoon of knuckled vengeance, but Sally proved to be as encumbering as the audience had anticipated. He had trouble connecting with his shots, whereas Sonny made Little Jimmy feel the error of his ways with every missed opportunity. To onlookers, it was less a fight than it was Sonny whaling on a crash test dummy. He was called the Sandman for good reason, and as Little Jimmy fumbled and lumbered, Sonny kept singing him lullabies in the face and body. By the time someone clang a ruler on a tin pencil case to signify the end of the first round, Little Jimmy was in bad shape.

"Aww, I'm just gettin' warmed up!" said Little Jimmy as he meandered back to his corner, though it took some effort from Sally to get him there. The mouthguard in his hand was lined with a very fine coating of blood, and his newsboy cap was crumpled somewhere on the floor.

"I dunno, Little Jimmy, seems like Sonny's a pretty good fighter. Maybe you should just call it quits," said Ram. "Sally doesn't look too happy to see you getting hit either."

Sally put both her hands around Little Jimmy's hand, pleading for him to stop, but he waved her hand away.

"No, I got this. Now I get his strategy. I'll just be smarter next round."

Another round and another 180 seconds later, although Little Jimmy's head had enlarged significantly, it was not due to a dramatic increase in intellect.

"Seriously, pal, I think it's time to hang it up," said Ram, and he gripped Little Jimmy's shoulder to help him discern the direction of his voice.

"No, no," he said, sluggish in movement and speech, "that ain't how a man does business."

"A man can't do any business at all if he's six feet under," reminded Ram.

Little Jimmy just lowered his head, resigned to his fate. Sonny might take the match, but he was never going to take his pride. In spite of Sally's tugging and whimpering, he made his death march to the center of the ring, ready to make his last stand. Sonny raised an eyebrow.

"Gotta say, I ain't even takin' no joy in this no more," he said with a sigh.

"Prize fighters, final round, and God help you if you bet on Little Jimmy!" said the ref. Even though Jesse Jawbreaker knew he should have already stopped the fight, he admired Little Jimmy's perseverance, and he decided it was not his place to intervene in a moment of such sterling machismo, no matter how negligent it made him as a referee. "Have at it!"

"Oh, no, you don't," interrupted Carl, breaking the perimeter of boys to get at them and inspiring many disappointed groans.

"Looks like you'se got yaself a reprieve from the angels, eh?" said Sonny, genuine relief spread across his face. "Ah, well. Seeya next bout, champ."

And Sonny would have taken his leave of the arcade, except Murdock blocked his way and pulled him aside. Carl similarly took Little Jimmy and Sally into a corner.

"What's going on here?" asked Ram as Fury and Wilson walked up.

"Well, being grownups and officers and all, it's our duty to discourage the kids from walloping each other, even though it's exactly the stuff we did when we were kids," said Fury. "Kind of fun to watch the differences in the captain and the lieutenant's technique, actually."

"You rearranged that kid's face, little man," said Murdock, arms akimbo to a timid Sonny. "What if we would have let that continue? You really could have put him on a stretcher, and the last guy we put on a stretcher in this town exploded in his ambulance! Is that what you wanted? For that kid to explode?"

"No, sir," said Sonny, hands together.

"And think about his poor mama! How would your mama feel if you came home looking like a piece of abstract art? It would probably melt her into tears, and that's exactly how that boy's mother is going to feel today. You're not the only person with feelings, little man, and I don't just mean the feeling of getting an anvil dropped on your chin. You get it?"

"Yes, sir," said Sonny, tearing up a little, not just from fear of Murdock but because he could actually imagine his mother in such a situation. He pulled a new lollipop out of his pocket to provide himself a distraction.

"Come now, you have better sense than that," began Carl, addressing Little Jimmy. "What was the point in that display just now? To defend your honor? Against some kid you barely know? Do you suppose when you go to get a job out of college, employers will be impressed by the fact that you gotten beaten within an inch of your life at an arcade when you were a kid?"

"Aww, nah, I suppose not," said Little Jimmy, watching Carl through narrow slits in his swollen eye sockets. Sally unwound the bandages on his bloody knuckles so that she could reuse them to nurse his face.

"That's right. And do you know what kinds of effects a pounding like you got can have on a growing boy's development? Nothing good, I can tell you that much. It is important to have a backbone and to take pride in yourself as a person, but not at the cost of common sense. Pick your battles, and know when to be the bigger man. You read me, son?"

"Yes, sir, I do," said Little Jimmy as Sally scrubbed him. He and Carl both knew that Little Jimmy would not change a thing if he could do it over again, except that he would try to get hit less. But Little Jimmy did understand what Carl meant.

"Hey, you're right, that was fun," said Ram to Fury. Sonny, Little Jimmy, and Sally all left the arcade soon afterward, along with several others who had had their fill of blood sports for the day. The Rumble Til Ya Crumble Arcade was nearly empty then, except for Ram and the police.

"Alright, I get a dramatic entrance, but this is ridiculous," said Fury. "Where the heck is Manuel, or the doppelganger that wrote a letter for him?"

And on cue, Manuel Salas himself burst through the front doors, off-balance and with eyes bulging. The difference since the last time Ram had seen him was that his body seemed to have been entirely replaced with a sleek, shiny robot body. His head was the only thing that still appeared human.

"Oh, finally!" cried Manuel, collapsing to his robot knees. "First my car broke down, then the cab took me to the wrong arcade, then I forgot I left a cake in the oven. I tell you, this is the worst thing that's happened to me since I exploded."

"Manuel, what the heck happened to you?" asked Ram. "You look like you got bit by a radioactive Tin Man."

"No, don't call me that name anymore! I am no longer Manuel Salas," he hissed. "Today, I am *Mecha Manuel Salas*! Still as foxy as before, but now with a sweet cyborg body! You see? Even when Gyakusatsu kills you, he makes you better! I tell you, the guy must have had a great upbringing."

"We get it—you're a conniving moron with a good medical plan," said Murdock. "Cut to the chase. Why are we here?"

"Hey, now, don't you go thinking you call the shots in this city anymore," said Mecha Manuel. "This city belongs to Gyakusatsu, and me by association. I think. Honestly, I've never asked how the organization works. But that's beside the point. The point is, I'm not afraid of any you."

Then he took a quick look around.

"That scary hot chick isn't here, is she?"

"No," said Ram.

"Then I'm not scared of any of you!"

"Tell us what you want," demanded Carl.

"Fine!" Mecha Manuel said, and he made his best effort to spread his legs out and pump his chest to appear menacing. "As it turns out, the good doctor Gyakusatsu is a fan of you guys in Lethal Enforcer. He really likes your sound."

"Gyakusatsu is a doctor?" asked Fury.

"Uh, never mind. You're not supposed to know that. I'm not even supposed to know that," said Mecha Manuel with a finger to his mouth. "Anyway, like I said, Gyakusatsu is a fan. In fact, he is *so* much of a fan of Lethal Enforcer that he could not bear to see you lose Battle of the Bands!"

"What does that mean?" asked Carl.

"Well, the Battle of the Bands you guys are playing is no ordinary competition, is it? It's right here in the city at The Bloody Wolf, the most vicious freaking venue on the planet! You guys don't even get a prize for winning. The prize is just knowing that you're the best there is, period."

"We *know* that," growled Murdock. "Spit it out already!"

"Okay. Gyakusatsu wants you to win Battle of the Bands and show the world that Lethal Enforcer is the best act in metal. That's all. But if you lose, my master will completely annihilate Ultratropolis."

A period of grave and absolute silence seized hold of the arcade then, aside from dozens of game cabinets blaring so much noise that it was difficult to hear what had been said in the first place.

"So, that's all I brought you out here to say," concluded Mecha Manuel, shrugging his shoulders and extending a hand. "I guess I'll be going now—unless you would dare try to stop me."

The police turned to Ram.

"Okay," he said, and he advanced on the lanky cyborg.

"Ha ha! Know my wrath!" exclaimed Mecha Manuel, and he suddenly pulled a cyborg boa constrictor out of his back. "Meet the Battle Boa, the ultimate fusion of animal and machine. That crazy hot chick won't be tossing him out any windows this time!"

Then he hurled the Battle Boa at Ram, only to have Ram catch it and casually throw it out a window and into the stratosphere.

"Awwwww," moaned Mecha Manuel.

He gave himself up without a fight then, and the police immediately resolved to have him placed with the worst of the worst at Ultratropolis Penitentiary until they could decide what else to do with him. Having revealed that Gyakusatsu was some type of doctor, Mecha Manuel must have known something more they could use in discerning his master's true identity, but the police were not sure how to extract that information. Mecha Manuel no longer feared death now that he was convinced his master would keep reanimating his gnarled corpse, and he would not feel any pain in his cyborg body if Ram suddenly decided to crush him into a paperweight, so violence was ruled out as a means of persuasion. It would take good old-fashioned interrogation to get the truth out of him, but that would have to wait.

Lethal Enforcer had suddenly been pulled into the spotlight unlike ever before. If the arcade was where boys became men, the place where Lethal Enforcer would perform was where men went to die. It would take everything they could muster to win.

"We need to make these last few days of practice count," said Carl to nobody in particular. "We are at the top of our game right now, but we need to make sure we stay there until Battle arrives."

"Don't sweat it, captain," said Fury. "What are the odds of us having a falling out between now and Battle?"

8

The Bloody Wolf had a fabled history amongst music venues for having killed more people since its conception than most nineteenth century coal mines did in their entire lifetimes. Had its original owners known they were constructing a deathtrap, they would have invested their money elsewhere, or they would have at least done a better job of marketing it. The Bloody Wolf began life as The Happy Pup, a venue established for families to gather and enjoy music from the community together. The business did well until the night that a mad dog inexplicably burst through the front door and mauled a boy's face off on his birthday. Children became too afraid to come around after that, so the owners changed the venue's name to The Mad Dog Club and altered their format to cater to metal enthusiasts. Once again, business picked up, until a pack of wolves lost in winter time decided to seek asylum at the club, resulting in the biting death of every person in attendance who was not wearing spiked leather. After that, the owners changed the name one last time to The Wolf Pack, this time promising a haven for aspiring rappers. However, the owners had forgotten to get rid of all the wolves that had never left, and a whole generation of rappers was lost in one fateful night.

In the end, the owners grew tired of wrongful death suits and sold the site to a man known only as Halstein. It was this man who christened the venue with its final name, The Bloody Wolf, when he single-handedly slew every freeloading wolf with a mighty axe he called Vidar. Afterward, the venue yielded to destiny and transmuted into the last and greatest bastion of true metal from around the world. Only then did concert deaths stop being treated as a tragedy and instead receive acceptance as just another part of the experience.

After all, to enter The Bloody Wolf was to step through the haze and look upon the abyss in its utmost clarity; it was a realm where language and perception untwisted to reveal the brutality intrinsic to all things. Insanity and fatality were inescapable for minds seldom equipped to face such truths, and yet that did not stop the possessed masses from materializing out of the nether in furious herds. Man and beast alike found themselves drawn beyond all sense of reason to The Bloody Wolf at one time or another, moshing and chanting together in a pit soaked with the remains of those who succumbed to their mortality. By its very nature, The Bloody Wolf was a citadel of death and carnage erected on the backs of monsters to bring hell to the world.

And those who survived became gods.

"Gods don't live in an apartment beside a strip club, Carl," said Fury, adjusting his boots.

"The whole reason you live there is because of the strip club," said Carl.

"Ah, that's right, I forgot."

Lethal Enforcer had arrived at The Bloody Wolf for Battle of the Bands, the most visceral of gladiator contests. Since the dawn of the electric axe and its mentor the PA system, combat had been revolutionized into a symphonic clash of wills that laid bare the rage of all humanity. For one night in Ultratropolis, metal bands selected internationally by Halstein himself would perform and pass final judgment on the whole of the Earth, the entirety of human existence teetering on the edge of ultimate inferno. Nothing would ever be the same afterward.

"Seriously, Carl, you're good at the dramatic speeches," said Fury.

"I will confess—I've been practicing."

The fate of the world hung in the balance in potentially more ways than one, if Mecha Manuel's secondhand threat was to be believed. The police doubted that any one man excluding Ram Van Bamf could really possess the power to destroy an entire city, but that did not make them any less anxious. It was Lethal Enforcer's civic duty to win.

"I'll be rooting for you, guys," said Ram with pumped fists. Ram had volunteered to be their security detail, which in itself guaranteed the band would suffer no intentional harassment. When a man working the stage lights accidentally bumped into Wilson, he apologized enough times that Wilson somehow ended up owning a new sports car and a farm in Puerto Rico by the time their conversation ended. While this was all a far cry from Ram's original plan of doing and attempting nothing to unravel the growing conspiracy, he thought it was for the best for the city.

As the many bands prepared in the backstage area, the ticketholders finally began receiving admittance. The Bloody Wolf had no capacity limit, because it was too difficult to calculate how many human occupants should constitute one lemur or elephant, both of which were just as eager and deserving to purchase a ticket as any human. In the end, it was decided that anyone and everyone could purchase a ticket for a concert, and nature would sort out who lived long enough to enjoy the show. The inherent fairness of the policy ensured the happiness of all parties involved, even the families tasked with shoveling up the distinguishable pieces of their lost loved ones afterward.

In spite of the danger involved, people from all walks of life found themselves drawn inexorably to the event, and there were many familiar faces in the crowd. Warden Warmaker exchanged gruesome anecdotes with Halstein over the very spot where the child lost his face so many years ago. Ruttiger and a recently released Fuzzy sat drinking at the bar while Elmo courted the bartender with hip gyrations thought reserved for gypsy dancers. Even a recovering Little Jimmy and Sally found a couple of open stools at the bar, though they had brought their own juice boxes from home.

"Nothin' like a good blast of Merry Berry," said Little Jimmy with a satisfying gulp, and Sally lovingly tightened her grip on his hand.

Ram peeked out from the backstage curtains to take in the audience. Everybody appeared to be the appropriate level of savage and deranged, nothing out of the ordinary. If Gyakusatsu was in the audience, he had no way of knowing yet.

"You've been doing a really good thing lately," said Fran, coming up on Ram from behind. She had been informed about the episode at the arcade as soon as she left her insurance meetings, and she was not about to miss any more of the action. Officially, Fran had been admitted to the backstage area as Wilson's groupie, prompting countless thumbs-ups and whistling between Wilson and the backstage people who got to admire her. Having an outfit for literally every occasion, Fran was now dressed like a trashy biker, except that her leather flat cap and denim short shorts alone cost a combined $2,500.

"What, standing around? Yeah, I've always been praised for my ability to do that. Thanks for noticing."

"No," and Fran smiled slightly, having become accustomed to Ram's unabashed stupidity by now, "I'm talking about you being here, now, helping me and the police with this mess. You may be freakishly, impossibly strong, but that doesn't mean you have any obligation to us or Ultratropolis. You could be anywhere else in the world right now, but you're not. You're here, trying to protect everyone."

Ram's first instinct was to take offense to being called a freak, but then he realized that this was the first time he had ever seen Fran smile without contempt or bloodlust, so he let it go.

"It's not a big deal," he said. "If Rambo were in my situation, he would do the same thing."

"Not likely," countered Fran with unexpected conviction. "Rambo would have already hunted Gyakusatsu back to his lair, killed him, burnt down his compound, and saved a third-world country."

If Ram had been caught off-guard by Fran before, he did not even know what to call this.

"Huh, guess you're right. Too bad I'm not Rambo then," he said with a hesitant chuckle. He stared at her for a few seconds, his face as blank as a petition to ban cleavage. "I didn't know you knew Rambo."

Fran's gaze began to fly in all directions, some nervous energy building in her.

"Why don't you go check out the crowd?" she blurted at last. "Have a good look around. The guys will be happy to get your 'OK' that nobody will impede their performance."

Before Ram could respond, Fran had already hurried away. She went to check on the police, who had little left to do at this point as they sat around their gear in a large open space. They would be the third of seven bands to perform, so it would still be some time before they had to set up their instruments.

"Ready to rock?" Fran asked, though she immediately regretted how corny she sounded.

"You could say that," said Carl with a half-polite, half-mocking smirk.

"We should play the new song," brooded Murdock as he strummed a few chords at a subdued pace.

"We tried, Murdock," said Carl. "But you only just showed it to us. There hasn't been enough time to practice it, and Lethal Enforcer gives it everything it's got or nothing at all."

"I know, Carl, I know," Murdock said with an eye roll. "Don't lecture me about my own band."

Fury, usually eager to distribute his unique brand of hip urban wit, was slow to chime in now.

"If I have to sit through another hour of the two of you, that's gonna require a drink or six. I'll catch you guys in a little while."

Fury nudged Wilson with an elbow.

"You wanna come?"

Wilson nodded, and the two of them disappeared into the many rooms and corridors of the backstage area. Fran was alone now with Carl and Murdock, who had both become uncharacteristically distant all of a sudden, and not just because they were standing thirty feet away from each other.

"Something the matter?" asked Fran in a loud voice so that they could hear her from either direction.

"No. All we have to do is go out there and win, so that's how it's going to be," said Murdock, though his gaze never left the floor.

"Yeah," grunted Carl.

Fran sighed with heavy, audible disgust. Any semblance of pleasance in her mood had just disintegrated like so many ray gun victims.

"We do *not* have time for this crap," she began, shooting her head back and forth between the two of them. "If you screw this up, people might die. If you lose just because you don't have the chops, fine. There's nothing you can do about that. But if you lose because you suddenly decide to implode, that's on *you*, and it's *all* on you. I don't know what happened, and I don't care. *Fix it.* I don't want to see this city buried because the two of you decided your bromance isn't working out anymore."

Fran stormed off, bicycle kicking the nearest vending machine as she left. Sweet and salty snacks spilled out all over the floor like someone had just cut open the fattest man at a buffet, and backstage workers rushed to commit as much theft as possible.

The first band, Murder Engine out of Germany, prepped to take the center stage. Halstein, himself a fan of each band performing, stood at the front of the crowd. He drank from a goblet of the finest pig's blood, while his friend Warmaker just enjoyed scotch. It was easy for Ram to find them in the crowd, as Halstein and Warmaker dwarfed everyone else in the audience aside from Ram himself.

"Ram Van Bamf! The toughest man I have never had to kill," declared Halstein as he and Ram exchanged a handshake so firm that nuclear fusion was achieved between their palms.

"Guess we should both be thankful, huh?" responded Ram.

With veins bursting and winding like a convulsing dragon and a beard that echoed the most victorious years of Odin, Halstein struck terror into the hearts of people who had never even met him. He was the unseen in nightmares and the guttural scream of the beast. He was fangs and claws and the death red moon. He was the price of humanity, the Other, the story of oblivion. Halstein was no landlord to The Bloody Wolf; The Bloody Wolf was merely another reflection, another consequence, of Halstein. Rage and fire coursed through his body like a life force. When the curtain closed on the cosmos, Halstein would remain, an insatiable Vidar in hand.

Ram and Warmaker got along great with Halstein.

"What have I missed?" asked Ram.

"Ah, nothing much, just swapping the same old war stories," said Warmaker as he stroked his rad 'stache.

"Warmaker dispatched the Vietcong and liberated the disenfranchised, while I rent asunder the jaws of the World Serpent and immolated the hydra, but we fought the same war. And though the universal fiend need only claim a new mask to be born again, the glory of conquest is a treasure worth repeated rediscovery," observed Halstein with a proud, bloody grin.

"Yeah, and I punched a dinosaur," said Ram.

"A feat of which even I am envious," said Halstein with eyes narrowed.

And then a blackness suddenly took the room. It could only mean one thing.

"Geh zum Teufel!" screeched a voice that sounded like a broken violin played with a knife.

Murder Engine had fallen upon the unsuspecting crowd. A snarling, hissing dissonance tore and bled through the speakers until the startled prey erupted into a mad frenzy. Ram, not unlike Warmaker and Halstein, remained as immovable as Excalibur in the rock while an ocean of lunatics gushed back and forth in lethal waves. Several of these berserkers and maenads would not survive to the end of the first hunt.

"Lethal Enforcer has some stiff competition!" yelled Ram so that the others could hear him.

"Indeed!" said Halstein, his wild white hair surrounding his face like a mane as he tilted his head back. His voice seemed to carry to every corner of the room without assistance. "But what Lethal Enforcer lacks in experience, it recovers with unbridled originality. There is no dark horse in this race, only untamable stallions brought up on a diet of that which the eagles did not peck from Prometheus."

"You talk so cool," said Ram.

Warmaker put a hand on Ram's shoulder.

"Van Bamf, I've been keeping an eye out," said Warmaker with an expression almost severe enough to be a scowl, "but nothing doing. It was good of you to tell me everything you've learned about this Gyakusatsu monster. He must be the person causing the whispers among the inmates. I've got my ears to the ground, both here and at the penitentiary, but I haven't learned anything we can use yet."

"Well, I wouldn't expect you to. The ground isn't known for squealing."

Warmaker took his hand off Ram slowly and lowered his head, disappointed with himself to have expected any other response.

"Thanks anyway, though, warden," said Ram. He nodded courteously to Warmaker and Halstein. "I should keep patrolling the area for suspicious activity. I'll catch up with you guys later."

Still unable to find anything out of place amongst the hordes, Ram decided to investigate the bar next. At its elevated position, the bar escaped the most immediate threat of the mobs, but getting there proved difficult. Knocking people over or brushing aside that one buffalo that seemed to have developed a taste for human flesh was no trouble; it was all the crying children clinging to Ram's legs and begging him to find their missing, dead parents in the crowd who proved to be a real hindrance.

"Look, kids, I don't have time for this. I promise to get you all adopted next week, okay?"

The children lit up with satisfaction at this proposition, and they dispersed in a chorus of jolly chirps. With his calves freed up, Ram proceeded to the bar. There was a narrow stairway along the wall leading up, the steps sticky and corroded like everything else at the venue. Fortunately, there were enough unconscious patrons juxtaposed along the steps that it were as if a vindictive grandmother had stitched together a human rug out of relatives who did not visit.

"So then I said to the cops in my cell, 'You call this food? I've had a better meal with my head shoved in dirt!' So that's when Murdock shoved my head in dirt. He sure did call my bluff."

Fuzzy finished his glass and slammed it down on the table, but amidst the anarchy it made almost no sound at all.

"It's more lenient than the place I would've shoved your head," said Ruttiger with a raised lip.

"You guys crack me up," said Ram as he puts his hands on their backs.

"Ram! I knew you'd turn up in a place that had free-roaming alligators," said Ruttiger.

"Well, I do like reptiles," confessed Ram.

"Reptiles?" repeated a middle-aged man on another stool. His eyes could not agree on one object of focus, opting to look in two different directions at any one time. He wore a brown leather coat to disguise the fact that he had not changed his clothes in days, a fact which was betrayed by his odor that smelled like a dozen sweaty butts in a race to dislodge the most diarrhea. "I worked wit' sum reptiles in MY day. BIG freakin' beasts, they were."

He was also drunk.

"Shut up, lush. It's bad enough that stuffing my nose with dirty diapers would be a step up from what I'm smelling out of you. Don't punish my ears too," said Ruttiger.

"Yeah, that's my department!" beamed Fuzzy.

"Aww, let's go easy on the guy," said Ram. "Maybe he's a down-on-his-luck sewer worker or something. You don't know."

"Sewers?" said the drunk, and he started to laugh in a measured, mocking cadence. "Nice try! Somethin' way worse 'an a REPtile down there!"

"Would you killjoys be so kind as to pipe down and let a silver fox work his magic?" said Elmo, who by now was standing on top of his stool thrusting his pelvis in a dance that had been banned in the Dominican Republic for its subversive content. "This bartender has two children and I think I am rendering her eager to have her third!"

The busty brunette bartender, suitably hypnotized by his movements at this point, could only agree with Elmo via her gaping-mouthed silence. A river of drool poured down her bra.

"I really gotta take a yoga class," reflected Ruttiger.

"Just as soon as they repeal that rule against letting wildlife into the class, right, Rut?" said Fuzzy, tugging on Ruttiger's forearm hair. Ruttiger responded with a quick swat to the back of Fuzzy's head. "You're not helping your case much acting like that, Rut."

"Sure I am, Fuzz. I'm building a case for temporary insanity," said Ruttiger with a sneer.

"I don't get it," said Fuzzy.

"Aww, gee, you guys, why you always gotta act like that 'round my girl?" said Little Jimmy, squeezing his empty juice box. "Pretty little thing like my Sally don't have to hear such verbal abuse."

Considering what he had just put her through, Sally snorted at the comment.

"Sorry, Little Jimmy," said Fuzzy and Ruttiger in unison.

"Hey, Little Jimmy," said Ram, "what are you doing at such a dangerous place? You and Sally should be at home on a night like this."

"Sally wanted to come," said Little Jimmy with a shrug. "And I do whatever makes my doll happy."

"Happy!" barked the drunk, apparently only able to talk when the right codeword was spoken. "How ePHEMeral a concept! Just ask my GREAT friend, the thief, the BUTCHER! Such a MERRY time he 'ad of flushin' me down the drain. B'bye job! B'bye friend! B'bye POWer!"

"Look, guys," said Ram, ignoring the drunk, "none of you have seen anything extra suspicious around here, have you? Nothing that looks like it could signal the beginning of a city or universe-dooming apocalypse?"

"You mean aside from Battle of the Bands?" asked Ruttiger, pointing at a man in the audience being ripped apart by that same mean buffalo.

"Yeah."

"Nope, can't say that we have."

"Huh, okay," said Ram with an extra pouty lip. "Well, if anything changes, just let me know. I'll be around."

He made a sudden stop.

"Say, do any of you guys hear a really high pitch noise? Like a dog whistle?" he asked.

"Humans can't hear dog whistles," said Ruttiger. "Well, except maybe you."

Ram nodded with a tight jaw and a concerned glare. This warranted a closer listen. As he turned back down the stairs, Fuzzy started on a new drink.

"Ram Van Bamf is a real class act, huh? Trying to keep the peace in a place like this," he said.

"Ram Van Bamf!" yelled the drunk with unprecedented ire. "Where? Where is he?"

Everyone stared at him like he was crazy, and when they remembered that he probably was crazy, most of them looked away.

"Ram was the big guy who paid us a friendly visit just now," said Fuzzy. "Boy, I dunno how you miss a guy like that."

"Well, it's EASY when your eyes pick 'n choose what 'ta SEE," snarled the drunk, pointing at his eyes that were currently looking at a garbage can and a defecating rat respectively. "Ram Van Bamf ruined my LIFE! Him and that OTHER guy."

"Yeah, well, Ram ruins a lot of people's lives," said Ruttiger without sympathy. "He did drop a mountain on some sexy lady's business the other day. Doesn't make him any less of a good guy."

"Mountain!" cried the drunk, and a frightening lucidity came over him ever so briefly, a sobering hatred washing away the madness. His eyes snapped into focus, as if he could have willed it to happen any time. When he spoke now, everybody listened. "If Ram Van Bamf would have died on that mountain, I would never have been reduced to this. I would still be a man—Dr. Marvin Drago. And I would have sent Gyakusatsu to Hell."

And then the drunk finally passed out, plummeting backward off his stool like a sniper victim. His skull broke his fall, which at least defended his liver from any further injury. Ruttiger kicked him in the face a few times to make sure he was really out.

"This is big," said Ruttiger. "Whoever this nut job is, Ram needs to know about him."

"No kidding. This guy just went from stinking to stinking *suspicious*!" said Fuzzy.

9

"It is so sad. Before all is said and done, I will have killed you all."

Whatever it was, it was constructed to appear feminine. Ram Van Bamf was staring down an enemy plated entirely in pearly white armor of cybernetic design, with pink luminescent tubes running up and down the inside of the arms and legs. The armor was sculpted in a manner to accentuate bust and hips, whether or not there was anything human housed inside, and it had long, sinuous prosthetic hair of an unnaturally rich gold. When it spoke, the voice sounded manufactured, but whether it was merely modulated or entirely invented was indiscernible. The face was nothing more than an expressionless mask, the mold of a female face that did not move. In spite of that, it stood tall and seductive, a temptress made of metal. In its own way, it was eerily beautiful, like a descending valkyrie.

"What's there to kill?" asked Ram. "There's nothing here."

He spoke the truth. They stood in a realm of empty white space as far as the eye could see, though physics still seemed to apply in some incomprehensible manner.

"You are experiencing a pocket dimension I have opened in space and time," it explained. "You stumbled upon it without any intervention on my part. And now I am afraid you will never leave, while I busy myself with destroying the city and killing all of the people you care for."

"Okay, fair enough. One more question," said Ram, cracking his knuckles, "what name should the undertaker put on your tombstone?"

"You may call me White Pandora, or merely Pandora, if you like," it said, "and our Emperor sends his regards."

Meanwhile, back in normal space-time, Fran watched a man pee on a wall.

"Um, the bathroom is right there," she said, pointing to a door directly beside the man.

"Sorry, honey, don't believe in bathrooms," he said. He lifted his cheap shades to look at her. "Whoa! It's you!"

He zipped up his pants and motioned to shake her hand, but then, recognizing his folly, he retracted the hand.

"Have we met?" asked Fran.

"Yeah, yeah! You stopped me on the street a few days ago to ask me about the fire on Mount Slipendie, remember?"

"Oh, yeah," she said, already plotting an exit strategy, "you're, uh, greasier than I remember."

"Thanks! You too, pretty lady. Those bazongas of yours look ready to burst out of that tank top."

Fran felt an abrupt, desperate need to find an overcoat.

"Do you work here?" she asked.

"I do tonight! The name is Chaz, and I'm the lead guitarist for Chainsaw Execution out of Las Vegas. I only got into town the day that we ran into each other. And now here we are again! Must be destiny, huh?"

"No."

"What are you doing in the backstage area anyway? Don't tell me you're the competition, because I don't think I could keep it in my pants if you told me you play metal."

"I do not play metal!" Fran gasped, recoiling into a capoeira stance by instinct. "I'm here on official police business. But I guess the short answer is I'm Lethal Enforcer's groupie."

"Lethal Enforcer! I love those guys, been a fan since the beginning," said Chaz. "Yeah, met them for the first time not too long ago, wasn't quite what I expected."

"What do you mean?"

Chaz had finally gotten her attention in a way that not did warrant her disgust.

"Ah, it's nothing. It's just that, well, you listen to *Lethal Enforcer*, and man, you don't just hear a thousand notes a minute. You hear brothers in arms, you know?"

Fran had never listened to Lethal Enforcer before.

"Sure."

"Yeah! Those harmonizing solos are killer. It's like, you close your eyes, and you can imagine one solo taking a bullet for the other solo, and the solo that survives goes and gets revenge. You know? Real brothers! But I wasn't getting that vibe so much when I met them. Felt more like Carl and Murdock wanted to put a bullet in each other."

"You noticed that too, huh?" said Fran, biting her lip. "I just don't understand. Last time I saw them they got along just as much as you would expect them to."

"Well, that's what a song can do to you."

"A song?"

"What, you don't know?" he asked, lifting his shades. "Yeah, man, it's all over a new song. Murdock wrote it, and from the way Fury talks it up, it sounds like *the* song. Some sorta crazy thrash metal masterpiece. A ten minute beast with solos that trade off between Carl and Murdock the whole time, but at the end of the song, their guitars join together into something that's supposed to melt your face into a crappy-tasting soup! Or at least that's how Fury sees it. Anyways, Carl doesn't think the band is ready to play it yet, and that's the problem."

"Really, that's all?" asked Fran, a little annoyed. "Murdock mentioned a new song before. Is he just being a crybaby that the others won't play his song?"

"Could be," shrugged Chaz. "But Fury told me that Carl's a quick study. Told me he can learn how to play pretty much anything in a day. And Fury's just a machine, he can keep up with anything. And Wilson... Well, can you imagine a guy *that* cool ever missing a note?"

"So you're saying Fury thinks Carl's just being unnecessarily cautious?"

"Possibly. So, maybe Carl and Murdock both have a leg to stand on."

Fran absorbed the situation. Maybe there was still time to fix this. She had to try.

"Thanks for the chat, Chaz," she said. "You're not quite the pig I took you for."

"Is that a good thing or a bad thing? Because baby, I can get greasier."

"Please stop talking."

Any stress Fran may have felt in her conversation was of little merit compared to the more literal variety Ram Van Bamf was experiencing at the moment. As it turned out, while White Pandora was allegedly not a killer robot, it was still a good facsimile for one. With thrusters in its calves and soles unsheathed, it flew across the white void at more than twice the speed of sound, a streak of pink lingering in the air behind it. Ram felt its right hook connect with him dead in the jaw, and he fell backward almost as far as Pandora had traveled to hit him, bouncing and rolling the whole way.

"Hey, you're fast," said Ram with an empty grin as he got back on his feet.

"Will that be a problem?"

"Not if you keep punching like a girl."

Pandora immediately fell upon him again, but this time Ram was ready. With preternatural instinct, Ram stopped it in its tracks, grabbing it by the throat.

"Also, you're actually not that fast."

Ram headbutted it in its face, launching it into the ground with such devastating force that it bounced several stories back into the air, and it continued to bounce up and down like a super ball dropped off a roof. By the time Pandora had finally hit ground and stayed there, sparks burst out of its concussing head like heavy coughs.

"Can we go home now? Just in case you're really human, I'd rather not hurt you anymore," said Ram, rubbing the back of his neck. "I think I overdid it as is."

Pandora snapped back to its feet with unexpected elegance.

"You have done nothing of the sort. And you are not going anywhere."

Slits in its forearms slid open as thin metal rods popped out. The rods unfurled into saucer-shaped guns, the concave sides pointing outward. The saucers caressed and enveloped Ram in a shower of golden light.

She spied Ruttiger a little longer, noticing the fur rugs on his arms.

"Wait a minute, you're not a kid. You're just a moron."

Ruttiger stared at the floor, massaging his hairy knuckles.

"Well, it's just that I have this love of sci-fi, and it's not every day you get to live out your dreams, and you should see the way those punks scatter when Sally takes a bite out of your shoulder, and please don't tell anybody about this because I've got a reputa—"

"Say, Ruttiger, weren't we supposed to be doin' somethin'?" asked Little Jimmy.

Ruttiger froze, a residual piece of pumpkin sliding off his cheek in the interim.

"Aww, crud."

He looked up toward the bar in the distance, stone-faced.

"Nobody ever tells Fuzzy about this."

Little did Ruttiger know that Fuzzy was having problems of his own. Dr. Marvin Drago was a wily sort in the first place, and being a drunkard only enhanced his natural state. When he roused from his stupor with an ache like his head had been used to kick a field goal, his first thought was to get revenge on the magic typewriter that had eaten his legs. The magic typewriter was Fuzzy, and revenge consisted of gnawing at his kneecaps.

"Oh, God! Talk about a *caps lock*!" howled Fuzzy, his hands on the drunk's face, trying to pry his jaws open.

"Did typewriters have a Caps Lock key?" asked one spectator.

"Kind of," responded another.

"Eh, let's give him that one."

"Yeah, wasn't that bad a joke, considering the pain he must be in."

"I am in so much pain!" cried Fuzzy.

He finally gave the drunk an elbow to the nose that forced him off, and Fuzzy used that opportunity to reach behind the bar counter and grab a large bottle of something that he hoped would hurt a lot if used like a billy club.

"Ha! I don' care HOW many'a my legs you eat, magic typewriter! I got SEVEN more!" said the drunk, pointing to his arm pits for no apparent reason. He dropped to the floor and scurried like a spider in Fuzzy's direction. Fuzzy, fearing anything that had more legs than himself, yelped and leapt on top of the bar counter.

"Get off the counter ya moron, unless you intend to grow some hooters!" said a chubby patron.

"You know, I would, but it looks like you already beat me to it, tubby!"

"Tubby? That's it!"

And now Fuzzy was fighting off both a crazed drunk and a man with a glandular problem. But at least he would have the soundtrack to war itself as his backdrop, as Lethal Enforcer had just taken the stage. Carl had commanded the audience to fall into order, but then he declared that the first order of business was establishing mayhem. From that opening speech, they immediately segued into their opener, "Police State," and chaos reigned ever afterward.

By now, Trizon the Destroyer had reassembled, if not just for the sake of Little Jimmy and Sally.

"So you're that businesswoman whose life Ram ruined a few days ago," said Ruttiger, swinging his fists in wide arcs in the hopes of injuring anybody unwise enough to enter his threat radius.

"Yeah," said Fran with a tentative quality, leaning her head from side to side, "but that's beside the point right now. In all of the craziness, I never realized Ram was missing, but you're right—this is serious. We need to find him."

"You're tellin' us, miss!" said Little Jimmy. "Who knew it'd be so hard to find a guy that leaves a footprint big enough to drown in?"

"I need all of you to think," said Fran. "Last time you saw Ram, did he say where he was going?"

"No, nothing like that. He was just making the rounds, doing a patrol for anything fishy," said Ruttiger.

Then Sally squeezed on Little Jimmy's hand a couple times in quick succession.

"Oh, you're right, Sally! This sweet thing o' mine!" exclaimed Little Jimmy. "Ruttiger, before Ram left, he asked if any of us heard a really high-pitched sound, remember? The kind that dogs can hear! But we couldn't hear it."

"Oh, yeah! Good going, kids!" said Ruttiger. "But we still can't hear what he heard, if he really heard something in the first place. What can we do about that?"

"There's only one thing we can do," said Fran. "We need to find a dog."

White Pandora had so far imitated dogs and every other animal it could recall in its efforts to destroy Ram Van Bamf, but he proved to be as indestructible as any report had ever suggested.

"Why do you still live?" it asked, so bored with trying to kill him that it had resorted to just slapping him in the face once every few seconds.

"Good genes, I think."

"This is quite tedious."

"No kidding." Ram thought things over for a minute. "Come to think of it, why are you still here, anyway? First thing you did was tell me that you wanted to kill everybody *else* in the city. You should be torching buildings and strangling the elderly right now while I stand here very slowly trying to punch you. What gives?"

"I lied."

"You lied? Really? Can killer robots do that?"

"I told you, I am not a killer robot."

"Well, what are you then?"

And then it finally stopped hitting Ram altogether. It jumped backward and revisited the elegant, fearsome pose it had assumed when they first met.

"I am White Pandora, first of the Abandoned, conceived by Gyakusatsu, for the service of our Emperor, in the name of the Control."

"Okay. I can pretend I understood that. Is Gyakusatsu the Emperor?"

"Gyakusatsu serves our Emperor, who maintains the Control organization. Someday soon, the Control shall reign over all things. You are the only obstacle."

"Sorry about that."

"I would be more inclined to forgive you if you would die."

"That's what a lot of people say after I accidentally kill their friends and family."

"All the same, do not fret. The night is young, even if this void offers no indication of such things. You may even yet break before the first rays of sunrise."

"Hey, speaking of rays, I notice you tend to zap me with your flashlights every five minutes, give or take."

"That is an accurate observation."

"Yeah, well, you forgot the last time."

And then Ram lunged at a speed that could rival light itself, not even daring to swing a punch, as that would have ripped Pandora's head clear off its body for miles. Rather, Ram used the weight of his body itself as a blunt instrument, striking with such catastrophic impact that Pandora blasted off into the blank sky like a pink rocket and disappeared. Unfortunately, without Pandora as a reference to establish his position in space, Ram had lost all bearing of himself and the universe altogether. He was alone in empty space, possibly forever, and he began to wonder if he had really handled that situation in the best possible manner.

Fran held no such reservations herself. She was perfectly confident the pooch she and the others had located would lead them straight to Ram.

"Are you sure this is a good idea?" asked Ruttiger.

"Of course," Fran said.

"But it's tugging at that buffalo's intestines like it's in dire need of a new jump rope, and the buffalo isn't even dead yet."

"Yeah, well, that's Murdercide for you," offered Chaz.

Although ferocious animals ran rampant amongst the crowds, there were few canines, and even less canines that had not already been slain by larger animals. But Fran had remembered what Carl said about the band Murdercide employing a pit bull as a vocalist, and she thought to borrow its services if possible. To that end, she had found Chaz and enlisted him to help her negotiate for the dog backstage.

"So, you would really dare approach us with the suggestion of granting you audience with the Black Lord of Blasphemy, the Dread King of Chaos, the Satanic Sultan of Sin?" asked a member of Murdercide. The entire band was present, though they wore a uniform of white clay mask over sweeping black robes that rendered them largely indistinguishable. The concept driving the band was that every living thing in existence deserved to die, preferably via murder, and as such, they masqueraded as lifeless avatars that haunted the land and mocked the living.

"Don't you think you're pushing it with the 'Satanic Sultan' bit?" asked Ruttiger.

"Are we?" responded another member.

Ruttiger turned back to the pit bull, who had moved on to consuming the buffalo's face. The horned brute emitted one final cry of eternal misery as it passed away, a fitting end to a mean buffalo.

"You may have a point."

"So whatdya say there, boys?" asked Little Jimmy, producing a squeaky chew toy that presumably had been in his pocket the entire time. "Can we play with your dog for a little while? We'll treat him real good! And we'll give him a nice scrub before we give him back."

"A scrub!" gasped a third member.

"He was kidding!" interjected Chaz, better versed in bargaining with the seedier element of humanity. "You know kids today! Buncha snot-nosed brats thinking they run the show. No, no, we'll treat the Sultan like crap! He'll be more pissed off than ever by the time we give him back. He might even kill one of you!"

A favorable murmuring arose amongst the members of Murdercide.

"What you propose pleases us," said one of them. "We shall grant you the service of our esteemed beast with the expectation that he shall be returned with a yet even blacker heart for our nearing performance. See to it that he returns in a timely manner, or the consequences shall be grave."

"You got it," said Fran, echoing the phrase of a certain someone.

"By the way," one of the band members added, "he answers to the name 'Cecil.'"

As it turned out, Cecil did not make a habit of eviscerating big game, but ever since Murder Engine took the stage, Cecil had begun to lash out in uncharacteristically savage ways, even above the standard of violence expected of an animal at The Bloody Wolf. It pleased Fran and the others to learn this, since this change in behavior coincided with when Ram had noticed the sound that drove him to his disappearance. If something fiendish was afoot, Fran was about to discover it firsthand, just as soon as Cecil put a paw on it.

All the same, Lethal Enforcer were themselves at that moment vying to be the most fiendish force in the room. The heat of the crimson spotlights and the intensity of the playing had drenched the band in a layer of sweat which, thanks to the lights, appeared more like sacrificial blood. They had entered into their single "You Fought the Law (And We Kicked Your Ass!)" with Carl performing at a whole new level of confidence. He fed off the energy of a crowd, and the more maniacal the crowd, the more commanding and charismatic he became. Each growled lyric became a fresh indictment on the lives of every soul moshing in the pit, and every hammer-on dropped like a gavel passing a death sentence. As their opener had promised, they had established a police state, and the only freedom that remained was the right to die fighting.

But the most perceptive amongst the audience recognized a dissonance.

"You say a fiend threatens the very being of the city itself, should Lethal Enforcer not triumph in this contest?" said Halstein, arms crossed, stray drops of lasting blood falling from his emptied goblet.

"That is how Ram describes it," confirmed Warmaker, his 'stache drooping.

"Then I should hope Lethal Enforcer exorcises its demons with haste. For its existing temperament would beckon Judgment Day before it would avert it."

Meanwhile, Fuzzy beckoned his own apocalypse as he systematically made a mortal enemy of every man, woman, and rodent at the bar. His only respite was that most of his assailants were too intoxicated to remember what he looked like for any extended period, causing multiple smaller fights to break out among people who all thought they were throttling the life out of Fuzzy. As it stood, the only person who had not suffered some sort of injury that would require surgery and a frustrating rehabilitation was Fuzzy.

"Say, what is all of this fuss over a Fuzz?" asked an approaching Elmo, grinning ear to ear.

"Elmo! Where have you been?" asked Fuzzy, his back against a rack of bottles.

"Where do you think I have been? I have been busy creating a child of which I have no intention to support or remember on its birthday."

"Well, that's swell for you, but I'm in the middle of the fight of my life—all fifteen of them! I think I'm winning a couple of the fights over in the corner, but I'm mostly losing. And I think I got killed in that one over there."

"That sounds just like you in a fight," said Elmo, nodding his head. "But where is our drunk, the supposed doctor?"

Fuzzy stopped completely for a moment, like a gagged gasket had broken the whole machine.

"You lost him, eh? Ruttiger is going to be feeling the anger with you."

"You got nothing!" shouted a processed voice in the distance, a pink flare fast approaching.

Suddenly, the sterile void to which Ram had become accustomed in an instant achieved volume and substance. In fact, it seemed they had returned entirely to reality, with the venue ceiling above them and Lethal Enforcer unleashing a supersonic cacophony below them. It only became evident that something was still wrong in that Chaz was still holding open a gateway, and also in that Ram and Fran seemed to be standing on thin air above the crowd.

"Whoa! Sweet trick, guys. Let me try that!" said Chaz. He relinquished his grip on the gateway without another thought, allowing it to snap shut. Then he took a step off the rafters, expecting to float, but instead he plummeted for forty feet toward an unsuspecting crowd.

"This is cool too!" he said while making the sign of the devil with his hand.

Much to the convenience of everybody involved, Chaz ended up landing on top of a charging Cecil, softening his final impact and knocking out the bruiser of a pooch.

"Oh, no! You killed him, Chaz!" said Ruttiger, who had been chasing the animal to no effect.

"Killed him? Nah, not the Sultan! He'll just wake up extra pissed, just like we promised Murdercide in the first place. All's well that ends well!"

"Then where are Ram and Fran?"

Chaz stuck out his lip and put a hand to his chin.

"You know, I might have dropped the ball just now."

He looked back up toward the rafters, but Ram and Fran seemed to have vanished. And yet Ram and Fran were still up there whether or not Chaz or anyone else could see them, along with a returning third guest.

"I thought a change of scenery was in order," said White Pandora, seemingly as healthy as ever, standing on nothing like Ram and Fran.

"What *is* that thing?" Fran asked, and she took a few weary steps back.

"Apparently, not a killer robot," answered Ram over his shoulder. "What did you do to us anyway?"

"Nothing," said Pandora with a shake of the head. "For all intents and purposes, you are still in the white space, but I have allowed the pocket dimension to overlap with natural space. I did this so that you could witness me kill Lethal Enforcer while they perform their final song ever."

"No! Why would you do that?" said Ram. "Gyakusatsu gave them a chance to win. Even a guy like me can see there's no sense in giving their hopes up just to kill them now."

"Well, then," said Pandora, "how long do you think you can stop me from killing them?"

And just like that, Ram Van Bamf and White Pandora fell into combat one last time as Lethal Enforcer entered into their closer, the thrash metal masterpiece conceived by Murdock. On either stage, carnage was fraught as hearts bled with determination. Never before had the strife of the human condition been so encapsulated in one space, even if it technically occurred over two dimensions. The force of the blows exchanged between Ram and his nemesis reverberated like a parade of earthquakes, threatening the integrity of the dimension itself, while Fran could do nothing but bounce and shake without anything to ground herself. She was a crowd of one, bearing witness to the most awesome clash ever imagined, while just underneath her, a crowd of thousands bore witness to the most heated battle ever fought on any battlefield.

Fury could feel a tingle in his bones, like he had surrendered his body to the heavens and his feet and drumsticks were commanded by lightning itself now. On his drums, he could invoke rain, thunder, a hundred kinds of natural desolation. And now he channeled it all into this moment, for this song.

Wilson was a stoic undercurrent, the rhyme and the reason belying a deluge. His fingers grooved up and down the fretboard like frogs across lily pads, an effortless exercise in serenity. It was then during this song that his shades took on a quality of truth, that his shades became the best representation of himself. Whereas eyes reflected fear and uncertainty, shades only absorbed, only perceived. Wilson had no use for eyes anymore.

Carl crashed into his final solo like a tsunami against a skyscraper, shattering eardrums and breaking spirits with equal abandon. Many in the audience had already begun to collapse, having drowned in the blitzkrieg of sound that rippled and echoed to inundate every corner and crevice of the building. Carl realized now that his fears had been unfounded. This was the song that would save Ultratropolis, and none of them were about to make a mistake now. All the pieces had fallen into place. Lethal Enforcer was in perfect sync. All that remained was the harmonized solo at the finale, where two axes would join forces to deliver a deathblow to all of creation, washing the Earth clean to usher in a new era of metal.

Murdock found himself lumbering through every chord, placing the weight of his entire body into every strum. He thought if he hit the strings hard enough that he could punish them all for even thinking themselves worthy of the song he crafted out of his own literal sweat and blood. As the harmonized solo approached, the intensity of his playing escalated beyond any boundary that even his bandmates understood. Murdock was set to explode, and he would take everyone with him.

Ram only wanted White Pandora to explode, but even then, he could not bring himself to make it happen. Being a man of principles, Ram Van Bamf could not intentionally destroy Pandora as long as any possibility existed that his enemy was actually a human being. But that did not mean he would not fight. Ram struck as hard and as quick as he could afford, but Pandora proved resilient beyond anything Ram had seen so far, compelled by some unknown force. Even worse, Pandora employed a minor grade version of the Gravity Compulsion Beam out of its own knuckles, slowing Ram down to a more manageable level. Ram knew he was in no danger of defeat, but survival and conquest were not the purpose of the battle. His only intention was to keep Pandora engaged until Lethal Enforcer finished their performance.

"Boy, you're a tough customer. You've practically got me on the ropes," bluffed Ram, who, to his credit, was making the best use of subterfuge as was physically possible given the limitations of his particular brain. "Keep this up and you just might have me beat."

"Then I must apologize that my interest in your demise has subsided for the moment," responded Pandora, looking down and away. "But your friends below us have a date with destiny."

The gateway burst back open of its own accord, and Pandora headed straight toward it. Fran instinctively lunged, capturing her enemy by the waist and pulling it aside just before it would have escaped through the exit. The stress of stopping an object moving at such a fast velocity nearly gave Fran whiplash, but she would recover. As far as Fran was concerned, White Pandora was just another idiot with an ice pick glued to a briefcase.

"You foolish woman!" it hissed.

It was almost over on both fronts. As Pandora advanced on a wounded Fran, Carl and Murdock entered into the final stage of the harmonized solo. To the onlookers in the crowd and at the bar, what Carl and Murdock were producing at that moment was nothing less than synchronized annihilation. Order and brutality had been woven together into one ultimate tapestry. In just a few more notes it would be complete. But Ram did not have the time to admire it. With Fran less than a second away from death, he could not afford to do anything but let his muscles do the thinking. Ram leapt forward, readying a terrible fist, and in that same instant, Murdock entered into the very last riff of the solo.

He played the wrong note.

And the next one was wrong. And the one after that. And so forth. To the shock of everyone in attendance, most of all himself, Murdock had choked in the execution of a solo of his own design, and a performance that would have gone down in history as the death and rebirth of metal would instead be remembered as just another botched gig by an unproven band.

Even though the song continued on to its conclusion, time had long since frozen for Lethal Enforcer. Carl could not comprehend how it could have happened. Fury was uncertain he could even trust his own ears, that maybe the mistake had been imagined. Wilson only concentrated on completing the song, unable to do anything further. But Murdock was dead inside. Thoughts entered his mind in the faintest whispers, and he finished the song as a matter of muscle memory, a sequence of mechanical, unconscious movements. It pained even Halstein to witness the self-destruction of such a good man on stage.

Ram had experienced a far different conclusion in his battle, having punched White Pandora so hard in its body that the pocket dimension itself literally shattered from the impact. Shards of a disintegrated reality rained down on the audience like a special effects trick while Pandora inexplicably disappeared in a blast of white light. With proper physics renewed on Ram and Fran, they fell toward the floor, and Ram took Fran in his arms before they hit the ground.

"We did it!" he celebrated, throwing Fran up and catching her on the descent again and again. "We won! We won!"

Then Ram stopped before Fran even could yell at him to do so. He realized that for the first time in the history of The Bloody Wolf, there was silence. A crowd of thousands had lost the ability to speak.

Fran and Dot sat in a cozy nook, but every nook was cozy and every seat was a nook at the Sale El Sol. A man who did not even work there played violin for the two of them, occasionally stopping to compliment them on their looks and give them foot massages.

"How does one conduct a Battle of the Bands in the first place? I cannot imagine what colorful criteria by which they judge."

"No kidding," nodded Fran. "I think under normal circumstances that a panel of judges would score the competitors. But at The Bloody Wolf, Halstein invokes some sort of ancient blood ritual and a dark god named Astaroth selects the winner."

"Ah, yes, Astaroth. I summon him every time I cannot choose between cereals at the supermarket."

Fran laughed at that, a genuine, toothy bit of catharsis that had been badly needed. She took Dot's hand into her own hands.

"Dot, until now, I had forgotten what it was like to have a normal, human conversation."

"Yes, I have always been exceedingly skilled in my execution of the mundane," Dot said, and she stopped to take a sip. "I think I would have made a fitting character for a Samuel Beckett play."

"But, I mean, can I really help that everything is a mess anymore?" asked Fran rhetorically. "Our lives are literally in danger at this very moment. There would be a wide-scale evacuation if we had any proof that the city was really as doomed as Manuel claimed."

"Fran, you know as well as I that Ram Van Bamf has provided constant proof of the inevitable demise of Ultratropolis for as long as he has been suplexing cars and displacing geographical features. If we will not leave for Mr. Van Bamf, we shall certainly not fret over vague threats from a reporter who once blackmailed the station janitor for his ham sandwich. We are a strong citizenry, all things considered, or perhaps just very foolish."

"Just like Ram," said Fran with a knowing grin.

"Has your opinion of him improved?" asked Dot, and she ducked to avoid being struck by a child's impromptu jazz hands. "I do not detect the same bitter sarcasm for his existence anymore."

"Ram, well," and Fran took a moment to really think about it, "Ram is an idiot."

"I see."

"But he's a really, genuinely good person," Fran continued. "He could conquer the world a hundred times over, but he hasn't, and I would like to believe it isn't just because he's too dumb to think of it.

His problem is that he's directionless. People tell him what to do, and he does it. But he doesn't seem to have any aspirations. I don't even know if he has *interests*. He just exists, like a force of nature, invisible until he acts upon us."

"And why, may I ask, should something such as that concern you? Is it not safer for us all that a man of such incalculable power chooses to stand idle? I use 'idle' as a figurative term, of course, considering your business only exists as an abstract concept anymore."

"It just doesn't seem fair," said Fran, and the violinist segued into a more somber composition to best reflect her emotional state. "Ram is human too, as far as we know. He's done things that no one else will ever be able to imagine doing. But I feel like he's never *lived* a day in his life. I could be wrong. I could be totally off-base. But that's how it seems to me."

"Fran, if ignorance is bliss, I can assure you that Ram is quite happy in his life, whether or not the quality of it is to your satisfaction."

Then Dot finished her cup, but a waiter had already refilled it to the brim before the cup had even left her lips. Even the violinist was impressed.

"All the same," Dot mulled, "it is nice to see one of us has found a man."

Fran spewed her coffee in all directions at the thought of what Dot had just proposed; fortunately, a nearby parrot swooped in and intercepted every spilled drop in midair with a large bowl clutched in its pedicured talons, singing a Top 40 radio hit all the while.

"Are you implying something about Ram and me?" asked Fran, frazzled as she allowed the bird to pour the captured coffee back into her cup.

"Yes, I am implying you find his combination of innocence and virility intoxicating, in so far as you are willing to overlook the defective machinery that constitutes his brain. Truthfully, I envy your ability to appreciate a person in spite of his flaws. I have always been too severe in that regard."

"Oh, listen to you, Dot!" said Fran with a nervous giggle. "Just because I've learned to sympathize with the idiot doesn't mean I have to fall in love with him. This isn't a movie where the two leads have to hook up to justify the R-rating."

"And listen to *you*, my dear," said Dot with a very big smile, the likes of which Fran had not previously seen out of her. "You refer to yourselves as 'leads,' as if you and Ram are the only two people in this entire crowded fiasco who matter. The city is at stake and you frame the story in terms of yourself and him. I wager if I search through your belongings long enough I shall find a heart drawing with 'R-plus-F' scrawled inside of it."

"Dot," said Fran, but a significant amount of time passed before she thought how to finish the statement, "I'm too busy for romance. And if I had the time for it, I wouldn't be going for Ram. I'd be going for someone successful, someone like—well, basically a male version of myself. A Dan, I guess."

"And I do not doubt that you believe that, but if we all married our preconceptions of the person we originally imagined in a spouse, I suspect our lives would not be nearly so interesting, nor would our notions of love be held in such high regard. To love someone is to acquiesce to the frivolous nature of the world, to decide that one captivating soul in the crowd is worth your continuous time and energy. I do not believe in 'destiny' or 'star-cross'd lovers,' and to my mind, it is in that lack of certitude that romance is born. The ability to objectively select one person to whom to devote your affections is what makes love so special in my opinion. Is it possible that you might select one person for your spouse, naïve to the fact that there are ultimately countless others on the Earth better suited to your needs and desires than the one you have chosen? Rationally speaking, probabilities dictate the answer is almost inevitably 'yes.' But as long as you are happy with the person you have selected, it does not much matter, does it?"

Fran did not know what to say, having just received a thorough education in one theory of the art of love. She felt embarrassed to have so little to offer in reply, and she suddenly wondered if she too had ever really lived a day in her life.

"Ram and me?" Fran said at last.

"If the parents are any indication, your child will be gorgeous, brilliant, and capable of physically dissembling the moon into its constituent parts should the need arise. I do not find anything undesirable in that."

Fran and Dot sat in silence for a while after that, sipping their coffee and soaking in the tranquility while it was still possible. After this, there would be no more peaceful days, and the hardships would only become ever more apparent and frightening. But for this moment, in this hush, everything was just right. The calm was welcomed like an old friend.

"You're going to find an incredibly guy, Dot," said Fran some time later.

"While I shall not impugn it, I will take note that you neglect to specify a time frame in your imperative," said Dot. "And although I do frequently imagine engaging in a whirlwind romance, it occurs at a retirement home and I succumb to heart disease twenty minutes later."

"No, no, Dot, it's going to happen soon. Who knows? Maybe your guy is here in this room right now."

The violinist straightened his bowtie and cleared his throat.

"Eh," responded Dot to the sight of him.

Then, unbeknownst to them, a new contender threw his hat in the ring.

"Man! This stuff gives me such a buzz I bet I could swim halfway across the Pacific Ocean before a shark bit my 'nads off!"

Chaz and his bandmates in Chainsaw Execution stood around the entrance, drinking their coffee out in the open so they could best admire the bountiful varieties of flowers outside. Until then, they had only ever seen flowers in tattoos and were as surprised as anybody to discover they existed in real life.

"Chaz? What are you doing here?" asked Fran, near enough to capture his attention without shouting.

"Fran! What a delight," said Chaz, and he hurried over toward her. "Me and the guys heard about the crazy Joe this place serves, so we had to check it out. And this is the Joest Joe I've ever had! I feel like I'm making out with him!"

"To which animated gentleman are we speaking?" asked Dot.

"This is Chaz and his band Chainsaw Execution," said Fran, and she swallowed with disbelief before she continued. "They won Battle of the Bands last night."

The bandmates all showed Dot their golden medallions with the words "YOU ROCK!" emblazoned on both sides.

"An appreciable feat, I am sure," praised Dot.

"You know it, honey," Chaz said.

Until now, he had been so infatuated with the cup in his hands that he had not taken the time to really look at anyone while he spoke. But when he finally saw her, it was like he had wandered into

11

The organ music and the regular human sacrifices were the first hint that the Tooth Decay Hooray was not all that it seemed. Nobody was sure where the music or the shrieks of agony originated, but since both seemed to rise up through the floors with such regular frequency, the children at the shop just assumed there were a bunch of very uncoordinated students learning to play organ in the basement. In a store where the aroma of melted chocolate constantly filled the air and even the walls were made of ice cream cake, a few frivolous screams for mercy were nothing more than a passing oddity at best. But the atmosphere was only the least intoxicating feature of the Tooth Decay Hooray; the candy itself was what left kids comatose on the floor, sugar leaking from every exposed orifice. Only the largest and most comically impractical candy in the city was sold at the Tooth Decay Hooray, and some parents set up a direct deposit system with the store so that their children could spend their allowances there faster. It was usually the negligent parents who agreed to direct deposit.

Nonetheless, sophisticated payment methods were sometimes required to afford the extravagant manner of treats sold behind the counter. Girls tended to pool their resources to buy a Variety Bouquet, a set of flowers made of dyed fondant with licorice for the stems and leaves made of peanut butter encased in chocolate. Boys meanwhile flocked to the aptly-named Mourning Star, a literal spiked mace molded out of caramel and nougat that was as delicious as it

102

was painful. Then there was the Achocolypse, a conglomeration of chocolates so fatal in combination that it came with a free inquest. Although survivability and rate of addiction varied from treat to treat, everything sold at the Tooth Decay Hooray was known to provide the most carnal pleasure a child was going to experience before puberty.

"Aww, it all makes sense now! No candy this big and delicious could get made without some sorta ancient evil magic," said Little Jimmy, holding a Mean Bean, a gigantic jelly bean that exploded into more jelly beans if thrown. "But, since we can't unmake the candy they already made, you mind buying me and Sally this here bean?"

Sally was an unwilling participant in the proceedings, having made it clear to Little Jimmy in private that they should stay away from any business most likely run by super villains. But his persistence was unyielding, so Sally acquiesced to stand by his side in his dangerous scheme, hand-in-hand as always. Little Jimmy thought her going with him was an even worse idea, not wanting to endanger her, but Sally refused to entertain any other notion. In the end, neither one of them was happy with the final arrangement, but there they were, all the same.

"Sure, Little Jimmy, whatever you kids want," said Ram Van Bamf. "The warden gave me a good payday for cracking the Grandma Grinder. I never stopped to count all of it, but the bag felt heavier than usual and the dollar sign was extra big."

Ram pointed to the Mean Bean as he addressed the counter clerk, an older man shaped like a matryoshka doll. His pink cheeks and gray eyes instilled a pacifying effect on all who entered his presence.

"One Mean Bean, please," Ram said.

"Ah, the Mean Bean! Can you imagine a world where all of the grenades and bombs were replaced with these?" the clerk said as he typed into a computer.

"I guess. It sounds like it would take forever to kill somebody with one though," said Ram.

"That is precisely the point, my burly friend. All the world's problems could be solved with the appropriate dose of sugar," the clerk said. Ram noticed his name tag called him Pietro. "Care for a complimentary box of chocolate ants? The ants are made out of strawberry jelly."

So they all took a break to eat. Little Jimmy and Sally each took hold of the Mean Bean with their free hands and broke it in half. Sally herself was more partial to the Gummy Armada, a faithful representation of the sixteenth century Spanish navy except that all of the sailors were bears, but she would have been embarrassed to eat an entire fleet in front of her beau. Falling on the side of dainty, she snacked on her half of the Mean Bean, yearning for sea bound gummies from a distance.

"Sure is a shame these guys are evil," mumbled Ram in-between munching.

"Tell me about it," said Little Jimmy.

"Who's evil?" asked Pietro.

"You," said Ram.

"Me?"

"Probably," said Ram.

"This whole city is on the verge of destruction thanks to some creep named Gyakusatsu. And we heard from a reliable source that the Tooth Decay Hooray has been a hive of scum and villainy for the last sixty years! We put two and two together and decided to make a crackdown," explained Little Jimmy.

"Well, actually, Little Jimmy here put it together," said Ram. "I'm kind of just hoping you guys are evil, because we don't have any other leads. Uh, do you have any leads?"

"Can't say that I do, no," said Pietro.

"Didn't think so."

Then bells at the entrance chimed, an afternoon breeze preceding Fuzzy and Ruttiger as they arrived through the doors made of rice crispy treats.

"So who do we beat up first?" asked Fuzzy, sending a fist into his palm in a slow rhythm.

"Oh, can it, Fuzz," growled Ruttiger. "You couldn't even keep an eye on one deranged drunk last night for Ram. You let everybody down! So if you want to help now, the best you can do is just shut up and maybe be a human shield if we need."

"Yeah, okay," said Fuzzy, head down, arms at his sides. His failure at Battle of the Bands had drained him of much of his trademark enthusiasm, and though Ruttiger would not admit to it, he found it unnerving to witness Fuzzy in such a state.

"Glad to see you could make it, guys," said Ram. "I just hope this all pans out so we didn't waste your time."

"Ah, no problem, Ram. I stop by this place twice a day anyway," said Fuzzy. Pietro waved at him.

"Should we really be talking so openly about busting this place's evil operation with the clerk right there listening to us?" asked Ruttiger.

"Oh, don't mind me," said Pietro, ringing up a girl's order. "You boys have your fun with your investigation. Would anybody like some pineapple upside-down cake? It's on me!"

So they all took a break to eat.

"Man, this is some good cake," said Ruttiger, at one point foregoing a fork altogether.

"Artwork, if I've ever seen it," agreed Fuzzy.

"We should probably investigate after this," said Little Jimmy.

"Probably," said Ram.

A short time later, and after Ruttiger had procured a napkin, they were ready for their inspection.

"Okay, let's get to work," said Little Jimmy after his final gulp.

"Well, look what I just found under the counter!" said Pietro as he lifted a tray. "Would you boys care for lamb chops and apple sauce? Free of charge!"

So they all took a break to eat.

"This lamb died for all the right reasons," said Ruttiger.

"Amen to that," said Fuzzy.

"We should wash this down with some chili dogs afterward," said Little Jimmy. "There's a real swell vendor just down the block."

"Let's go there now!" said Ram.

So they all took a break to eat chili dogs down the block.

"A dog like this should be sold in stadiums," said Ruttiger.

"They should sell it at my house," said Fuzzy.

"Ain't nothin' like a good dog," said Little Jimmy.

"Boy, this is really shaping up to be a great day," said Ram. "Anybody wanna go to the park and feed the raccoons?"

"Let's go!" said Little Jimmy.

And they would have gone to the park, except Sally was squeezing Little Jimmy's hand so hard by now that he felt like he was losing an arm wrestling match.

"Yeesh, never took you for a homebody!" said an antsy Little Jimmy. But her pursed lips and glare got him to stop and think further. "Oh, that's right! The candy store!"

believe I was stupid enough to think you all worked here? It's not like I attended graduate school in Pennsylvania."

Speakers throughout the various towers began to blare with warnings such as "Black Protocol: Activated!" and "No littering in the abyss! Keep our black hole beautiful!" The people in the coats dispersed through the various exits in a hurry as lights flashed red and black.

"Well, now you did it, Sonny!" said Little Jimmy. "Way to doom us all!"

"Ah, lay off o' me, will ya? This woulda happened no matter what we did," said Sonny, and he took another long lick. "At least I got you'se guys some info. Ever heard o' this Dragon character before now?"

"I don't think so," shrugged Ram. "I wish Fran were here. She'd know what to do right now."

"You're absolutely right. I would," said Fran, hand at her hip, standing at the foot of the escalator.

"Fran! How'd you know to come here?" asked Ram.

"Ran into Chaz, told me you were coming here. It wasn't difficult to follow your path of destruction to this place. The organist filled me in on what I needed to know. If I'd have known he'd be so cooperative, I wouldn't have said all those terrible things about his grandmother."

"Lady, there'll be time to buy him a condolence card later," said Sonny, "but right now we got an alarm system and death rays 'ta worry about."

As red lasers began pelting and grazing the room like a grading pen on a dyslexic's spelling test, Fran and the kids took cover underneath a table. Ram, not wanting to accidentally annihilate the entire tower and send them all plummeting into the cavernous abyss, lifted couches and threw them in the direction of the death rays with as little muscle as he could muster, which was still more than enough to smash the weapons into thousands of little pieces.

"Hey, Fran, I know we're in a tight spot right now, but there're some people above us who're in worse shape," said Little Jimmy, and Sally nodded her agreement. "That's where all the yellin' is comin' from. They're bein' used as experiments or somethin'. We need to save them!"

"Save *them*? How 'bout us?" said Sonny, and he took a fierce bite out of the lollipop, taking a large chunk of it. "That sleaze ball said those experiments are planned 'ta end anyway. Right now we oughta focus on ourselves."

"So you just wanna turn tail and run? Coward! I knew you'd show your true colors eventually," said Little Jimmy.

"Hey! The Sandman never runs, unless he has a hot date 'ta get to," said Sonny. "All I'm sayin' is, if we're gonna explore this place, we need 'ta go *deeper*. There's no time to be goin' *higher up*."

"Fine! Be my guest and get lost down there," said Little Jimmy, "but I'm goin' upstairs to save those victims. There won't be any blood on my hands, at least not until I rearrange your face during our rematch."

"Big woids for such a small boy!" mocked Sonny with a leer. "Fine, fine. I'll help you wit' your pansy plan, just 'cause I know a couple o' cadavers will show up in the mornin' wearin' your clothes if I don't come to keep you'se guys alive."

"Well, actually, boys, you both have a leg to stand on," said Fran, who had been thinking the situation over while Little Jimmy and Sonny argued. "We have to save the innocent victims, but at the same time, there won't be another opportunity to surprise these people here. If we leave and come back, anything especially incriminating might have been removed by then. This is our only chance to do a real investigation."

Suddenly, they all felt a large jolt when the table under which they hid was struck by a death ray that had loosened from the ceiling. Fran bumped her head when she jumped from being startled.

"Sorry about that," said Ram. "On the plus side, that was the last one."

"I never expected 'ta get killed by a death ray," said Sonny, and he put his hands on the laser as he slipped out from underneath the table, "especially not by gettin' hit in the head by the gun itself."

It was an unusually light weapon, enough so that any of the kids could carry it, even if it was as long as the children were tall. The gun shimmered navy blue, very angular in design but comfortable to hold, and a large green button was set in the side of it, meant to be pressed by the thumb. Quickly seduced by its allure, Sally pressed the green button, initiating a blast that left a new hole in the wall.

"Still functional! We can use it," said Little Jimmy.

"You lunatics will ruin everything!" said the same scruffy man in a coat, who had apparently not left the room at all. He took a luger out of his coat pocket. "I will not stand for this."

In a fit of fright, Little Jimmy pressed the trigger button on the death ray again, but much to his added horror, it did not react when aimed at the man in the coat. Then a loud shot was heard, and Little Jimmy turned whiter than a country music festival. He looked down at his shirt, and not noticing any holes or loose kidneys, he turned his attention to Sally, and then finally to Sonny. They were all unharmed. But the man in the coat dropped his gun, falling over on one side and not moving afterward.

"I guess we've learned one thing about the death rays," said Fran as she holstered her Beretta. "They won't fire on anybody who they think works here."

Having finally distinguished that none of them had been hurt, Sally could feel the little wet beads forming at her eyelids, and as the rivulets began to gush, Little Jimmy tightened his grip on her hand and put his free hand around her shoulder.

"I know, doll, I know," said Little Jimmy. He bit down hard on his lip to stop from bawling himself. Even Sonny had a difficult time shrugging off the trauma, unaccustomed to gunfights that did not occur with an upbeat orchestral score and surround sound.

"This is, this is for real, huh?" he said at last.

Ram and Fran shot the same concerned glance at each other.

"What the heck were you thinking bringing children down here anyway?" asked Fran. "They'll have nightmares for years now."

"It was Little Jimmy's idea to come in the first place. I didn't think it would be fair to tell him to stay home," said Ram, looking away. "I thought I could protect them all."

"You can protect them from a lot of things, Ram, but not from this," said Fran, and she pointed to the kids, whose eyes were in turn glued to the lifeless body that had only recently been threatening to make the same of them.

"Take the kids and go back up. I'll investigate this place on my own," decided Ram, his lips exhibiting even more pout than usual.

"But I, well," said Fran, conflicted, "okay, yeah, the kids need to go back up. But then I'll be back. I want to do this with you."

Ram shook his head.

"This is dangerous. More people are probably going to die," said Ram. "I won't let you be one of them."

Fran only gazed at him for a while then. As far as she could tell, this was the most emotion she had ever seen out of Ram Van Bamf, and it would have been endearing if he was not telling her to go away. She noticed at one point that Sally was looking to her, her big baby blues filled with dread that felt all the more violating on such a pretty face. Now was not the time to argue, Fran decided, but she would not have the chance to say as much.

"You really should listen to the man, little lady," came a voice that sounded processed. "Because I plan to kill every one of you in short order."

The first attack came before any of them ever saw the assailant. A force unlike anything any of them but Ram could have imagined tore through the entirety of the tower, stirring up such a quake that one of the supports that anchored the tower to the Earth above snapped like a guitar string.

"What was that?" yelled Little Jimmy as they all felt the continual reverberations of the shockwave.

Without wasting any time, Ram grabbed the kids by their collars and threw them into the nearest elevator, which would take them directly to the next level up in the tower.

"Ram! What are you doing?" said Fran, but before he could respond, it was already too late.

The floor underneath Ram and Fran collapsed as the entire lower half of the tower broke off from the rest and began a rapid descent into the abyss.

"Ram!" screamed Fran, and she reached out for him.

By the time Ram had gotten a hold of her wrist, he had run out of time to save her. The velocity required to throw her upward to safety would have killed her upon impact, so instead, they just fell. As they dropped further and further away, Fran thought the towers increasingly resembled skyscrapers against a surreal inverted skyline. She felt like she was falling up. But even if they had not been falling at all, Fran would have felt weightless wrapped in Ram's arms, and she was not afraid of what would happen next.

hints as to which direction would actually take them somewhere. Sonny was not sure if he could even find his way back to the elevator at this point. Little Jimmy wondered if they should leave a trail, but they had nothing with which to make it, and he and Sally began to regret eating their Mean Bean so quickly.

"That does it! I dunno why I didn't think o' this sooner," said Sonny. He pointed the death ray at a wall and fired. Instead of creating the usual hole, the laser ricocheted off the walls and went bouncing down the hallway till it finally angled upward and crashed into the ceiling.

"Yeesh! Laser-deflectin' walls too? It's like we're in a maze!" said Little Jimmy.

Then they all stopped and looked at each other.

"We're in a maze," Little Jimmy and Sonny said simultaneously.

"It makes perfect sense. If the victims ever somehow escaped, they would get lost in the maze for long enough to get recaptured," said Little Jimmy.

"Those are some high walls, too," noted Sonny. "All three of us together wouldn't be the height o' these walls, so we can't cheat neither."

"This is serious. If we stick around too long, we run the risk of gettin' captured ourselves," said Little Jimmy, and he stopped to lean on a wall.

"We shoulda just followed the geeks in coats outta here when we had the chance," said Sonny.

"I'm gettin' real sick of that attitude of yours!" said Little Jimmy.

"Whatchu' gonna do about it, champ?"

"I can do plenty about it!"

But before they could come to blows, a portion of the wall slid open, revealing the first actual room they had seen in several minutes.

"Whoa! How did that happen?" asked Little Jimmy.

Sally squeezed and tugged on his hand with palpable impatience, using her other hand to point to something toward the bottom of the wall. Little Jimmy and Sonny leaned in toward it, only after long study arriving at the same conclusion that Sally had reached by herself in much less time.

"I see. Not only is this a maze, but gettin' inside the rooms themselves is a puzzle too!" said Sonny.

"Yeah. The patterns of colored symbols at the bottom of the walls distinguish what's just a wall and what is actually a door. When the red symbols bunch up, there's your door, simple as that. So you just touch the fake walls in the right place to make them open," said Little Jimmy. "How come we didn't notice that?"

Sonny shrugged.

Sally, still holding Little Jimmy's hand of course but otherwise ignoring the both of them, continued into the room that she had discovered. Knowing the little that she did about the Control, she was expecting to find alien test tubes and emaciated victims pinned by heavy straps to bloodstained tables. She was prepared for mad scientists with rusty hacksaws and funny accents. Instead, Sally found three men and a woman in lawn chairs, staring at her. They did not appear particularly mutilated, though the woman seemed a little chilly, if the rubbing her shoulders was any indication.

"Crap, it's about time," said one man, standing up to stretch his legs.

"You're not the hardened group of mercenaries I was expecting, but I guess I'll take what I can get," said another.

"It's because I started screaming louder. That's why they finally came," said the woman.

"What the heck is this?" said Sonny, almost offended that these people were not caught on the cusp of life and death.

"We thought a perp named Dragon had been usin' you as his lab rats in a dastardly experiment," said Little Jimmy.

"Yeah, we were, but they were pretty rad experiments," explained a man. "We never got to see Dragon's face before he disappeared. I heard he got canned? But anyway, the dude gave us powers! My name's George. I've got super durability. Harry here can eat *anything*. Seriously, we've lost count of how many wrenches we've shoved down his throat. Uh, Rodney doesn't need to breathe anymore if he doesn't want to. So that's pretty impressive! And Stacey can regenerate from stuff. We found that out when Harry accidentally ate half her face."

"It's not an afternoon I care to remember," said Stacey.

The kids all exchanged disturbed looks.

"So if these experiments are so dandy, why was you guys screamin' loud enough for us 'ta hear ya all the way from the soiface?" asked Sonny.

"With Dragon gone, they didn't know what to do with us!" explained Rodney. "We were getting worried they just intended to people who actually believed he could have stopped the fire were pretty angry about it.

"I'm with you, Rut!" said Fuzzy, the creases appearing around his eyes again as his goofy grin encompassed the rest of his face. "What do you got in mind?"

"We make a stink! We make a great big delicious stink!" said Ruttiger. He ripped his shoe off of his foot and threw it at a window with all the strength of a washed up minor league baseball pitcher, breaking a substantial hole in it. "Break all the windows! Nobody will care about the smoke—that won't get anyone's attention, not with all the treats in the Tooth Decay Hooray mesmerizing everybody within a mile with their smell. No, we fight fire with fire! I need you to take all the baked goods you can reach and throw them in the fire! *All* of the baked goods! Grab some mitts and rip the unfinished ones out of the ovens. Even grab the bags of sugar! Whatever! Just throw it all in the big fire! Throw it all in the same spot though."

"Huh? You want us to help burn the place down faster?" asked the middle-aged woman.

"You bet your butt I do! Don't you see? All of these baked goods roasting at the same time in the same spot is gonna produce one heck of a delicious smell! But it's not gonna last long, that's for sure. It'll only take a minute or two for it to just smell like burnt crap like a senile grandmother would hand out at Christmas. So move fast! A big whiff of our burning baked goods is our only chance at getting people to notice we're here!"

"Of course! It's so simple," said Fuzzy. "The irony is that normally the bakery would smell even better than the candy store itself in the first place! It isn't till I got my hands on the place that it all started to smell like a broken toaster."

"Fuzz, the last thing I need to be reminded of right now is how little you deserve to survive this disaster," said Ruttiger.

The bakers divided the work. The ones with the best arms threw whatever was handy at the windows, if they could even find the windows through the black smoke, while the others filled their aprons with anything edible, dumping it all on top of a tall, wheeled rack filled with cookie trays that had already been caught in the flames. They did most of this on their knees, as much of the oxygen in the room was gone and any more smoke inhalation than they were already suffering meant certain death. Ruttiger stood frustrated all the same, convinced there was some way to get the door to the candy shop open. After all, it was only a door with a handle that required pushing. But there was just too much fire in-between him and the door.

"That is some sweet-smelling smoke," said Fuzzy with a sniff. "To think, out of everything here, it might just be the bags of sugar that save our lives."

"Yeah, but it would help so much if we could just get that door open," said Ruttiger. "Kids will be the first ones to pick up on the smell, and it's a no-brainer that all the kids are inside the candy store, not standing around outside the candy store."

"Ah, Rut, are you about to suggest the human shield idea *again*?" asked Fuzzy with considerable dismay.

"Nah, nah," said Ruttiger, and then he threw up his hands, "but mostly because I don't think that would work. Nothing can get us through those flames now."

Fuzzy tugged Ruttiger's sleeve.

"Then just rise above the flames," Fuzzy said with a chuckle, pointing a thumb over his shoulder.

Ruttiger followed the thumb, and it took him to one of the cookie racks he had jump kicked across the room. It was on its side, but it could be turned back on its wheels with ease and mounted.

"The rack! Good thinking, Fuzz," said Ruttiger.

"The rack?" repeated Fuzzy, eyebrow raised. "Uh, yeah. *That's* what I was pointing at."

He and Fuzzy lifted the overturned rack and set it upright, ignoring the nearby inspirational poster of dough in an oven that read, "RISE TO THE OCCASION!"

"You're lighter than me, so I want you to take a deep breath and climb on top of this rack. Then I'm gonna give it a good kick and hopefully propel you into the door. You'll be home free, and then you need to get us help," said Ruttiger. "And if you screw this up, I will haunt the crap out of you."

Fuzzy did exactly as Ruttiger said, and in short order, he was riding a rack. Ruttiger had given it his best kung fu movie kick, and Fuzzy was surfing over a sea of fire, a glimpse of the eternity that lay ahead if he were to fall off. But the kick was a success, and Fuzzy found himself and the tray crashing into the door. The tray pushed through the door, knocking it open, whereas Fuzzy hit the wall directly above the door head first and lost consciousness. The door stayed open since the tray was lodged in the doorway, but Fuzzy fell to the ground beside the door, the fire closing in around him already.

"You have *got* to be kidding me," said Ruttiger, and he almost wished the fire would just kill them all.

Ram Van Bamf could have saved them all with a single heavy breath, extinguishing the flames and ensuring the propagation of baked goods for decades to come, except that he was preoccupied with the hammer headed for his face. Ram slid to one side with appreciable time to spare, but he left himself open for a furious punch from behind by White Pandora, blasting him through the wall of the tower. Fortunately, rather than plunge back into the abyss, Ram ended up colliding with yet another tower, breaking his fall.

"Oh, no. Ram wasn't kidding," mumbled Fran, hunched over in a corner, "this fight really will kill us all."

A loud boom and a flash of crimson were all that preceded Black Death as thrusters activated within its shoulder pads, allowing it to move between the towers with speed that almost resembled teleportation to human eyes. Pandora meanwhile had the luxury of actual teleportation as it used gateways to close the distance between Ram and itself in an even smaller fraction of the time. Ram would have a fierce battle ahead of him, but for the moment, Fran was alone and free to explore her surroundings. As she hopped in the nearest elevator en route to the lowest levels, Ram continued to fend off fists and hammers.

"Seriously, guys," Ram said as he continued dodging attacks with modest effort, "what gives? Why would you risk destroying your own house just to take a few swings at me?"

"Gyakusatsu has no further need of Dragon's research or facilities anyway," said Pandora.

"Call it a controlled demolition," elaborated Death as it swung its hammer like a baseball bat.

"And are you a not-killer robot too?" asked Ram as he took a step to his left.

"Does it matter?" responded Death, and it swung again.

Pandora unsheathed the saucers in its wrists to use the Gravity Compulsion Beam, but Ram had been paying particular attention for the attack and surprised Pandora by lunging straight toward it. Before the beams could fire, Ram crushed the saucers in his hands, destroying them in an instant. He took a brief moment to soak in the satisfaction of having robbed Pandora of its most devastating weapon, which was all the time Death needed to finally strike Ram in the spine with its hammer. Rather than find himself rocketed into space by the momentum of the attack, as had been the case whenever Pandora struck him, Ram did not move an inch from the blow. But the pain was incredible.

"What just happened?" Ram thought he said aloud, but he was so disoriented that he had no way of knowing for sure. He could feel all of his bones and internal organs convulse and rattle as if someone had set off dynamite inside of his body, but his skin was as pristine and unmarked as ever.

"Now you know my gimmick," said Death, stopping to admire its handiwork much as Ram had just done. "The Pluto Hammer utilizes space age gizmos to redirect and centralize the force of my assaults onto your internal workings. It is the perfect weapon for a man with impenetrable skin."

Ram Van Bamf had never felt genuine pain in his entire life until now, though the magnitude of pain he was experiencing at that moment was more than enough to kill every soldier who ever fought at Verdun. But much to his disappointment, Ram soon discovered that even literal gut-wrenching torture was not all it was cracked up to be, and he found himself recovering already. Nonetheless, it excited Ram to think that if the Control could continue producing enemies at this level of quality, he might someday face a challenge deserving of the full extent of his strength. But that day was not today.

"I guess you guys aren't so smart if your best plan is to go for my guts," and Ram paused to pat his abs, which were so firm that they doubled for a bomb shelter, "because my guts can take a heck of a beating."

Recognizing that his enemies expected him to retaliate on Death, Ram instead targeted Pandora again, whirling around with his signature speed to grab it by the wrists before Pandora could even react.

"If you're human, I can't kill you," said Ram, "but I can break you."

Then Ram squeezed, and just as he had crushed the saucers, he had now crushed Pandora's wrists, rendering its hands useless. Pandora screamed in a manner that indicated either horror at its disfigurement or agony at the pain induced by the loss of its hands. In either case, the scream did not support nor discredit the notion that a human being was encased within the cybernetic armor. Artificial intelligence and touch sensors of suitably advanced design could allow a robot to mimic how a human would react in such a situation, which in itself would increase a robot's combat efficiency against Ram by making him more hesitant to fight back, and Ram was not unaware of any of this. For all that Ram lacked in basic human intellect, he made up for in preternatural combat instinct. Of the three of them, Ram Van Bamf was the only genuine killing machine.

"You have only inspired my rage. You will pay for this!" said Pandora, resembling a raptor with its forearms extended and its hands limp.

"Shut up," instructed Ram, and he backhanded his wounded nemesis in the face with enough energy that Pandora fell through the floor, out a wall, and into the darkness of the abyss. With one threat out of commission, he turned his attention back to Death. "It's just you and me now, big guy."

The cobalt light choked and stuttered out of the face of the black goliath.

"I am the manifestation of the void. I drink from the pool of life. The human soul is my plaything," said Death, clenching its fist. "You pose no threat to me."

As Ram and Death traded blows and dramatic taunts, Fran found herself at the very bottom floor of the tower at which she had become stranded. She was alone, but she stood before an enormous control console with an accompanying LED monitor that stood two stories tall and wrapped around the circular wall like a home theater. The screen was currently inactive, and Fran did not know where to begin trying to start it up, let alone what consequences might result from her interference.

"A giant computer in the basement of an upside-down tower. That's gotta be important," said Fran to herself. She eyed up the myriad buttons, keys, and switches that appeared all over the console, hoping one of them would just be labeled "ON" or "POWER." It was entirely possible one of the devices did possess such a label, but there were so many of them to inspect that it would be a while before she would find it.

Then White Pandora fell through the wall and smacked its head on the console, and machines whirred as the screen activated and the computer came to life.

"I don't know whether to consider this convenient or not," said Fran once again to herself, though this time she had the benefit of pretending she had said it to Pandora.

"I am the very model of a modern major general," babbled Pandora, head jerking and trembling of its own accord. "And I am a material girl!"

An image of a red padlock finally materialized on the computer screen, with a box to enter a password underneath. It took Fran a few seconds just to find a standard keyboard on the console; it was under Pandora.

"Care to give me a hand?" asked Fran, not even realizing she had just cracked a joke about Pandora's current handicap.

"Experiencing critical system error. Initiating system reset," came a different, even more modulated voice from the head of Pandora. The pink luminescence in its body ceased, and Pandora went limp as it rolled off the console and hit the floor. For all intents and purposes, Pandora was unconscious.

"Or take a nap. Whatever," said Fran with an eye roll. "It's not like Ram and that grim reaper are about to tear this entire facility apart or anything."

It was at that moment that Fran noticed an entire tower passing by her through a window as it descended into the abyss. Fortunately, it turned out to be nothing more than additional collateral damage, as Ram and Black Death had already relocated to yet another tower as their combat continued. While Ram still withheld a great deal of his strength, Death could absorb damage much more capably than Pandora, and it possessed improved reaction time to better allow it to roll with Ram's attacks and avoid their full impact. Death also used the reach advantage provided by its hammer to force Ram to maintain a distance, limiting the types of attacks Ram could employ. Although Ram was much faster than Death on average, Death had the benefit of its thrusters to nearly match Ram for speed in brief spurts when necessary. To the untrained eye, it was an even match.

"How many different towers have we fought in now?" asked Ram as he tore out a piece of the wall and threw it.

"Three, or perhaps two and a half," responded Death, smashing the wall with its hammer.

"But we didn't do any actual fighting in the tower you broke in half," said Ram.

"We are right now."

the count of ten to get up. If you look like a train wreck, if you look like the gum stuck to the bottom of my shoe, I'm stopping the fight. I mean it this time. Okay, let's have a good fight."

"Where the heck did you come from?" asked Sonny.

"I was in the neighborhood," explained Jesse.

"Oh."

"Prize fighters, first round, have at it!"

As the most electrifying bout in the history of escalator street fights raged underneath him, Ruttiger had to hide the emotion in his face when he saw a large group of kids crowding around the bakery entrance, sniffing and cooing. The more alert children had already begun to drag the still immobile Fuzzy to safety, though some of the hungrier kids had singed their eyebrows trying to get at the goods. In any case, Ruttiger discovered at that moment that salvation was sweeter than any candy.

"Great, you rescued the moron who caused this! Now get some big buckets of water and call us the fire department," he said.

No sooner did he say that did one child arrive holding the hand of Pietro, who himself was wielding a water hose. The gushing splash of deliverance suddenly blanketed the flames, and the jubilant cheers of corroded bakers rivaled the carbon monoxide for the most unexpected thing to engulf a bakery on any day of the week.

"Pietro! Where did you find a water hose?" asked Ruttiger.

"I always keep a functioning fire hose beside the veal scaloppini in the pantry," said Pietro. "It just makes good sense."

"Why not have a functioning sprinkler system instead?"

"The Tooth Decay Hooray is not made of money, sir. It is made of ice cream cake."

"Huh, can't argue with that logic," conceded Ruttiger.

"The fire department has already been summoned. Let us hope they arrive before the establishment at large melts!" said Pietro as he began to whirl the hose in a more random trajectory.

With a small path having been cleared, Ruttiger and the many bakers scurried across the floor to freedom, leaving the smoldering inferno behind them. It was both comforting and surreal for them to witness the rampant destruction from a detached perspective. Every now and then, one of them would feel the urge to kick Fuzzy back into the room, but in the end, no one had the guts to go through with it. When Fuzzy finally regained consciousness, Pietro thought they should check him for brain damage.

"With Fuzz, it's hard not to find the brain damage," said Ruttiger.

"And with Rut, it's hard to find skin!" said Fuzzy, once again pulling at his forearm hair.

"Fuzz, listen, I mean this," Ruttiger began, and he put his face so close to Fuzzy that their noses nearly touched, "you are a buffoon. So far, you've let a potential super villain escape, you've burned down a bakery, and you nearly just killed the both of us. We were supposed to be helping Ram save the city, and instead, you just took out a small part of it! The fact that I let you anywhere near me anymore must mean I'm off my rocker, or maybe I've just got a death wish. Who knows? Point is, this is your last chance. Do *not* screw up again."

And before Fuzzy could respond, the bakery fell through the Earth. As it turned out, when someone decided to build a network of hanging towers over an abyss underneath the surface of the planet, certain portions of the surface were more stable than others; the bakery occupied one of the less stable surfaces. A fierce blaze evidently presented all the structural damage required to send the entire facility hurtling into the void.

"And I thought the hole your friend put in the store was unfortunate," said Pietro with a sigh.

Ram had long since lost count of the number of holes he had made that day, but he was genuinely surprised that he had not obliterated at least a whole city block amidst his battle with Black Death. He thought it must have meant he was learning some small measure of self-restraint, which he reasoned was a better late than never addition to his arsenal. But even with that restraint in place, Death found itself proving no match for Ram.

"I do not understand. How can any living thing be so powerful?" asked Death, weary and leaning on its hammer for support.

"Good genes, I'm pretty sure," said Ram.

In a sudden fit of rage, Death beat the handle of its hammer on the ground, which only served to break even more of the floor.

"My only function is murder," said Death. "You disgrace my very existence by persisting!"

"Personal trainers say the same thing about me," said Ram with a nod.

Death turned its head and pointed out the window.

experimentation victims to approach. "The goal of the Control appears to be domination on as wide a scale as is feasible. We're dealing with bad guys, plain and simple, but their M.O. is starting to become apparent. Gyakusatsu seems to know robotics, if White Pandora and Manuel are any indication. But Dragon apparently preferred a genetic playground, especially if he was the one who created an abnormally gigantic fire-breathing dinosaur, but even if he was not, we have live proof of his interest in tampering with the genetic code of living beings."

"Yeah, and now it doesn't hurt when trucks run me down!" said George, his face and clothes covered in black skid marks.

"I can drink and digest milk for the first time in my life without the specter of lactose intolerance looming over me. Dragon is a hero!" said Harry.

"Let's, uh, let's not start making Dragon out to be a good guy," suggested Fran.

"But I don't need to breathe anymore! I've been holding my breath since last Monday, just for the heck of it," said Rodney.

"Are these all things that people normally can't do?" asked Ram.

"I have a railroad spike penetrating through my skull at the moment, and I don't mind at all!" said Stacey, pointing to the entrance and exit wounds. "I don't even know when it got there."

"Anyway," said Fran, and she shooed the four of them away with heavy shoves, "all I'm saying is that we should be grateful Dragon is out of the picture, at least as a force of opposition. If his research would have continued, who knows how much worse he could have made our situation than it already is."

"Is that everything then?" asked Ruttiger with a nod. "We send Chaz to pump Manuel for his knowledge of the G-guy, and we search the slums for that drunk from the other night. Sounds simple enough."

"Actually, Ruttiger, while you and Fuzzy were being treated by paramedics, Little Jimmy told Ram and me about a very interesting discovery made at the facility," said Fran. "I don't suppose anyone in this room has ever heard of a man named Moose Tantrum?"

"Yes, of course," came a voice from the front of the store. "He was my father."

Everyone turned in their seats to find Bolivia Tantrum, accompanied by Dot and Pietro. Bolivia stood not unlike White Pandora, tall and defiant of everything around her. Cascades of jet black locks fell over her crimson trench coat, and her emerald green eyes were so piercing that they were almost a source of light in themselves. Bolivia was middle-aged, but she had received enough skin treatments to appear not much older than Fran.

"Dot! Gorgeous as always!" said Chaz, leaping out of his seat. Dot looked off in the opposite direction.

"Bolivia? Dot? What's going on here?" asked Fran.

"We are something of double agents, I'm afraid," said Pietro. "Dot and I have our day jobs, but we also report back to Ms. Tantrum from time to time. I suppose it's not as great a shock in the case of Dot, all things considered."

"When you told me of the neighborhood watch over the phone, I was obligated to inform Ms. Tantrum," explained Dot. "I am sorry I did not inform you of my sophisticated relation with my employer sooner, but it was necessary. I should hope you will forgive me, Fran."

"That depends on whether or not you're a super villain!" exclaimed Fran.

"Super villain? What are we talking about here?" asked Carl.

"We found a wild room on the top floor of a tower at the facility today," said Little Jimmy, his entire face puffy as if someone had lodged a blowfish onto his head. "The place looked kinda like a log cabin, with bearskin rugs and a fireplace and everythin'! And we found a portrait of no foolin' Moose Tantrum over the fireplace, with a plaque underneath readin' that he founded somethin' called the 'Defense' in nineteen fifty-two!"

"That's right. The Defense was to be my father's finest creation," said Bolivia. She held a hand out as if reaching for an apple from a branch, but then she clenched the hand into a fist. "I considered it nothing more than a waste of time."

"Tell us everything. This is serious. If you're behind this nightmare, we need to know now," said Fran.

"Well, if you must know," said Bolivia, and she took a seat herself, "the Defense was founded to fight aliens."

"Our enemy is an alien?" asked Ram. "Boy, Halstein is gonna be extra jealous when I tell him I punched out an alien."

"The aliens never existed," hissed Bolivia. "That is why it was all a waste of time. My father, Moose Tantrum, used all of the money accumulated from DOA, as well as other ventures, to fund the creation of the Defense, an organization which would explore

"No," and Fran rolled her eyes, "I mean, what do you want to *do*? What are your goals in life? What do you hope to accomplish?"

Ram closed one eye, ravaged by profound contemplation and internal strife as he penetrated the innermost chambers of his psyche to lay bare a definitive truth about his very existence.

"I dunno," he decided at last. "What about you?"

Fran lowered her head, which, along with the sighing and the eye rolling, had become one of her most natural reactions to conversation with Ram Van Bamf.

"I want to provide affordable and fashionable clothing to the world," said Fran. "I also want to crush all the competition, become the next Oprah, and be renowned as the most beloved business juggernaut of all time."

"Well, maybe I can do that too," said Ram.

"You can't."

"Okay, then maybe I can help you with your thing."

"That's sweet of you, Ram," said Fran, running a hand through her hair, "but that's my dream. It's not fair to you to dedicate your whole life to someone else's dream."

"Why not?"

Fran stopped walking. Ram noticed just in time, as he could have torn her arm off as if it were a butterfly wing if he had kept walking.

"What do you mean, 'why not?' " asked Fran.

"Why can't I dedicate myself to other people?"

"Because then you're not a person!" said Fran. "Then you're just a servant, or a robot, or a monkey butler or something. People have *hopes and aspirations*, Ram. What are you passionate about?"

"Nothing," Ram responded immediately. When he saw the disturbed wrinkles that had formed in Fran's forehead, he felt the need to elaborate. "But, but that doesn't mean I don't care."

Fran did not know what to say. She knew that she should pity him, but her desire to get angry was stronger. Ram was the only man for whom Fran had ever held strong feelings, and the fact that Ram was apparently nothing more than a monkey butler was crippling to her pride and common sense. Fran felt like an idiot, which, in spite of providing her a new commonality with Ram, was not a sensation she appreciated. And yet even in her anger and embarrassment, her adoration for Ram had not waned.

152

Elsewhere in the slums, sweat rained down on beggars as Fuzzy dangled by the ankles from the top of a five-story tenement. The beggars did not mind the showers, as it was refreshing to get drenched in a human body fluid that was not tears or urine, but Fuzzy himself was not so keen on the sky being underneath his head.

"Are you sure this is the best way to look for Drago?" asked Fuzzy.

"Of course it isn't," assured Ruttiger.

He could not hold Fuzzy by the ankles all day. Soon, he would have to pull back and set him down, but that was an eventuality worth postponing.

"Say, Rut, what do you call it when a big ape in flannel dangles a funny man over a rooftop?"

"I dunno, Fuzz. What do you call it?"

Some seconds passed, but Fuzzy did not answer. He did not have an answer.

"Guess you don't have any punch lines today either, huh?" remarked Ruttiger.

Just as Ruttiger was about to rear the funny man to safety, Fuzzy began to fidget and point a finger.

"There! That's him! Drago!" exclaimed Fuzzy.

Ruttiger yanked Fuzzy to the rooftop and tossed him aside.

"Hmm, yeah, yeah!" said Ruttiger, a hand over his brow. "That is him! He's wearing the same bum clothes from the other night, and he's really tugging on that manhole. Also, it looks like he just got done biting somebody on the kneecap, so that's gotta be a good sign too."

Out of the blue, before their eyes, an assailant on the street with a pink afro and shades lunged at Drago, knocking him over and quelling any effort to lift the manhole. In one swift and elaborate motion, the assailant produced handcuffs from his sleeve and cuffed Drago's hands behind his back, and Drago had not even see the man's face yet.

"The *heck* is going on down there?" exclaimed Fuzzy.

"Only one man moves with that kind of grace," observed Ruttiger.

Fuzzy and Ruttiger hurried down the splintered and condemned steps of the tenement building, tripping over empty bottles and discarded children in their rush to stop Drago from being carried away. What they did not realize was that when most men ran in the slums, it was to get away from a woman demanding child support, and by instinct, a pack of feral single mothers started chasing them down the steps. By the time Fuzzy and Ruttiger hit the street, they owed forty-seven thousand dollars in back payments.

"I'll see you in court!" cried one woman.

"I'll see you in a grave plot if you don't shut your trap!" said Ruttiger, shaking a fist.

The afro-wielding assailant had already heaved his resistant captive much further down the block than Fuzzy or Ruttiger could have anticipated. Even more unpredictably, the assailant stopped at the next nearest manhole, lifting it open with no difficulty. Drago jumped from side to side with joy, nearly losing his balance when he realized his captor intended to help him. Using his yellowed teeth and pasty lips to grip the bacteria-soaked rungs, Drago climbed down the sewer ladder into the murk below, escaping from one stinky place into another, and the assailant followed after him.

"Hey, aren't manholes supposed to be notoriously difficult to lift in real life?" asked Fuzzy. "And sometimes require special tools?"

"Yeah, well, these are the slums. Manholes in the slums are just made out of recycled 'get well' cards of people in the hospital who didn't make it," explained Ruttiger.

"Oh, I guess that's why the last manhole was dedicated to the life of my grandpa," said Fuzzy with a puss.

"The better question, Fuzz, is—why is that guy helping Drago?"

Suddenly, a single scream penetrated and inundated the sky like a thunderbolt. What followed in its wake sounded like inconsolable blubbering, a song of guttural weeps punctuated by shrill whimpers. The beggars and bums, who had long considered themselves accustomed to the primal noise of suffering, were now looking to the clouds, to the source of the sorrow. Then they found it. Against the sun, in one of those rare moments where there was even a sun to find, hovered a spider. As it descended on the Earth, its cybernetic nature became apparent, ultramarine blue armor hugging a small frame. Four thick, wiry appendages originating in its back simulated arachnid legs, each one powerful enough to support the rest of its body with poise and agility. Although shorter than White Pandora, it could walk on its arachnid legs to achieve a height taller than that of Ram Van Bamf. White luminescent tubes ran along the inside of its body and down the insides of its arachnid legs, leaving a dreamy coiling afterimage for anyone who would try to track its movements.

On its head, the unmoving mask of a face was present, as seen in Pandora, except that four pairs of eyes dominated much of the face and crown. Two fist-sized pairs sat around the sides of the top of the head, while two more pairs sat more traditionally on the face, with the pair in the middle being the largest. The beast had in itself the potential to be the stuff of nightmares, but in its current pitiable state, no one could make heads or tails of it.

"The itsy bitsy spider's been taking its vitamins," noted Fuzzy, in fierce combat for control of his bladder.

"Something tells me its being here where Drago is isn't a coincidence," said Ruttiger. "Fuzz, I'm sure Ram has already noticed that thing and is on the way, but even still, I want you to go get him and Fran. Bring them to Drago's manhole."

"Sure, Rut, but what about you?"

"I'm going in after them," said Ruttiger, putting his fist into his hand.

Knowing that he could not convince Ruttiger to change his mind, Fuzzy swallowed with a loud gulp and rushed off in the direction of Ram and Fran with as much speed as he could afford without alerting the single mothers.

"Too bright, too hideous!" cried the spider in a very high modulated pitch, hands on the sides of its head. It stood on the ground now. "I can *see* your agony. Is it worth it?"

In a blast of movement almost too quick to discern, it leapt off two of its arachnid legs at an arced angle, spiraling sideward and crashing through the asphalt into the sewers underneath. Ruttiger could not tell if the machine knew the location of Drago and was tracking him or if it was simply crazy and trying to escape daylight. In either case, Drago and his captor were not safe anymore, and Ruttiger needed to catch up with them before the machine did.

"Just gotta be brave, gotta be like Trizon," muttered Ruttiger as he lifted up the manhole Drago had used.

The sewer system in Ultratropolis had been renovated to exactly resemble the variety seen in every cartoon produced since 1987, because that was the only kind the construction workers had ever seen and they honestly had no idea how a sewer system was supposed to function anyway. This worked to the benefit of Ruttiger, who had been brought up on cartoons and comic books, though he had never felt any dire urge to divulge such details of his personal life. Everything about this place seemed familiar to him.

The weak lighting, the sooty bricks, the community of surface-fearing mutants that kept giving him dirty looks—it was as if each one were saying, "Welcome home."

Ruttiger proceeded down a perfectly circular bricked drain tunnel, trusting the lingering stench of Drago to show him the way. Eventually he arrived at a filtration station, where sewage divided down two corridors that provided no space for walkways. There were more stairs and ladders to climb, but Ruttiger noticed the stench did not continue in any of those directions.

"Great, looks like I get to go wading in liquid crap," said Ruttiger as he dipped waist-deep into sewage. His nose told him Drago had taken the corridor on the left, so that was the direction he selected. "At least Fuzzy isn't here to crack some brain dead joke."

Then the spider exploded through the wall behind him, launching bricks in a wild trajectory that nearly took Ruttiger's head off. Its eight eyes immediately locked on to him.

"Your struggle, I wonder, could I end it?" it asked.

"No thanks!" replied Ruttiger as he tried in vain to waddle away from the spider through the waste.

"I can't decide," the spider said, shaking its head with frenetic speed. "Should I kill you all instead? Will you be happy then? I need to know!"

"The last thing that will make me happy is getting mauled by a big blue spider, trust me," said Ruttiger, wiping sweat from his brow. He had not looked back at the spider even once since it had begun stalking him.

"Big blue spider? Yes, accurate," it said. "I am Blue Widow, third of the Abandoned, deplorable nurse to a world of dying patients, or just Widow, if that is too much of a mouthful. I have a mission to complete. But dare I?"

"No, no, just go get a latte," said Ruttiger. "Missions suck."

That was when he found himself abruptly lifted out of the sewage, his head almost running into the ceiling. He was being held by the back of the shirt collar by one of Widow's arachnid legs, which had grasping mechanisms of various sizes and thicknesses for lifting anything as small as a pebble or as large as a house. Widow reeled Ruttiger in toward it.

"Do you want to find the answer to human suffering with me?" it asked, face to face with him.

"It really doesn't matter how I answer, does it?"

Blue Widow launched down the corridor on its arachnid legs at a speed that dwarfed Ruttiger's pace fifty times over, though it continued to hold Ruttiger, who simply hung helpless. The very fact that he was even still alive and actually being brought to Drago faster was enough for Ruttiger to feel grateful. And if he did have to die, murder by spider robot was inevitably going to trump the death stories of anybody else he bumped into if there was an afterlife.

Before he could daydream any further, Widow bashed through another wall, and suddenly Ruttiger understood exactly what was going on. Beneath them was an enormous facility, as technologically advanced as anything employed by the Control, very neatly hidden within the sewer system. Drago and his captor stood at a computer console at the threshold of the facility, which Ruttiger curiously noticed did not seem to have any doors.

"So, uh, I take it this place is why Drago's been searching manholes," said Ruttiger, still hanging. "But that doesn't explain one thing. Why are you helping Drago, Wilson?"

The captor, never one to be taken by surprise, discarded his pink afro, revealing the unbelievable and shocking truth that he was indeed Wilson. He cleared his throat as he was about to speak and tell what was inevitably a tale of tremendous exploration and triumph.

"Oh, wait, I get it," said Ruttiger. "After Battle of the Bands, you heard about this suspicious Drago character from me, and when the police disbanded, you decided to go after Drago yourself. You realized acquiring one piece of the puzzle might make all the others fall into place, and this was your best lead. After days of study and observation, you tracked Drago down and deciphered what you believe are his true intentions, and now you are doing your best to save the city in your own unique way by helping Drago with something. Is that it?"

Wilson gave him the wink-and-a-gun.

"I thought so," nodded Ruttiger.

Widow descended to the level of Wilson and Drago in a slow, graceful leap that defied physics. It dropped Ruttiger upon touching ground, and though he landed on his feet, the distance of the fall hurt his joints in the impact.

"The pain approaches critical mass," said Widow, and it flung itself across the way to rest on the side of the facility wall. It skittered

I was wrong, because Gyakusatsu mocked me with its location when he kidnapped me. And worse, he intends to release my creation to facilitate the destruction of this city. If I cannot be victorious as the vital lifeblood of the Control, then I shall be sure to spill as much of the Control's blood as possible! My intention here is to kill my baby, the Dragon Slug, before it falls into the hands of Gyakusatsu."

"Hmm. Your story explains a lot," said Fran, "but there's still plenty that makes no sense, specifically Gyakusatsu's intentions in all of this. How much did Lethal Enforcer losing Battle of the Bands ever have to do with any of this?"

"Heck if I know," scoffed Drago.

"Fine, then answer me one more thing. Where is your headquarters? Where are Gyakusatsu and the Emperor?"

"The Doomsday Fortress, of course," he replied.

"You have a Doomsday Fortress? Seriously?" asked Ruttiger. "That's, uh, kinda cool, actually."

"Where is it? How do we get there?" asked Fran.

"It's on an island that will not appear on any map or satellite, and beyond that, its specific location on Earth is unknown even to Gyakusatsu or myself. We used portal technology to get to and from there, but the location of the portal to the Doomsday Fortress changes once every week to ensure security. I am of absolutely no use in finding the Doomsday Fortress."

"Terrific," said Fran with an eye roll.

"There!" declared Drago, which startled the others, who had forgotten he had still been working the entire time. "It is done. My delicate Dragon Slug is not long for this world. The incubator shall cease all life-bearing functions momentarily, and my baby will die in the quiet from which it was spawned."

Then a giant killer monster exploded out of the top of the incubator.

"Talk about a *breach birth*!" said Fuzzy, having been itching to get off a good one-liner.

"Fuzz, I will kill you right now!" warned Ruttiger without any of his usual tact, and then he grabbed Drago by his filthy coat collar. "What did you do, *Dragon*?"

"This is not my doing!" said Drago, struggling to make Ruttiger release him. "The spider! Its *eyes* must have done something to my machine! The Dragon Slug was supposed to die."

"Well, anybody have a really big shoe to stomp it with?" asked Fran, hand on her hip as the emerging monster crushed its way over the incubator walls.

The Dragon Slug was in many respects a massive, four-story tall bundle of blubber, except that its sour yellow skin secreted an acid potent enough to disintegrate even titanium in seconds. Whatever was dissolved by the acid became subsequently inhaled through pores and assimilated into the body of the monster, allowing it to grow and devour without end. Both of these facts were stumbled upon by Fran and the others almost immediately as the Dragon Slug consumed the facility from which it was born and moved on to digesting the sewer system.

"We need Ram," said Fuzzy.

"Ram? Ha! Foolish apes!" mocked Drago. "The Dragon Slug was designed specifically to be indestructible. This is judgment day for us all."

"Not today!" said Fran, and she fired her Beretta into the monster, just desperate to take action in any futile manner possible.

Before she could get off many shots, the Dragon Slug twisted its body into an elongated shape, pushing down on its own body to build energy before untwisting to spring itself up toward the surface like a giant sentient pogo stick.

"Pretty spry for a blob monster, huh?" said Ruttiger.

"Follow me. We're getting the heck out of here before the sewer system collapses on top of us," said Fran. Her phone, tucked away in a pocket, began to ring, but she ignored it. "And by the time we reach the surface, I expect one of you to have gotten an idea on how to kill that thing."

Ram, who had until now busied himself with suplexing as many cars as possible onto Blue Widow in an effort to stop its red eyes, had not been expecting a giant monster to jump out of the Earth, but he was also not that surprised about it either. He had always assumed some sort of mythical creature had been biding its time inside the planet, feeding on its thermal energy, waiting for the right moment to strike an unsuspecting humanity. Now was as good a time as any for it to happen, all things considered.

"The human mind is so fragile under light pressure," said Widow, resting on the side of a tenement building. "As it stands, I do not think any of them will survive."

Beggars, bums, and everything in-between had been rolling in the streets shrieking ever since Ram had forced Blue Widow back to the surface. Under the gaze of the red eyes, people who had been hungry were now starving; people who had been cold were now freezing. The fear of tomorrow that nagged at the unconscious mind of every soul in the slums had transmogrified into an insurmountable terror, a nearly literal fanged demon that would eat them all if the Dragon Slug did not catch them first. It was clear to them all now that debts accumulated could surely never be paid off, and their children would never rise above the poverty provided to them at birth, especially not with those cats everywhere. The only decision left to make was whether to kill themselves or each other, and in most instances, it appeared that they chose the latter course.

"These people are going to tear each other apart because of you. That makes you even worse than either one of the other not-killer robots!" said Ram.

"I am Blue Widow. I can only mend the suffering utilizing the meager methods I have at my disposal," it said. It turned its attention to the Dragon Slug, which had in no more than thirty seconds consumed an entire tenement building, killing at least a hundred people. "This is why the Control exists, Ram Van Bamf. Once the Emperor reigns, all people will be safe and happy! And then the suffering can subside. But while ogres and demons exist, there can never be peace."

"If you care about these people, then stop killing them!" said Ram.

"I could say the same of you, ogre!"

"Hey, the only people I've killed lately were the ones at the Hottie Body, and it's not like I don't feel bad about it."

"There are only two acceptable reasons to kill—to punish and to pacify. The demon kills to punish. I kill to pacify. You kill for no good reason at all. That lack of motivation disturbs me."

"Could you hurry this up, please?"

"The only way to free the slum dwellers of my influence is to kill me. But if you spend that effort extinguishing me, the demon will likely have already grown too large to be stopped. However, if you devote your energy to slaying the demon, I can guarantee the deaths of thousands in the slums by their own hands. You can't save everyone, Ram Van Bamf. Will you save a few lives over the many now, or will you allow society's downtrodden to be obliterated for the greater good?"

Ram shook his head at the trite utilitarian dilemma.

"It might be human nature to get angry and pop a guy in the nose, but it's not human nature to take a bite out of his jugular," said Ram. "You won't kill anybody with those big red eyes of yours."

And then Ram was off, forgetting Blue Widow altogether to go whale on a giant monster. As it turned out, his fists, which could generate enough force at any given moment to make water vapor detonate, were doing very little to affect the Dragon Slug. His hands stuck inside of its acidic blubber like a finger into butter, accomplishing nothing and just leaving Ram with a somewhat icky sensation. Although the Dragon Slug could never digest Ram, the worst case scenario was that it digested the whole rest of the planet, which was not as thrilling a proposition in real life as it was in science fiction movies.

"Well, I'm out of ideas," shrugged Ram.

"That's okay, Ram. The cavalry has arrived," said Fran with gritted teeth, hands over her ears, trying to overcome the intensity of emotion born of the red eyes. She and the others had made it back to the surface in one piece, all of them soaked in sludge but otherwise determined. Wilson appeared particularly like the hardened hero of an action movie, an urban Rambo if ever there was one. "But I'm not the one with all the answers this time. Ruttiger, go ahead."

"Gladly!" he said, though he had a tick in the muscles in the left half of his face that would not go away. There was a part of him that wanted to just throttle everyone around him, to prove he was man enough to survive any robot or monster or crazed mob, but he tried to ignore it, just like he did all the other crippling emotional pain in his life. "So, I saw this, this movie about a blob monster once. Real old movie. It's not like I'm into that sort of thing or nothing. It was just the only thing on, honest. And, and the way they stopped the blob monster was to freeze it! You need to put that monster on ice, Ram!"

Ram took one look at the monster, squinted an eye, and nodded.

"You got it."

If Ram were capable of gripping the Dragon Slug, he could have hurtled the monster into outer space and been done with it. But barring that possibility, and considering the dearth of novelty giant-sized refrigerators in Ultratropolis, Ram could only look to himself to bring the Arctic to the city. When Fran and the others realized what he was going to attempt, they retreated underneath an overhang at the entrance to a tenement. It was a few seconds before the growing vacuum in space became apparent to the naked eye, but once the process had begun, there was no stopping it. Ram inhaled enough gas and particles out of the air to construct his own atmosphere inside of his lungs, and he could have inhaled even more than that, except that he would have suffocated the entire planet of its oxygen supply.

Finally, Ram exhaled, and a blast of subzero particles erupted from his lips like a blizzard on Saturn, enveloping the entirety of the Dragon Slug in frost twenty meters thick and unleashing several metric tonnes of icy particles into the air. In that moment, the city underwent such a complete transformation that a snowman sculpting contest had already been held, judged, and written about in the newspaper. It was plain to see that an early winter had abruptly descended on Ultratropolis, snow sprinkling and blanketing the city like a mother with her baby at bath time.

"Ram did it!" said Ruttiger. "Except now we have to worry about polar bears going through our garbage again."

He shooed away a couple of cubs that had gathered around a trash can.

"Humph! You think such a rudimentary trick will stop such a glorious bioweapon?" mocked Drago, who could do nothing to harm anyone now that Wilson had cuffed him again.

"Wait a minute. Ram's 'trick' is doing a lot better than just caging a monster," said Fran, grinning and touching her face. "The freezing cold is killing Widow's power over us."

"Hey, you're right," said Fuzzy. "My hands and face are so numb that I don't even care how much I want to ball up into the fetal position and die!"

"Exactly. The physical stimulus has counteracted the psychological stimulus, and now they're cancelling each other out," said Fran. Her phone started ringing again, but once more, she paid it no attention. "Did you know this would happen, Ram?"

"I didn't know it wouldn't happen," he responded, looking elsewhere.

"Boy, Ram sure showed you what's what!" shouted Fuzzy, pointing an accusing finger at Blue Widow, still on the side of a building. "Guess this is one spider that got washed out by the *snow!*" Ruttiger, tired from his ordeal through the sewers, decided to let that one go.

"Do you suppose that Ram has cured human suffering?" asked Widow as it abruptly glided across space to stand face to face with Fuzzy.

"Uh, nah, course not," mumbled Fuzzy, in the midst of an impromptu bowel movement. "Unless you think he has. Then sure!"

"Leave Fuzzy alone, Widow," said Ram, stationary but ready to leap into action.

"Yeah, what Ram said!" said Fuzzy, suddenly regaining his confidence with the knowledge that his brawny protector was watching over him. "You know, I can sympathize with your late husband. I'd wanna be dead too if I had to be married to you!"

Then Widow lowered its head, and one of its foremost eyes turned powder blue while the others remained red.

"I was going to let you all go," it said. Then its hand formed a fist. "But it seems I have been poisoned by the urge to pop you on the nose."

Fuzzy started running long before he knew what was actually coming for him. A projectile missile that had until now been wholly concealed launched from the tip of one of Widow's arachnid legs, targeting him at a fantastic speed but following an almost arbitrary trajectory. This lack of precision allowed Ram to intervene, smacking the missile away, but no sooner had this been accomplished that three more missiles were fired. Ram intercepted and deflected each one in turn, saving Fuzzy from the death that many people believed he almost certainly deserved at this point.

"Thanks so much Ram, really," slurred Fuzzy, who even when factoring in the bakery inferno had never faced down his own mortality so hard. "Sometimes I wonder if maybe I bring this stuff on myself!"

"*Jesus Christ*, Fuzzy! What have you done?" yelled Ruttiger, pointing at something behind them.

Ram and Fuzzy turned around to find that each of the deflected missiles had subsequently struck the exact same point in the frozen prison housing the Dragon Slug, bearing a substantial crack in what was before a fortress of ice.

"Oh, how strange a coincidence that they should converge in such a way," said Widow with a shake of the head.

That was when the yellow tentacle burst through the fracture, homing in on Ram and engulfing his entire body with such a velocity that the gust produced by its movement was enough to knock Fuzzy off his feet. Then the blubbery appendage recoiled as quickly as it struck, reuniting with the central blob mass and trapping Ram inside the girth of the Dragon Slug.

"Checkmate!" said Drago with a flexed fist, even if the fist was behind his back. "Gyakusatsu too will die in its infinite maw!"

"My mission is terminated," said Blue Widow, the color dissipating from its eyes. "The future is already written. The Control will quash the suffering in this world—this is my pledge."

And then Widow seemed to fall through the ground as a portal materialized to retrieve it, leaving Fran and the others alone to deal with the Dragon Slug, which was already pouring out of the hole in the ice in massive puddles of blubber.

"You've killed Ram, Fuzz! You've killed us all! You've killed the whole freaking planet!" screamed Ruttiger, grabbing and shaking Fuzzy by the collar of his lime green sweater. "You are a worthless moron! I've let you hound me with your stupidity for how many years? And for what? I dunno, I guess I just felt sorry that there could be someone as wholesale pathetic on the planet as you. And this is the repayment I get for pretending all this time that you're more than a third-rate bozo? Well, no more of that! If I'm only gonna be alive another fifteen minutes, I'm gonna be *damn* sure I spend them the way I want to, and you aren't any part of that! We're through, Fuzz! We're *through*."

Ruttiger pushed Fuzzy aside and stomped off back toward the others. Fuzzy wanted to follow after him, but his legs felt heavier than cinderblocks and he had not taken a single breath since Ruttiger put his hands on him. At first, he did not even notice the blatant cascade of tears pushing down his face, each drop hoping to fall off his cheek and flee him like seemingly every person who had ever met him. Fuzzy was suddenly all alone in the world, for however much longer there was even a world.

"The Dragon Slug is already consuming and killing again, and Ram is stuck in the super villain equivalent of a tar pit right now," said Fran. "I don't think we can win this one, let alone survive it."

"It's a delight, isn't it?" asked Drago rhetorically. "Those little experimental apes of mine you retrieved from the Tooth Decay Hooray were all a precursor to this beast! The slug's invulnerability, its ability to consume anything, its durability in any environment! It all stems from those apes, along with innumerable other experiments. The Dragon Slug will kill us all, and it shall do so carrying the torch of my genius and superiority!"

"Just shut up," said Fran with a casual right hook to his face, rendering him unconscious. The beggars and bums that had been freed of the influence of the red eyes now ran past her in droves, all hoping to escape the monster that promised to unite the whole planet as a singular blob. "Even if he did know something that could help us, he wouldn't have ever told us."

"Heh, leave it to Ram to be the one guy to survive this whole thing, even though he's in the worst position of all," said Ruttiger, speaking in monotone. "I guess it makes sense that the guy with the toughest stomach is the most indigestible."

Fran nodded with a grimace. In situations like these, up till now an answer had always provided itself, even if the answer usually ended up being Ram Van Bamf. But now she was coming up empty at every turn. They were all going to die and the Earth was going to be destroyed, and doomsday had not even officially arrived yet. This was as fundamental a failure as she could possibly imagine.

Then Wilson took off his shades.

"Oh, of course!" gasped Fran, having grasped exactly what Wilson was trying to convey. "The Dragon Slug can't eat Ram. But I bet Ram can eat the Dragon Slug! Good thinking, you guys."

And so Fran and Ruttiger risked their lives by getting closer to the center of the blubbery mass, yelling and waving their arms, hoping to get Ram's attention and hoping he could hear them through the thousands of pounds of acidic lard. Fortunately, Ram Van Bamf could hear the idle gossip of decrepit old women from upward of one hundred feet away, and hearing a couple of screaming, jumping people was of no difficulty at all. When the words, "Eat, you idiot! Chew as fast as you can!" arrived at his eardrums, he knew in no uncertain terms what he had to do.

By the time Ram had swallowed his last gulp of giant mutant blob monster, a hole in the city nearly the size of the entire slums had been carved, a couple thousand left dead, at least half of them homeless or impoverished, though the damage had spilled into the better neighborhoods of Ultratropolis before being stopped. The day was in every sense a grim catastrophe, and Dingus salivated at what it could mean for his next reelection bid if he gave a great FDR-style infamy speech about it. But the damage was both real and surreal, having established the horrifying destructive power of the Control even amongst its rogue agents.

"This needs to end," said Fran, staring at devastation that went on as far as the eye could see, only pacified by the gentle fall of snow. "The Emperor and Gyakusatsu must be stopped now."

"How do we do that?" asked Ram, smacking the side of his head to dislodge some spare acidic blubber from his ear canal.

Then Fran's phone rung for the third time, and this time, she finally answered. It was Carl on the line. The call lasted all of ten seconds before Fran dropped the phone in shock.

"What is it?" spat Ram, instinctively trying to shield Fran from an enemy that was not present.

"Carl and Fury have gone up and down Dingus's notebook finding the name of the person who has been acting on behalf of the Control to influence dealings in Ultratropolis," Fran said. "And all of the evidence in that book points back to only one name—Elmo."

15

Once any possibility of an error had been ruled out, Carl and Fury put in the call to the police station to report their findings, and Elmo was apprehended immediately on a list of charges so long and varied that even the mafia was offended by his gall. Nonetheless, Elmo maintained his vehement innocence, going so far as to strip naked without provocation in front of the attractive female officers and demand a cavity search. Even after passing three polygraph tests and performing a stirring rendition of *Primo* for the children at the orphanage on the outskirts of the city, he still found himself imprisoned at Ultratropolis Penitentiary, where he would spend the last few days of his life if he did not confess to crimes of which he had no knowledge.

"What? What did I do?" asked Elmo, shifting with discomfort in his cold steel seat in the interrogation room. "And is it not customary procedure to have a trial before you put someone in a jail where the accepted currency is severed fingers?"

"Funny thing about trials and procedures is," and Warmaker paused to crack his knuckles, "they're easy to forget when the perp in question is responsible for the apocalypse."

"Please, warden, I know nothing. All I know is hair. And dames! Where are all the dames around here?"

"Look, you wrinkled old fart, this is how it's going to be. You confess to everything, you tell us everything you know about the

Control, or I set you loose amongst the inmates in the penitentiary. You won't survive thirty minutes, let alone till doomsday."

"I am begging you, warden, do not do this! You will learn nothing, as I have nothing to relate. Unless of course you are wanting knowledge of the spicy variety. In this department, I am an excellent instructor. If you provide me with a woman, I will be happy to begin a floor demo."

Then Warmaker threw Elmo out a window. Fortunately, this window was installed for the express purpose of delivering prisoners to their respective cells faster via an elaborate system of tubes. Most of the prison guards were unaware of this fact and used it to discard their concealed beer bottles, and by the time Elmo reached his cell, there were enough glass shards stuck in the folds of his skin that he was declared legally dead for six hours. When the coroner noticed how many times she had to ask the cadaver to stop cupping her breasts, suspicions of a mistake arose and Elmo was returned to his cell.

"Nice shape to that one, mmhmm," thought Elmo aloud in his bunk, groping the air, reminiscing over love lost.

"Elmo! What are you doing here?" asked Chaz in the cell across from him.

"Eh? Who are you?" asked Elmo. Then he snapped his fingers. "Ah, you are the one Warmaker got to—"

"Confess to cannibalizing all those foreign chicks! Yep, that's me. I've just got a hard-on for flesh!" corrected Chaz in a hurry. "Ain't that right, Louis?"

Louis Goodie, whom the public still knew as the Grandma Grinder, nodded his head in the bunk above Elmo.

"That is correct. Chaz is a savage displaced in modern times," said Louis with a plastic grin. "But do not look to me to protect you! I am quite the animalistic killer of people myself—grandmas, in fact!"

"Yeah, well, sometimes a broad has it coming," shrugged Elmo, unimpressed. "So boys, tell me, what kind of place is this? I was led to believe this is a super maximum security prison, the most secure in the nation. Should we not all be in separate bunks, with minimal contact with each other or the outside world at large?"

"You'd think so, but no," began Chaz. "As it turns out, this place is more like a really, really long death row than it is a prison. Everybody here is getting the chair, so if the guards let us loose a little to go nuts on each other, it doesn't affect society one way or the other, right? The guards are loaded to the teeth with weapons and armor too, so it's not like they couldn't shoot me into a piece of Swiss cheese if I tried anything."

"Yeah, well, I'd like to see them try and put a hole in *me*! I'd like to see anyone take a shot at Mecha Manuel Salas!" he declared, sitting in the bunk above Chaz.

"Oh, robot reporter, right," recalled Elmo. "Why don't you just break out?"

"Why should I? Gyakusatsu will be around to pick me up in a few days when the world ends anyway!" explained Mecha Manuel. "I consider this a well-earned vacation."

Then a stray bullet nicked him in the neck.

"Missed again," mumbled a voice in another cell.

"Yep, a well-earned vacation," Mecha Manuel repeated.

"You were singing a different tune before I got here, man," said Chaz, standing up to pat his bunkmate on his metal knee. "Even a vacation can get to be the pits without a bud to gab with, right?"

"You know it. We should've been pals years ago! Who knows how many schemes we could've pulled off together? Chaz here could convince a nunnery to invest in his devil worship t-shirt business under the pretense that the devil hates seeing his face merchandised."

"Well, it was just the one time," said Chaz with modesty.

"You two look like you could share your deepest secrets with each other!" suggested Louis. "And I am not just saying that as part of a ploy devised by the warden."

Louis gave Chaz a wink and a thumbs-up.

"Whatever. Just let me sleep away these tragic final days of what was once a proud and virile stallion," said Elmo, lying down on his bunk.

"Well, what exactly did you do to end up here, old-timer?" asked Mecha Manuel.

"They think me in league with you! The police claim to have a notebook from the mayor implicating me in every kind of crime you can think of, except for outright murder. They believe I am the conduit through which the Control operates in Ultratropolis! But how can that be? I am but the humble neighborhood barber!"

"Huh, to be fair, the only person I ever knew in the organization was Gyakusatsu himself, so for all I know, you're the mastermind behind everything," said Mecha Manuel.

"You're the man, Mecha!" said Chaz.

"More like the *metal* man!" pointed out Louis.

They shared a heartfelt round of laughter.

"Is not prison life supposed to harden a man?" mused Elmo, observing his companions from an appreciable distance.

They were left to stew in their cells again until lunchtime, which consisted of all the food that the local high school had planned to throw away.

"Hey, anybody else get a cyanide capsule in their mystery meat?" asked Mecha Manuel.

"Missed again," mumbled that same voice from another cell.

"I do not believe this chicken was ever fully cooked," said Louis. "Or killed."

The chicken marched off his tray in a huff, but it left an egg behind for all the trouble.

"The prison calls this sustenance? Pills and mobile poultry?" asked Elmo.

"They call it lunch. They don't make any promises of sustenance," said Chaz with a smirk.

"I cannot live like this, even if for a brief period! I must unravel this mystery," said Elmo, rubbing his temples. "I need to determine why my name appears so many times in relation with serious crimes."

"Well, you better do it quick, old-timer, because you probably won't live past the next fifteen minutes," said Mecha Manuel.

"What? Why?"

"Time for the Playground, children!" called a guard. "Eat up quick. You don't want to be left behind."

In due time, the prisoners fell into single file and proceeded outside to the prison yard, where all laws and rules were abolished as long as nobody attempted to flee the grounds. Left to their own devices, the prisoners might have been expected to bask and prosper in the anarchy, but in reality, the Playground was a place where the rules were better enforced than anywhere on the planet. From the chaos of the void, the Four Kings of the Playground had arisen to wrench order. Each king claimed dominion over one wall of the yard, and there was peace among the kings, though they vied for extended power behind the scenes.

"And to which king do we pay homage as subjects?" asked Elmo.

"Well, Hammer is King of the West, so we tend not to trade baseball cards 'round that wall," said Chaz.

"I accidentally stepped on the King of the North's toe with my cyborg foot on my first day, so we stay the heck away from there too," said Mecha Manuel.

"I like Wesley, the King of the South. He's the only one who doesn't refer to me as a 'pretty girl,' " said Louis.

"Wesley is a mastermind type," explained Chaz, putting a shoulder on Elmo. "He's no bigger than you or me, but he's brilliant and a good showman, so he's got a lot of muscle at his command. The other three kings are all bodybuilder types. Avery, the King of the East, does let us on his turf too, but only because he saw a weird sci-fi movie once and now he's developed a phobia of robots. He's too afraid to tell Manuel to leave."

"His subjects do not share that fear, however," said Louis, pointing to the large group of Eastern subjects wearing "KILL MANUEL REPEATEDLY" t-shirts.

"Okay, so we remain at the southern wall for our security," said Elmo.

"Actually, I've got a surprise for you guys," said Mecha Manuel.

"Yeah?" said Chaz.

"Today we are helping Hammer usurp the Kingdom of the South!"

"Wha?" uttered Chaz. "Hammer just got done kicking your ass! When did you agree to help him take down Wesley?"

"Yesterday. His brutal attempted murder of me today was all a well-crafted cover! The deal is that I help him take over the Playground, and then I get to live like a king for the duration of my time here. I use 'king' figuratively, of course."

"But why bother, pal? It's not like there are many days left to go," asked Chaz.

"Because I'm used to living it up, baby! Gyakusatsu got me spoiled. Mecha Manuel Salas is not the type to settle. I take everything I can get! And right now, Hammer's offering the most."

"So how shall we proceed with this operation?" asked Elmo. "Who are the players? What is the timetable? Threat analysis? Does the eagle soar at the witching hour?"

"Uh, I don't know how to answer any of that," said Mecha Manuel. "But I have to hand it to Hammer—he's smarter than he looks. He's already told Avery that I'm in Hammer's pocket, and so

Avery has agreed not to intervene today if something were to happen in the Southern Kingdom. No matter what's going on, the King of the North would not dare cross the center of the yard and risk the wrath of both the West and the East, so we don't need to worry about him either. This is an operation purely between the West and the South. All we have to do is separate Wesley from two of his three main bodyguards. The one that remains, Brody, is a defector. I'm going to 'injure' Brody so that he can't help, and then I break Wesley's bones with my sweet cyborg body! That's when Hammer rolls into town and takes over during the ruckus that ensues. It's a pretty simple plan, really."

"The problem there is that Wesley never leaves the sight of any of his bodyguards," said Chaz. "He's always with all three of them. There's nothing we can do about that. We should call it quits now before this cold war turns hot, and we're the ones left to roast."

"Chaz is right. If you want to talk excitement, let's all play a high-stakes game of hopscotch!" said Louis.

"Pay no attention to those fruits. I know how this is going down," said Elmo, a grave expression sapping his allies of any lingering joviality.

In short order, Mecha Manuel was requesting an audience with the King of the South, and much to his surprise, the audience was granted almost immediately. Wesley stood at the center of a triangle, with two bodyguards in front of him and Brody behind him. Chaz and Louis stayed just behind Mecha Manuel, though Elmo stood beside him, leaning one elbow on his shoulder.

"Ah, Manuel, our most vocal subject," said Wesley with a slow and deliberate tone. He wore horn-rimmed glasses and spent most of his time with his arms crossed. "What can I do for you today?"

"This one's a kicker, your majesty. You're gonna love it," said Mecha Manuel, though deep down inside, he wanted to strangle Wesley right there for not referring to him by his full name. "See the old sack of crap hanging on to me for dear life? His name is Elmo, and he works for the same guys I do, except he's way higher rank! This guy can make you a made man in our organization after the impending doomsday. You'd like that, right?"

"Continue."

"Okay, well, Elmo'd love to help you out with that. The problem is he's sick! The guy could croak on us any second, but the guards don't care. Heck, I barely care myself, but what can I say?

I'm loyal to my employers. But word on the street is you have a stockpile of pharmaceuticals. Let Elmo in on that, and he'll take care of you like you've never seen. What do you say?"

Wesley bit his lip.

"Your proposition is," and he paused for dramatic effect, "intriguing."

Suddenly, Elmo shrieked as if all the women in the world had volunteered for mastectomies, and he grasped his arm.

"Mamma mia! I think he is having a stroke!" said Louis, hands on his cheeks. "And I am not just saying that as part of a ploy devised by Elmo!"

He winked and gave a thumbs-up to Mecha Manuel.

"Ah, heck! No time to debate, Wesley. Are you in or are you out?" asked Mecha Manuel.

"Fine! I'm in. He can have all the drugs he requires, assuming he lives that long," said Wesley.

"Elmo's fragile. Moving him is like lifting fine china from the rich couple's house you've been casing—it requires finesse!" explained Chaz. "You better get your best goons to carry him to the goods."

"Very well. The drugs are maintained at a secure location inside the prison. We shall all go there," said Wesley.

"All of us? Are you crazy?" said Mecha Manuel. "Do you know how long Avery has been eying up your kingdom? If you leave your dominion now, you won't have a dominion to come back to! I'll stay here with you. With his fear of robots, we know for sure he won't attack, even with your bodyguards gone."

"You are a wily sort, Manuel," said Wesley. He batted a hand. "Banner, Tomas, take the old man to the drug stash. Brody shall remain with me."

"I'll go with Elmo, to watch out for the poor old man," said Louis, this time with full sincerity.

Chaz could feel his heart pounding like a Las Vegas brothel as Louis followed the bodyguards carrying Elmo back into the prison. Going undercover was no big deal, but hurting people to maintain that cover was another issue entirely. Wesley seemed like a good person as far as convicted death row murderers went, and Chaz wondered if there was a way out of this situation.

"So what's it like being a cannibal?" asked Wesley, making small talk.

There was a television set to very low volume hanging from the ceiling, and Warmaker pushed a button so they could hear it better.

"Not a trick, not a joke," began the DOA-13 reporter. "Mr. Trillionaire himself will be making an appearance in Ultratropolis tomorrow evening to host a private event entitled the Enchantment Over the Sea Ball. The event will be held atop his very own blue whale, and the rumor is that only society's elite have been invited. Could this spell the beginning of exciting new days for Ultratropolis? Time will tell! In the mean time, remember—murder is the best deterrent."

"Tomorrow," repeated Chaz.

"Yes," said Warmaker. "That's two days before doomsday—unless the timetable has shifted."

16

The blue whale helmed by Mr. Trillionaire to accommodate the Enchantment Over the Sea Ball was such a hit with all of the other wealthy business moguls that they were already vying to secure their own endangered species to host their future events. Those in attendance at the ball ranked among the most affluent in Ultratropolis, with a disproportionately high number of philanthropists included in the proceedings. But underneath the lavender twilight, with a cadre of the finest musicians performing acid jazz compositions along the flanks of the hefty mammal, the ball was anything but dry. The sea breeze stung the skin at times, considering that the artificial winter created by Ram Van Bamf had no intention of dissipating, but the shifting of waves along Duround Beach and the full moon in the firmament provided ample stimulation to divert the senses from the chill. Fran found it ironic that they had used the cold as the distraction to save so many lives only three days previously.

"This whole night is so beautiful it could almost bring a girl to tears," she sighed.

"Too bad the guy's evil, huh?" said Ram.

It was never in question that Fran would receive an invitation to the ball, and as a matter of good sense, she selected Ram to accompany her as her guest. They were situated at a small private table toward the center of the whale, and though there were a handful of other private tables, it was otherwise larger tables that

"You know, it occurs to me," said Fran, in-between forkfuls of an expensive cut of some random meat, "that we have never been properly introduced."

"To who?"

"Each other."

"Oh. Okay. We can do that. You start."

"Alright. My name is Francesca Lunardo," she said, teeth on full display, hand extended.

"My name is, heh, Ram Van Bamf," he said, reaching over the table with no effort to shake her hand. "It's a, uh, pleasure to meet you."

"The pleasure is all mine, I'm sure."

"So, the portal to the Doomsday Fortress," Ram began, and he did not notice when the expression on Fran's face instantly turned sour, "we know where it is, but Elmo says it'll zap closed right away if anybody actually sees me trying to get in through it. If something goes wrong tonight, we're going to need a plan to get into that place."

"Well, let's just worry about that tomorrow," she retorted with a weak grin.

"Okay."

Ram had consumed the contents of his plate almost immediately, freeing up his time and energy to absorb the atmosphere better than anyone else. Unlike the other guests, he had ridden on the backs of any number of vertebrates in his time, and so the whale and the sea did not interest him. Instead, he could not help but be transfixed with what was right in front of him.

"You look really pretty," said Ram. He squinted, trying to think. "Like the moon, all big and bright. I mean, I'm not saying you're as big as the moon. Just pretty."

Something electric abruptly coursed through Fran's chest, only to be superseded by a knot in her stomach, which in turn gave way to an unexpected bout of euphoria.

"Thank you, Ram. That's the sweetest thing anyone's ever said to me," she said, though she felt a little depressed when she considered the truth in her words. "Really, it is."

Ram massaged the side of his face with one finger while chuckling.

"What is it?" Fran asked.

"I was just thinking back to that time at the TV station. You were so good at making Dot think you were this pitiful thing, when it's so easy to see that you're as tough as they come. That story about speed dating was really clever. You're really something."

Then Fran clutched the silk tablecloth with enough strength to throttle a turkey.

"Ram," and she chose her words with studious precision beyond that point, "while what you are saying is very kind, I did not fabricate the speed dating component of my story to Dot. Speed dating really was the reason I survived the destruction of the Hottie Body."

Ram reacted with the same incredulous raised eyebrow that a young child would employ if told Santa Claus was more of a convenient marketing tool than a man who braved chimneys for a living.

"You? Really?" he squeaked.

Fran felt a burning compulsion to leap off the side of the great beast and swim off into the night, never to be seen again, but she knew she could never bear to ruin such a gorgeous gown like that.

"Yes."

"That's crazy," said Ram, though he meant it in the nicest possible way. "A woman as strong and smart and pretty as you could get any guy she wants."

"For one night, maybe," added Fran, eyes on her plate.

Still confused, Ram did not push the matter any further.

"This whale must have been a gift from Dragon in better days," Fran said, opting to change the course of conversation herself this time. "Even as far as blue whales go, this one is much too big to occur naturally in the real world. You could say it's a cousin to the dinosaur you fought."

"Do you think it can breathe fire?"

"That wouldn't be very practical. But if it's borrowed any genes from the electric eel, we might all be in for the shock of our lives."

"Heh. I guess that would make it more of a killer whale."

They paused to appreciate each other's attempt at humor.

"Can you think of any reason at all why Mr. Trillionaire would decide to throw a ball only a couple days before he goes and tries to level the city?" asked Ram.

"No, but I wouldn't be surprised if this entire event is just a trap to lure the two of us into a vulnerable space."

"And you're not afraid of that?"

"Not as long as I'm with you."

Fran was reluctant to swallow the last bite on her plate, as if the plate were a clock and emptying it meant that the better portion of their evening was over. She pushed the food side to side with her fork like a cat undecided on what to do with its kill. Eventually, the easy simplicity of it got to be mesmerizing and she could see why cats did it so much.

"Are you gonna eat that?" asked Ram at last.

"Do you want it?"

"No, but I'm waiting for you to finish it so we can dance."

"Dance!" she parroted.

"I've never tried it before," he shrugged. "I thought maybe you wouldn't mind showing me."

"Okay."

They took to their feet and approached the area of the whale unofficially designated as the dance floor. Ram might have been able to master slow dancing given a patient teacher, but it was a moot point, as slow dancing would not suffice for much of the unorthodox style of music being performed. Acid jazz demanded a somewhat faster tempo of dance than was generally expected of a ball, and its irregular time signatures rendered many basic dance steps inapplicable, all of which ultimately seemed to agree with and complement the nervous excitement that defined the evening. Fortunately for Ram, nobody else in the business elite present seemed to have the best idea of how to dance to such music either, and so anything that resembled moving to the rhythm became an acceptable practice.

"Am I dancing yet?" asked Ram, gesticulating not entirely randomly.

"Close enough," said Fran, blessed with more natural rhythm, though she seldom made use of it.

When the cadre embarked upon a slower but not necessarily less frenetic piece of music, Fran took Ram around the waist, as she could never reach his neck. Ram in turn placed his gentle mitts over her shoulders, and they began to sway together at a pace that might have seemed silly if not for the fact that dancing on the back of a blue whale negated all concepts of silliness in the first place. Finally, Fran allowed herself to just collapse onto his body, holding him the way she had when they were falling down an abyss together. For the first time in her life, her inhibitions had wholly subsided. And that was when the most dangerous words she had ever spoken breached her mouth.

"I love you."

The music and the dancing continued unfettered, but as far as Ram and Fran were concerned, the entire universe had frozen over, perhaps never to reanimate. Fran suddenly began to perspire in places she did not even think were possible for a woman, and her heart assaulted her sternum with such a vengeance that it could have replaced the drummer in a black metal band. Ram only stood in place, as impenetrable as ever, save for the small opening provided by his hanging lip.

"Thanks," he said after a few eternities.

"Thanks?"

"A lot," he clarified.

Fran flung her hands off Ram as if she had just remembered he was sick with the plague.

"Do you," and Fran exhaled through her nose, "not have any feelings for me?"

"Sure I do. Good ones," he said, rubbing the back of his neck.

"And?"

"I dunno."

Fran felt then how a prisoner dragged through the streets to his execution must feel. Never in her life had she felt so vulnerable and embarrassed, so completely sapped of her self-worth, and it did not even matter to her what could have been going through Ram's mind at the moment. She laid herself bare for him and he did nothing but put an axe to her neck. For a wound like this, there was no remedy. But she would self-medicate all the same.

"So I'm not good enough, am I?" she yelled, drawing the attention of everyone within earshot, though the opinions of these people meant absolutely nothing to her now. "Useful for playing 'Save the World' with, but not fun enough to take for ice cream?"

"I don't think the whale has any ice cream," said Ram.

"I'm pretty enough to get in bed with, but not gentle enough to hold after it's over?"

"Whose bed? I don't even know where you live."

"I'm just scary and mean, aren't I? You think I'm just like Pandora!"

"Well, you are right now."

signify calamity. She wondered if there was even time enough to warn anyone.

"The Abandoned!" she cried. "They're here!"

While the businesspeople had by now tired of the screeching of a mad woman, Ram swung around with a grimace that could have knocked the Earth off its axis had he had been looking down. Nonetheless, it was already too late. A red laser beam carved through the blue whale like it was being served for Thanksgiving, tearing the beast widthwise into two massive halves. Fran was flung from the back of the severed lower half into the icy waters of the night, along with all the others unlucky enough to have been situated on that half.

"Fran!" screamed Ram with fists clenched so tightly that they began to exhibit black hole behavior.

Before he could dive after her into the water, he felt a blow to the back of his neck, and since it was as if a freight train had just run over his spinal cord, it was evident that he had been struck by Black Death. Unable to respond quickly enough, Ram was flung into the air by something unseen, where Blue Widow materialized to catch him by the ankle with an arachnid leg.

"Let me go! Let me go!" growled Ram, unable to reach the point where he was being held from his dangling position.

"Didn't like my first trick much, huh?" asked a modulated voice from behind Ram. "Well maybe you'll like the next one. It's a real scorcher!"

Although Ram could not see who was speaking, he could see all of the people underneath him scurrying to stay afloat on the sinking whale. The blowhole had become the new center of the recently deceased mammal, and the cigarette company executives suddenly felt vindicated, if ephemerally. But they were all inevitably doomed, especially when fire suddenly began to rain down from the heavens.

"Yes! Burn, you bunch of two-faced monsters!" came that same voice. "Hey, what do you call an impromptu barbecue at sea? A heck of a good time, that's what!"

Unable to bear lying idle any longer, Ram finally just punched the air itself with enough energy to send a shockwave through the sky, rocking Blue Widow out of its grip of Ram. As he fell, he finally caught sight of his unnamed new nemesis. In the vein of its brethren, it was plated in ruby red cybernetic armor, with yellow fluorescent tubes running along the insides of its moderate frame.

Not quite as tall as White Pandora but broader across the shoulders, it seemed to exist as a totem to rage, with a chalk white face that was molded permanently into the caricature of a scowl. Thick black eyebrows acted like cliffs descending into a flared nose and jagged teeth, while on its crown it wore a hat with bells. Essentially, it was a clown, a very angry one.

There would be plenty of time for revenge on that one later, but at the moment, Ram had to concentrate on his landing. He decided he needed to hit the water, because if he targeted the whale, he would only succeed in sinking what was left of it in a nearly literal cannonball drop. But then serendipity provided a better target.

"Hey, remember me?" asked Ram as he crashed into the back of Black Death, gripping it by its cape. Without any further consideration, he took Death's arm and pulled it back with enough force to break it in one clean tug, and the hammer that it had been wielding was lost to the waters. "Next time, it's your neck."

And then he released Death, jumping off its back to make a much gentler landing onto the sinking whale, which incidentally was now also burning.

"No! It wasn't supposed to be like this," choked Jerry in-between sobs. "I thought he understood! I guess I was just being naïve again."

"What are you talking about, Jerry? You're the Emperor, right? Call them off!" said Ram, closing in on him immediately and having no choice but to ignore the rest of the people.

"Unfortunately, the Emperor no longer holds executive privilege where we are concerned," said Blue Widow, descending upon them. "Gyakusatsu maintains singular control now."

"Forget privilege and control! These are *human lives* we're talking about!" pleaded Jerry.

"Nothing more than cows to the slaughter, I assure you!" mocked the clown as it too closed in upon them. "Or is it fish to the filet? Who can say? Ha! Listen to me! I could go all night!"

"But we would prefer if you didn't," grumbled Death, holding its useless arm, scanning underneath the water for any sighting of its hammer.

"Shut up! I've had enough of that. I am Red Jester, greatest of the Abandoned, furious punisher of worlds! And I intend to laugh at everyone's expense."

"This thing reminds me of someone," mused Ram aloud.

"That is enough," said a repaired White Pandora, making its presence apparent for the first time. "We are to complete our mission and return to the fortress. There is no need of theatrics beyond this point."

That was when Jerry nearly had a heart attack at his not very old age. He stared upon Pandora with a mix of awe and disgust, as if it were a Goddess perverted. Even Ram wondered if Jerry had finally just snapped.

"No, no, no," said Jerry. "You can't do this. Please, Leonora, you have to stop!"

And White Pandora, now known to be both alive and human, did exactly that. She froze so instantaneously that it became apparent she had never been made aware that Jerry was the Emperor, neither before nor after Leonora had made the transformation into a cyborg.

"I, I," she stuttered, "I am not Leonora."

"Wait a freaking minute," said Ram. He pointed a finger at the clown. "Fuzzy, pal, is that *you* somewhere in there?"

"Fuzzy is a smoldering corpse used to fuel something infinitely greater than he ever was!" he responded with a shaking fist.

Then came one of those rare moments in life where a man experienced perfect clarity. Even without definitive evidence to substantiate it, Ram could somehow stare upon Black Death and Blue Widow and see through the spectacle and the facade. They were Murdock and Sally, an honest cop and a precious little girl respectively. Gyakusatsu had mutilated them all to fit his purposes.

"I can't hurt you guys," gasped Ram.

"Great! Now close your eyes, because this is gonna hurt you a lot!" exclaimed Red Jester. In only a few seconds, a fireball burning like a small sun grew from his hands, large enough to encompass the entirety of what remained afloat of the whale. "See you all in Hell, courtesy of Gyakusatsu!"

Ram could have stopped the fireball, but Pandora must have tagged them all at some point with the Gravity Compulsion Beam, as he and the others were all helpless in the end when the inferno fell upon them. There was an explosion, and then there was darkness afterward.

By the time Ram was conscious and mobile again, he was hundreds of feet deep in the sea, and his only motivation was to find Fran. He swam and searched and scrambled for hours, until the sun had risen to greet the sea, and yet there was no sign of Fran. As the first families began to set up camp along Duround Beach, Ram finally ceased his search, emerging from the water like a mythical creature, terrifying all of the families back into their cars and back to their homes. Although he was soaked from head to toe, his lungs filled with water, it was not the sea that coursed down the cheek of Ram Van Bamf now. And in this moment of absolute defeat, the time had come for Ram to face the truth.

Fran was gone, and for that, Keiji Kojima was going to die.

17

The face of all evil lived in a ranch house beside an orphanage. Happy garden gnomes littered much of the front lawn, defending violets and lilies in a flowerbed from mischief, and passing cars would slow down to admire the gnomes and the flowers both. A nearby stone bird bath reserved a patch of green for itself, though it invited all-comers to bask in its warm delight, the morning sun reflected in its waters. Too far on the outskirts of Ultratropolis to have suffered through the unexpected winter, the home remained a pristine reminder of a world from a safer time. Ram would have felt better about demolishing the house and extirpating Gyakusatsu from the plain of the living if the place were covered in skulls and pentagrams; even a swastika would have been great. But because Ram Van Bamf was a man of certainties, he resolved to knock on the front door.

"Yes, hello," answered an elderly Asian man, barely five feet tall when he hunched, though his smile was convincing. His accent was apparent but not problematic. "What bring you here this morning?"

"I'm here to kill you."

"I'm sorry, my hearing not so good," replied the frail man.

"Who is it?" came a female voice.

"I do not know. I think he here to inspect for mildew."

"Are you Keiji Kojima or not?" asked Ram.

"Keiji!" echoed the woman, who had now come into view, equally as wrinkled and fragile as the man but otherwise of a pleasant disposition. "Keiji is our son. He not here right now, but he be back soon. Please come in."

"Uh, okay."

Ram removed his boots at the door and turned sideways to fit through the doorframe. The aroma of springtime hugged every corner of the home, due in no small part to the liberal distribution of scented candles. Ram wondered if it was not just a ploy to mask an odor of decomposing flesh in the garage, until he saw that the garage was just filled with letters of gratitude from children in developing countries whom they sponsored. Everything from the refrigerator to the Hello Kitty reciprocating saw was environmentally friendly, and reusability was such a concern that the Kojimas only consumed recycled meats. Even the kitchen cabinets had been carved out of a tree that died of old age. On the surface, the home appeared to stand as a temple to thoughtfulness.

"My name is Nobuo, and this is my wife, Yoko," said the man as he offered Ram a complimentary glass of lemonade. "How you know Keiji?"

"I don't," Ram shrugged.

"Oh. You here for interview? He very special boy, been interviewed before," said Yoko.

"Uh, sure. That's it," said Ram, pleased with his abilities of subterfuge.

"Oh! Very good. Yes, very good. We help you," said Nobuo. "We love to talk about our son. Who you do interview for?"

"That really great news place."

"Ah, I like that one!" said Yoko.

Ram had them eating out of the palm of his hand.

"You come into den. We tell all about him," said Nobuo.

Ram quickly found that it was not so much a den as it was a shrine to their son, a chronology of a life recorded in photographs that sat or hung on every available surface in the room. At any age, Keiji Kojima was a handsome yet reserved sort, frequently looking away from the camera but wielding a humble grin. His hair was always very short, never changing in style, and he wore glasses with thin rectangular frames at every occasion. Ram thought Keiji might fit the bill for a closet serial killer, but calculating megalomaniac seemed out of his scope.

"Keiji born the year that Luke Skywalker first appear on big screen. That good omen!" joked Nobuo.

"We try many years for child, and we finally get blessed with Keiji," said Yoko.

"Was he born here?" asked Ram.

"Yes. My parents and Yoko's parents all emigrate here from Japan. Yoko and I both in late teens by that time. Yoko and I meet here, get married, have Keiji much later."

"So your parents worked for the Defense then?" asked Ram.

Nobuo and Yoko exchanged a startled glance, and Yoko suddenly felt an unconscious need to tighten her robe.

"You know of Defense?" asked Nobuo. "You very good journalist! Thought nobody knew about them. Heh."

"Anyway," said Yoko, directing Ram toward a picture of Keiji as a boy with a toy stethoscope, "our boy show interest in medicine from early age. He always wanted to help people, fix problems. He not even like when he see pet being ignored by owner. Keiji care about everybody, big and small."

"Which is good, because Yoko and I small people," said Nobuo with a chuckle.

"Keiji at top of his class throughout schooling. Everything he set out to do, he do! Nothing impossible for our boy. He valedictorian, he get scholarship to top university, he go to medical school. All while doing volunteer work! He work at soup kitchen, he read to sick in hospital. He even dress up like Mega Warrior from TV show for kids on Halloween."

"His favorite Mega Warrior always the green one," noted Nobuo, lifting a picture frame of Keiji in costume to illustrate his point. He was precisely imitating a pose that could only have been achieved through hours of dedicated practice.

"When Keiji finish medical school, he come home, pay off our debts. Legally, he own house now. We live with him, not other way around. Such a thoughtful boy. But he leave again for a few years, when he go to Japan to continue his studies. He come home again though, and he here ever since."

"He love orphans too much to ever move away for good," said Nobuo, this time displaying a picture of Keiji surrounded in children.

"Orphans?" queried Ram.

"Yes, yes, at orphanage next door," said Yoko. "Keiji dedicate thousands of dollars to Ultratropolis Orphanage. Employees refer to him as 'patron saint of orphans.' He over there right now. Keiji best son we can imagine. It make me cry sometimes."

"Yes, but sometimes he too good," sighed Nobuo. "He spend all his time helping everybody else. We wish he settle down and find nice girl, but he too busy with work. He so good-looking, like Takeshi Kaga! He find beauty of a woman, for sure."

"Does any of this help with interview?" asked Yoko.

Ram Van Bamf, emptied glass of lemonade in hand, had never been the most difficult person to confuse, but an orangutan with an axe could have burst through the floorboards and he still would not have been more baffled than he was at that moment. Either the intel gathered by Chaz was inaccurate, or the orphan-loving, soup-delivering son of immigrants was Satan incarnate. Both propositions were too much for Ram by himself, and his heart filled with burden at the thought that Fran was not going to walk into the room and tell him what needed to be done. It killed Ram to know he could never see her face again, except in static photos, the vaguest and most desperate form of time travel, no more useful in elucidating a life than the endless images of Keiji. There was even a part of Ram that missed Jerry, in spite of the bizarre circumstances of his demise, but Fran had done nothing at all to deserve her fate. All Ram could do now to honor her memory was follow the example of strength she had left behind, which meant he had to keep moving forward, in spite of anything and everything in his way.

"It might," responded Ram finally.

"Actually, tell you what," said Nobuo, "Keiji only goofing off with kids in playground behind orphanage right now. You can go there yourself and talk."

"Yeah, okay. Sounds like a good idea. Thanks for the lemonade."

"You seem like nice boy," said Yoko. "You and Keiji become fast friends."

They saw Ram to the door, where he recovered his boots and departed on cordial terms. He had by now concluded that Nobuo and Yoko Kojima really were as sweet and genuine as they seemed, even after all of the other implausible revelations to which he had been privy in the past twenty-four hours. Of course, none of that discounted the possibility that maybe the orphanage itself was a front for evil, and that all the orphans were actually just killer robots. That would explain why Keiji invested so much money in the institution, and it would divert all suspicion from his actual goal of total domination. Nobody ever suspected a man who donated to orphans, considering how easy it was to ignore even a child who did have parents. This line of thought renewed Ram's suspicion of Keiji, and as he approached the short chain-link fence that enclosed the orphanage playground, he hoped that maybe Nobuo and Yoko could just replace Keiji with a cat if he never came home again.

"Hey," said Ram, Keiji Kojima in plain sight, children hanging off of him. "We need to talk."

Upon setting eyes on Ram Van Bamf, Keiji appeared puzzled, but not afraid, and Ram found that unusual. That detail aside, Ram was almost disappointed that his presumed mortal enemy did not cast a more imposing visage, but a person could really only look so menacing surrounded in children who were still breathing. Even at this relatively early hour of the morning, Keiji wore a white lab coat, perhaps to inspire the trust of the children, and he looked unremarkably like any physician on television.

"Children, please excuse me a moment," said Keiji, his voice soft and steady. "It appears this gentleman has business with me."

"Hey, Ram Van Bamf! Remember us?" snarled one girl. "You promised to get us adopted after The Bloody Wolf iced our parents, and we all see how that turned out."

"Oops," said Ram. "Got a little sidetracked, sorry."

"All the same, children, please give us our privacy," said Keiji. "Thank you."

Ram stepped over the fence, accidentally catching his boot on it and uprooting the fence in its entirety. He shook his leg until he dislodged it, though by then the playground had been destroyed and at least one of the kids had been castrated. After some cleanup and a promise that women found scars sexy regardless of their location, Ram and Keiji met face to face. They stared at each other for quite some time, Keiji with narrow eyed-curiosity, Ram with pursed lipped-anxiety. In the end, Ram leaned over and extended the undersides of his hands.

"Are you Gyakusatsu?" he asked.

"I am afraid I am unfamiliar with the soul, if you are referring to a person," said Keiji. "In Japanese, that would translate to 'massacre' or 'slaughter.' I should certainly hope not to be associated with such a person."

"The Control doesn't ring any bells to you? The Emperor? Dragon? Pandora? Any of that?"

"Once again, I regret I am unable to attach meaningful associations to the names you offer."

"But you're all I've got!" exclaimed Ram, suddenly taking Keiji by the shoulders. "Mecha Manuel Salas said you were Gyakusatsu!"

"Manuel Salas? The deceased newsman?"

"No. Well, kind of. He blew up, but then he got better. And he told an informant that Gyakusatsu is a guy named Keiji Kojima."

"This very well may be the case, my enormous friend, but I am not the Keiji Kojima you seek."

"But the only other one in the city is dead," sighed Ram.

"Yes, my grandfather is very dead," confirmed Keiji. "He was my namesake."

Ram plopped down into the grass, displacing enough of the Earth in his descent that hills grew around him.

"I don't know what to do," he said, holding his head in his hands. "Fran always had a plan. She was great at telling me what to do. Everybody's pretty good at telling me what to do, actually. But Fran was the best, and she's gone. Now the city's doomed and Gyakusatsu's gonna get away with everything and a bunch of my friends are gonna spend the rest of their lives as killer cyborgs with cool outfits but no scruples."

"It sounds like you carry quite the burden, imagined or otherwise," said Keiji with a raised eyebrow.

"No kidding. I know where the gate to the Doomsday Fortress is, but I don't know how to get inside. That's almost worse than not knowing where it is at all."

"And the Doomsday Fortress is where the incorrigible Gyakusatsu resides?"

"Yep."

"Is your signature strength not enough to overwhelm the variety of gate this villain employs?"

"Heh, I *wish* it were a regular old gate I could smash with my face. Ram Van Bamf Syndrome would take care of that no problem."

"Mmm, Ram Van Bamf Syndrome, yes," mused Keiji, suddenly glum in tone and expression.

"What? Oh, is it about the playground I just totaled?"

"Actually, no, it was not that at all. But I should refrain from speaking further on the subject."

"No way, pal. It's people keeping too many secrets that got the city in this mess in the first place," Ram said, crossing his arms. "If you've got a secret, it's time to spill it."

"Well, yes, I suppose it is a secret, but amongst doctors, it is really more of an inside joke, even if it is in bad taste," began Keiji. He placed a finger over his mouth for a moment, pondering how to proceed. "Ram, it may disturb you on a foundational level to hear what I have to say, so I ask that you restrain yourself in advance. And yes, I do appreciate the irony of what I am asking."

"You got it."

Keiji nodded.

"Ram Van Bamf Syndrome is not recognized in any medical text. It has no basis in neurobiology. No one suffers from it. In other words, the syndrome does not actually exist."

Ram was so dumbfounded by the news that Keiji decided to elaborate purely out of a desire to alleviate his shock.

"As I understand it, years ago, the authorities and the world at large discovered a youth capable of feats of strength previously reserved for the wildest of science fiction. I refer to you, of course. So the authorities were presented with two options. They could attempt to cage you for your lifetime, risking a struggle that could end the world faster than a showdown with Godzilla, or they could simply disregard you completely. When a doctor diagnosed you with Ram Van Bamf Syndrome, which the authorities used to say you could not be held legally accountable for your actions, the government was able to take a moral high road while simultaneously washing its hands of any responsibility over your actions. Of course, the doctor who diagnosed you was merely acting under instruction of the government, and he hoped he was doing everyone involved a great mercy. The whole thing is a very hush-hush story only to be whispered amongst students in medical school.

"Honestly, I find the ruse to be beautiful in its simplicity and frightening in its implications. Ram Van Bamf Syndrome has given you free license to spend your life doing anything you desire, and both legally and philosophically, nobody on the Earth need ever claim responsibility for the things you do. You are a man devoid of original sin."

Ram did nothing for a long time. Keiji flashed a light in his eye when he stopped blinking, and content with the dilation, he concluded Ram was still alive in the clinical sense but might have been brain dead otherwise. Ram Van Bamf was like an abandoned building project in his current state, full of squandered potential and too expensive to remove; Keiji could buy a moon for how much it would cost to euthanize him. But finally, the golem roused from his self-induced coma in the grass, feathering off the moss that had begun to grow around his shins and taking to his feet.

"So, Fran was right?" he asked, continuing the conversation as if nothing had happened.

"Pertaining to what?"

"Fran said it was a problem of scale. She didn't think Ram Van Bamf Syndrome really mattered. She just said I make mistakes like everybody else, except when I make a mistake, continents get rearranged a little bit."

"Precisely!" said Keiji. "Now I wish I would have known this Fran. She sounds quite fascinating."

"Gyakusatsu's brainwashed henchmen killed her. I came here to kill you."

"I, um, hope you have reconsidered those plans in light of recent developments."

"Yeah," consented Ram with a puss and a nod. He rubbed the back of his neck. "So, when I threw Mount Slipendie, that was all me, huh? It wasn't a syndrome. It was just me acting without thinking about the consequences. And that's all it's ever been, right?"

"That is correct. And society has played the collective role of enabler to your frivolous impulses. We all share the burden of the consequences."

"But," and by now, Ram had broken out into an unnatural sweat, even hyperventilating, "if I always could have stopped myself from doing the dumb things I do, and I still didn't, that means I just didn't care. That means I'm—"

Then Ram Van Bamf stumbled into a self-realization that trumped any other revelation of the day, and this was one genie too powerful to punch back into its bottle. Keiji held his breath, still not afraid but genuinely concerned for him. Ram interlocked his fingers and faced the ground, the portrait of a defendant on trial, but when he finally finished his thought aloud, he did so like a juror.

"I'm selfish."

Ram was ready to be cuffed and taken away for this fatal flaw of character, to which Keiji could only respond with the same grin

18

"Got your package right here."

The mailman pointed a pudgy thumb over his shoulder at a large box on a flatbed trolley.

"But it is barely nine in the morning," responded the robot on guard duty. It had knives for fingers and guns for knives, and its head was a bundle of dynamite with a face.

"What's your point?"

"My insinuation is that this residence has never received mail before four in the afternoon. The time discrepancy is most unusual."

"Yeah, well, they don't pay me to be consistent."

The mailman lifted on the handle of the trolley, allowing the box to slide off into the grass. Then he took the trolley and meandered back through the entrance portal, back to Ultratropolis and away from whichever secluded island paradise housed the Doomsday Fortress. The robot should have reported the oddity of his timing to Gyakusatsu, but since it seemed impossible that a life form as pathetic and slack-jawed as the mailman could intend deception, the robot saw to it that the package was delivered to the mailroom. Ram Van Bamf, snug inside his box, had counted on this, and now the first phase of his plan was complete. He had infiltrated the seat of the Control.

Although it may have seemed counterintuitive at first, even super villains needed a valid mailing address. Otherwise, world leaders would have nowhere to ship their treasuries and attractive anchorwomen after being conquered. All the same, it was not easy for Ram to convince the mailmen to go along with his plan, especially since it demanded overnight shipping and early morning delivery, both of which left the postal workers hysterical with laughter. Even his explanation that Ultratropolis would face irreparable devastation if they did not help was met with a long bout of hooting and high-fives, as impending death was a welcome relief from the constant failure that punctuated their daily lives. But when Ram asked what would happen if any of them survived and had to continue delivering mail to the post-apocalyptic warzone that remained, the grim silence that answered was enough to convert the postal workers to Ram's way of thinking.

Through the peep hole in his box, Ram had received a brief glance of the grandeur of the Doomsday Fortress. True to its name, the front of the compound was sculpted to resemble a colossal skull, with enormous eye and nose sockets sealed by one-way mirrors, allowing workers to see outside and no one to see inside. Unlike the decrepit head of Black Death, this lofty skull was white and gleaming, and its top row of teeth fed into the ground to become the outer wall where the heavy gear-driven front doors were situated. Surrounding the skull around the generally rectangular perimeter of the fortress were crimson walls made of the same sturdy metal seen underneath the Tooth Decay Hooray, with small circular windows like those found on a submarine, presumably to heighten security even further. Crouching gargoyles the size of small homes abounded along the tops of the walls, the mouth of each one housing a beam cannon powerful enough to finish off Tuvalu once and for all. Several round towers of uneven heights protruded from deeper in the fortress, designed to appear as if they had been constructed out of thousands of interconnected bones, and they were topped by pentagonal sea green spires where the fingers of a massive skeletal hand ran along each edge.

Even though Ram had had to absorb all of this visual information in an instant, he could see everything had been crafted by a meticulous hand. The Doomsday Fortress struck a delicate balance between seriously-designed complex and impractical cartoon castle, perfect for both inspiring fear and subsequently backing that fear up with ideas that actually worked. Everything Ram had ever observed suggested he was dealing with a shrewd mind.

Then again, the Doomsday Fortress was under new ownership. Until recently, it had been the central hub of Jerry Trillionaire, who had burnt up and exploded on the back of a whale. How much differed in philosophy between Gyakusatsu and the Emperor remained to be seen, though it would be difficult to discern at any rate, as Ram had never understood what drove Jerry to create the Control before or after his unceremonious obliteration. Even Dragon might have had a hand in the design of the place. This was Ram's best and only opportunity to finally uncover the truth of everything, while hopefully averting apocalypse and avenging Fran along the way.

To that end, it was time to enact the second phase of the plan. As far as Ram could discern through the peephole, the mailroom of the Doomsday Fortress was a mailroom like any other, except that all of the parcels came with warnings like "ULTRA FLAMMABLE" and "IF YOU CAN READ THIS, IT IS ALREADY TOO LATE." Ram himself was wedged between a DIY neutron bomb assembly kit and a cage of self-aware bobcats who had developed a system of writing.

"The critics would have a field day with this sensational drivel. How could a leopard and a lynx ever find love in this sociopolitical climate?" said one robot, flipping through the pages of the latest completed bobcat novel. It threw the book back at the cats. "Try again. This time—less Austen, more Fitzgerald. Maybe keep the Dickens."

The felines all snarled at the robot in unison, until one of them finally slumped over and began clawing up a new Page One.

"I think it's pretty good that a cat can write a book at all," said Ram.

"A small mind *would* think that," replied the robot.

Then they stopped to stare at each other.

"You do not appear to be a machine," the robot said with modulation replicating skepticism.

"I don't even remember stepping out of the box."

"All human personnel have been dismissed from their duties within the Control as of two days ago. Your presence is cause for alarm, in the literal sense."

"You mean it's all just jerk robots like you now?"

"The jerkiest."

"Good to know," said Ram, and then he punched the robot's dynamite head off. The explosion that ensued knocked the animal cage door off its hinges, freeing the bobcats to take their message of love and hope to the world. Sirens began to blare and red lights started to flash as soon as the robot had been destroyed, and the other robots in the mailroom immediately attempted to stab Ram with their guns. Unfortunately for them, Ram Van Bamf was sturdy enough that just the act of propelling their weight against his frame was enough to compromise their internal structure, and so the rest of the robots exploded while Ram stopped to rub faces with the last leaving bobcat.

"Such a cute kitty," he sang.

Content that all innocent animals—human, bobcat, or otherwise—had abandoned the facility, Ram proceeded into his wanton destruction of the Doomsday Fortress. Walls were smashed. Floors were demolished. Unsaved files were exited. He launched one of the bone towers at a passing asteroid without it even being on purpose. Billions of dollars in damage occurred every passing second, and for once, Ram did not have to feel guilty about it afterward.

Somewhere between congesting the plumbing and playing roulette with the air conditioner, Ram happened upon a door with a label reading "PSYCH RECORDS." Agreeable to the prospect of acquiring psychic powers, he pushed the door open with a finger instead of a boot. Inside the small space was a single computer with a touch screen. The two buttons present on the screen read "Command" and "Staff," and since Ram wanted to command the psychic powers, he selected the former button. Two more buttons materialized, labeled "Dragon" and "Gyakusatsu" respectively. Perplexed but undeterred, Ram pressed "Gyakusatsu," though all he received for the effort was an error message. Out of options, he resorted to selecting Dragon. An audio recording cued up immediately.

"In the opinion of this psychiatrist," began the recording, "the man we know as Dragon is a textbook psychopath. In our sessions, he has demonstrated a consistent lack of empathy or even basic interest in other human beings. He perceives the world in purely antagonistic terms. Everyone and everything is an obstacle, and his usage of the term 'ape' to describe nearly anyone other than himself suggests an ego that borders on a God complex. Perhaps a God complex is a requirement in an organization such as this, but the fact remains that Dragon is dangerous.

"By his explanation, his mother died in childbirth, and he was left to be raised by a disinterested father who beat him regularly whenever he was not shipping him away to boarding schools. Such a tale is no revelation considering Dragon's present personality, but the fact that he recalled the story with a smile on his face was unnerving. He spoke of the beatings he received as if he were recounting a father-son fishing trip. Speaking speculatively, he may be a sadomasochist, or perhaps his beatings merely embody the most perfect representation of his antagonistic philosophy—punch or be punched, so to speak. At any rate, it is my recommendation to you, the Emperor, that Dragon should be removed from his position and placed in further psychiatric care immediately. It is for the good of the Control and humanity both. However, I should note one curious incongruity—Dragon has nothing but good things to say about Gyakusatsu."

Then the recording ended. No less confused, and certainly disappointed to not have developed new cognitive abilities, Ram lifted the computer and chucked it through the wall, not paying what he had heard another thought. Then his casual dismantling of the fortress continued, much to the horror of the guard robots.

"Could you please stop doing that?" asked one robot, so desperate that it had evolved the ability to appeal to a sense of mercy.

"No," said Ram, who had no mercy for mean robots, and he dropped a bathroom on its head.

"All the same, we really must insist that your rampage end here," came a vaguely feminine voice Ram had heard many times before.

He was unsurprised to find the Abandoned behind him, White Pandora defiant at the forefront and the rest of them at her flanks amongst the wreckage. Black Death stood erect with a hammer apparently retrieved and two functioning arms, while Red Jester was already nurturing fire between his hands. Blue Widow only struck a somber pose with her arms crossed, all six of them.

"Look, guys, I need you to come back to your senses," said Ram. "I don't know what Gyakusatsu did to you, but you're not operating under your own free will anymore. You need to snap out of it."

"The individuals you attempt to reach are long gone," sighed Widow. "They drowned in the amniotic fluid of our birth. All that remains of them now is their pain."

"And if you will not fight us, you will die just as they did!" said Death.

It began that abruptly. Pandora summoned a portal beneath Death, and he immediately reemerged behind Ram, greeting him with his hammer. Jester bolstered the offensive with a fireball that was smaller and yet exponentially denser than the one launched out at sea, spearing Ram in the stomach with the energy of a minor earthquake. By then, Pandora had already caught Ram in the Gravity Compulsion Beam, and so he did not even budge from the intensity of the fireball or any of the subsequent beatings delivered by Death.

"How disappointing that our final battle should end with so little challenge," said Pandora.

"Come on, Leonora. Don't talk like that!" said Ram, wincing each time a new blow made contact with the various regions of his massive body. "I only met you for five minutes and even back then I could tell you had a good heart! You can stop this."

"Shut up! Leonora is dead!" cried Pandora, punching Ram in the face. Then she put a hand on her cheek. "And it was the happiest thing that ever happened to her."

"The stooge just doesn't catch on, does he?" mocked Jester. "Here's a riddle for you, Ram. What bakes in the morning, boils at noon, and fries by sundown? Ultratropolis, today!"

"What is it Gyakusatsu's planning? What is the doomsday event?" asked Ram.

"Does it matter, if you do not survive long enough to see it?" asked Pandora.

The Abandoned persisted at chipping away his endurance in appreciable strokes while Ram continued his struggle to move.

"Is this all you have?" asked Widow, though there was an odd sincerity in her modulated tone.

"What do you mean? I can't move," said Ram.

The eyes of Blue Widow suddenly began to burn red as they had in the slums, though apparently only for dramatic effect, as Ram felt nothing out of the ordinary.

"Ram Van Bamf, the fate of everything is contingent upon your actions. We, the Abandoned, are the embodiment of human error. You have the power to extinguish us. But dare you?"

at the Kojima residence. Photos of Nobuo and Yoko at a younger age with their respective parents were prominent, along with a photo of a university in Japan. An image of Jerry Trillionaire wearing one of his many masks was present in one area.

"My grandparents, as you might have deduced, were recruited in Japan by Moose Tantrum to work for the Defense," began Gyakusatsu. "My parents were quiet about the profession of my grandparents, considering the sensitive nature of the organization, but I was not a fool, not at any age. I came to know the organization well merely by keeping my ears to the ground, though at the time it struck me as little more than a curiosity. I had no interest in working for the Defense back then. Helping to create a militant force to fend off an imaginary extraterrestrial threat did not strike me as a productive use of my time. To this day, I consider myself a humanitarian first and foremost, and to that end, I went to medical school following high school graduation.

"But upon receiving my license to practice medicine, I found myself unsatisfied. A doctor helps individuals. I wanted to help everyone. So I tried to expand my perspective. At the time, the first rumblings were rising in the medical community of the potential for robotics in medicine. Not simple prosthetics, mind you—I mean a unity of man and machine. A Darth Vader, if you will. It was a distant dream at the time. As far as the world at large knows, it still is a dream. But not to me. *I* cracked the code. I singlehandedly engineered and programmed so many new kinds of machines that they will someday fill tomes with the knowledge I have acquired for the world.

"Of course, it would be beyond believability that a doctor simply dreamed up such innovation. No, I returned to Japan, the land of Astro Boy and Mega Warriors, to study robotics after my time at medical school had finished. It was there, immersed in my native culture, that I quietly began to achieve the impossible, connecting all the dots of my predecessors in meaningful ways that had never been explored. It came to a point where I did not know what to do with my advancements. My discoveries were too expensive to market to the public. Only the very rich could afford the physical augmentations I had developed, and that too worked against my goal of doing work that could be used to improve the whole of the world.

"Frankly, I wanted to be Mr. Trillionaire. On a whim, he went and invented something that improved the quality of life of every person on this planet. Even some animals use his creation! But I was not Mr. Trillionaire. I was only Keiji Kojima. So I returned home, to Ultratropolis, to medicine, to my friends at the orphanage next door. Imagine my surprise when I received a letter in the mail, detailing that 'in light of holding dual doctorates in medicine and robotics engineering,' I had been invited to interview for a position in a new organization called the Control, which sounded suspiciously similar to the Defense in the letter. I think you know what happens next.

"Through a series of tests, my genius became evident, and it was only when I, along with Dragon, was selected to run the entire operation that I learned my employer was none other than Mr. Trillionaire himself. Of course, even then, before the codenames, our identities were a closely guarded secret. I was Mr. X, and Dragon was Mr. Z, and it was an official requirement that we remain masked for our own security. But Jerry trusted us and only us with his true identity, because it was the only way he could make us believe in the mad goal he had in mind.

"Mr. Trillionaire wanted to save the world from itself. He wanted to create a force that could end war and unite the world permanently—the ultimate gesture of peace, achieved through militarism. I was instantly enamored at the concept, enamored by my idol. And with his bank account that replenished at a rate that was difficult to even fathom, I would have all the money I ever needed to make every development I had ever conceived into a reality. I knew it was my destiny to work with Mr. Trillionaire to create a perfect world—at any cost to myself.

"That was when I constructed the android Keiji Kojima, a perfect facsimile for myself at the time, except he held no knowledge of the Control, and he is incapable of ever causing harm to another human being. He actually does know that he is an android and not the real Keiji, but he is programmed to believe he is the proper son of Nobuo and Yoko Kojima all the same. It was never my intention to construct him just so I could work in isolation. I created him to make my parents happy, to give them the son they deserved. That android is the humanity I discarded."

New images replaced the old ones. The Doomsday Fortress appeared in various states of construction. Several dinosaurs

reminiscent of the Tyrannosaurus rex on Mount Slipendie took up one monitor. Ram Van Bamf himself appeared on one display, accidentally headbutting a condominium into what was until that moment the world's oldest living woman.

"Freed of my obligations to my former life, I was left to my own devices to fulfill the wishes of Mr. Trillionaire. Dragon, Mr. Z, whatever you want to call him, he and I got along quite well in the beginning. We found it mutually refreshing to enjoy the company of such stupendous intellect, but over time, it became obvious that Mr. Z was an unabashed misanthrope. He did not want to use Mr. Trillionaire's money to save the world. He just wanted to build monsters. He was the caricature of a super villain, with no regard for human life and genuinely desiring nothing more than to invoke chaos and death. Frankly, he scared me. And Mr. Trillionaire continued to fund him! He had little choice. There was no other mind that could do what Mr. Z could with genetics, not even mine.

"So we continued to work. But no matter what manner of genius we conceived, it was never enough to address the elephant in the room—you, Ram Van Bamf. Nothing Mr. Z or I could construct was powerful enough to stand toe to toe with the strongest natural force on the Earth, and that was when I got to thinking. That was when I got to thinking that if the Control was going to topple a force of nature, it would have to become a force of nature. As a body of scientists working in isolation, we at the Control were little more than a cabal of geeks with a high budget. But what if we embraced fiction? Mr. Trillionaire wore a mask to hide his face. I wanted us to wear masks to erase our faces. Do you understand? If the Control were to brand itself as an anonymous nightmare, with no head to chop off and limbs that stretched forever, we could exist as an entity that not even you could topple. I convinced Mr. Trillionaire to construct the Doomsday Fortress and to have us don our more colorful codenames of Gyakusatsu and Dragon, operating for our newly christened Emperor.

"Stripped of the last trace of Keiji Kojima, my mind filled to the brim with ideas too glorious and perverse to have ever considered before. Fiction inspired me to take what was once imagination and wrench it forth into reality. In a flash of genius that could have just as easily been labeled boyish wish fulfillment, I sought to create my own set of Mega Warriors—human beings empowered by technology. And that was the origin of the Abandoned. But putting

a human in a machine suit and expecting it to stand up to you was preposterous. It would require unconventional sources of power to fight you. To that end, I chose to employ the human mind as a battery."

"Human misery, you mean," interrupted Ram, having been itching for a good place to shut him up for a few seconds. "All of the people you abducted to be your monsters were people coming off of a bad break, well, except for Leonora. Maybe she was in cahoots with you the whole time, I dunno. But the point is, how could you do that to those people? And how could you possibly have known that all these people who were so close to me were going to up and lose their marbles?"

"How pleasant, to see you using higher brain functions," said Gyakusatsu as screens changed to display the blueprints of the armor of the Abandoned and photos of their respective human occupants. "Firstly, I am sure you have noticed the unique ability of Blue Widow to literally *see* human suffering in a manifest form, a highly specialized form of synesthesia. That was a system I developed myself, a computer program that can read the brainwaves of any passing person and radiate a physical signal according to the emotions that person is experiencing. I also inserted that program into a satellite in space that monitors the entire city of Ultratropolis, which, ironically, was paid for and launched on the city dime, thanks to having a man as... *agreeable* as Dingus in office. Each time a worthwhile blip appeared in my system, I dispatched someone or something to abduct the person displaying the high emotions. In truth, we ultimately collected dozens of worthwhile specimens for the Abandoned project, and we simply released everyone we ended up not needing—after inducing amnesia in them, of course. It was just dumb luck when we found so many people with close relations to you, except in the case of Murdock. I always wanted to use him."

"Because he's huge," concluded Ram.

"How astute! Yes, Black Death required a powerful supporting frame, and Murdock was one of the few people who could fit the bill. That was why I bluffed doomsday would result from Lethal Enforcer losing Battle of the Bands in the first place. It was my best, albeit desperate, effort to create a tension capable of causing a rift between Murdock and his best pal, Carl, which, as you know, is the type of trauma that best produces an Abandoned. Their victory or defeat as a band was never of any consequence to me—doomsday would

occur either way. Battle of the Bands was all about acquiring Murdock, and in the end, I succeeded, with another bout of great luck."

"Then what was the point of Pandora showing up in the first place?" asked Ram.

"Simple. If necessary, she was to hit Murdock with the Gravity Compulsion Beam from the rafters in order to render him incapable of finishing their final song, in the process planting the seeds of the emotional strife I required of him. As it would turn out, he accomplished all of that on his own. And through the power of serendipity, Black Death was born with only a modicum of intervention. Pandora's clash with you was nothing more than an exercise in collecting combat data for the final battle, as were most of your contrived encounters with the Abandoned."

"That all sounds unnecessarily convoluted," noted Ram.

"If you think that's bad, try reading a comic book."

They shrugged at each other.

"So, Murdock, Sally, and Fuzzy. You seized their emotions, snuffed out their personalities, and turned them into monsters all for the sake of fighting me. That's it?"

"Yes, essentially. I developed an interface that allows my machines to harness brainwaves into a focused, self-replenishing source of energy, which allows the Abandoned to operate as they do. But Pandora and Death are more like prototypes compared to the others. They are not powered by emotion so much as by anguish and a general feeling of emptiness. Widow, by comparison, is fueled solely by sorrow, and Jester generates power from anger. I have found specific emotions are capable of a more interesting spectrum of abilities than the wholesale despair brought by Pandora and Death."

"I still don't understand Pandora. How does Leonora fit in all this?"

"Well, allow me to finish my story, and you will soon come to understand," said Gyakusatsu. "Not long ago, a rather simple idea occurred to me. I resolved that if the Control merely made a display of its full power to the world at large, then countries would gladly lay down their arms and surrender. But that would require *quite* the display of power. I suggested a doomsday scenario—we destroy Ultratropolis, the home of Ram Van Bamf. If a man stronger than a nuclear arsenal cannot defend his home from the Control, then what

chance does the rest of the world have? While I could tell it frightened Mr. Trillionaire to enact such a plan, he agreed it was the path that would require the least casualties in the long run, and so the Control conspired toward doomsday from that day forward.

"Only one thing ever got in the way—Mr. Trillionaire's personal feelings for Leonora. She worked for the Control in something of a paperwork capacity, but she had no idea that her friend Jerry was also her employer. As far as she knew, Jerry was just another drone like her. Leonora is as miserable a human being as there ever was. Having been ostracized her entire life for her beauty, she was at the end of her rope when she came to me, Gyakusatsu, head of the Abandoned project. She volunteered to become White Pandora. Do you understand what that means? Pandora was Leonora's suicide.

"Needless to say, Mr. Trillionaire was none too pleased when he finally discovered what I had done to his beloved. He called off everything. The doomsday plan was kaput. He did not outright dissolve the Control—he was not *that* mad with grief. But I could tell his heart was not in it anymore. That was when I knew I had no choice but to take over the organization myself.

"Agreeing to make Mr. Trillionaire give Dragon the axe was no difficulty at all. As you have inevitably heard out of his own mouth, I set Dragon up for failure with the Mount Slipendie episode, and Mr. Trillionaire was all too happy to have a reason to cut off that evil lunatic from his endless cash flow."

"You're lying. Dragon wasn't all bad. He tried to *stop* you from using the Dragon Slug to attack the city!" said Ram.

"What sense does that make?" retorted Gyakusatsu, flailing a hand. "While I was all too happy to receive and make use of Dragon's research upon his termination, I wanted nothing to do with his monsters. I dispatched Blue Widow to seek and *destroy* the Dragon Slug so that it could not interfere with the doomsday scenario. That she proved to be an unreliable spaz was not part of the plan. But the most frightening thing is that the slug was one of Dragon's *less* destructive unfinished creations. I myself am not even sure if all his worst monsters have been properly exterminated. And if Dragon tried to claim it was not his fault when the slug went and ate two thousand people, then I should give him credit for being a most gifted actor. But I take no credit for a random atrocity."

Actually choosing to believe Gyakusatsu, all Ram could think was that it was a good thing Marvin Drago was in police custody at the station.

"At any rate, that takes us to two days ago, on the back of a whale," continued Gyakusatsu. "I never wanted to kill Mr. Trillionaire, my idol, my friend. But I needed his money, and once he made it absolutely certain on that whale at sea that he was getting out of the business of world domination, I had no choice but to act. If he did not have the stomach to go through with creating a perfect world anymore, I would complete his vision for him. I dispatched the Abandoned and hoped to end his life in as quick and clean a manner as possible, but you know how that ended up. And finally, all that remains is doomsday, closer to two hours from now."

"What is doomsday?" asked Ram.

Gyakusatsu bent over and retrieved his mask fragments from the ground, reassembling the façade on his face.

"You will have to fight me for that information," he responded.

Ram snickered, rubbing the back of his neck.

"You may be a crazy weirdo, and I do need to get revenge for what you did to my closest friend, but I don't think it's in your best interest to fight me."

Then Gyakusatsu, across the room from Ram, threw a punch where he stood, and the air displaced by his fist traveled across space like a whirlwind to throw Ram into the wall.

"Where the *heck* did you learn that?" asked Ram as he pointed at the indentation his body had left behind.

"Did you honestly expect I would not reserve the best machinery for my own body?" he responded.

Then Gyakusatsu disappeared. But before Ram could even attempt to perceive what had just happened, thousands of blows began to pelt his body in a violent invisible rain. Each wallop connected like a weak swing of Death's hammer, and not even Ram could withstand an attack such as this indefinitely.

"How are you doing that?" roared Ram, and the ferocity of merely his muscles contracting was enough to send a tremor through the room that stopped Gyakusatsu in his tracks.

"Elmo's razor, of course," he said with a grin Ram could not see, patting his chest. "It is a power source greater than any emotion, and the only object ever proven to be up to the task of facing you."

"The razor is *inside* of your body?" asked Ram.

"No, but within my body is a conduit that interacts directly with the razor via wireless energy transfer, another one of my great technological innovations. I have become a true cyborg, sustained by a perpetual energy source that resides in a secure location far away from here."

"So you mean you're gonna kill me with the thing that a senile old man uses to scrape my face once a month?"

"Well, it sounds less dramatic when you frame it like that."

Gyakusatsu disappeared again immediately afterward. In truth, he was shuffling around the room at a speed approaching that of light, marginally quicker even than Ram Van Bamf could move. Ram knew he had run out of options. Merely subduing Gyakusatsu in his current empowered state would be impossible. Ram Van Bamf had to go for the deathblow, and he had to do it now.

"What are you doing?" mocked Gyakusatsu, his voice coming from a hundred different locations. "Why do you stand still? Can't you see that even you are capable of dying?"

"It's not my death I'm afraid of," said Ram, and he closed his eyes.

He could have easily stomped his foot into the ground and sunk the entire island into the ocean, or he could have screamed and produced a sound wave that would send the sea and the sky into a frenzy, conjuring up hurricanes in all directions. But that could not guarantee that Gyakusatsu would not survive. What Ram Van Bamf needed was one concentrated blow, guided by the same preternatural instincts that had maintained him in many of his battles with the Abandoned. It demanded time and patience that he could ill afford, but Ram could eventually begin to sense the distinct movements of Gyakusatsu as he danced around him. He attacked Ram in a tornado pattern, spiraling around him, moving up and down the sizable girth of his body to strike. Gyakusatsu himself probably believed he was attacking in a randomized manner, never realizing that his style of fighting was just as structured as his manner of plotting world domination. As far as Ram Van Bamf was concerned, it would be his last mistake.

Ram threw one punch, and the fight was over. He had actually botched his timing by the most incredibly minute fraction of a second, his knuckles ingraining themselves into Gyakusatsu's ribs instead of his chest, though it proved to make little difference. The impact of the punch was like the rage of God upon the Earth, obliterating the Doomsday Fortress, effacing the sky of every cloud, and spawning a ring of tsunamis that grew ever taller and more vengeful as it raced away from the island. A tropical paradise had been reduced to a barren rock at sea, save for a few odd pieces of wreckage wedged in the rocks. Gyakusatsu lay in a heap before Ram, blood and sparks alike flowing from his broken body. Fragments of his mask had embedded themselves into his face, and his trench coat had long since disintegrated, revealing a twisted mess of skin and metal underneath.

"I guess that's one way to stop the clock," sighed Ram.

"No," whispered Gyakusatsu, vocalizations having become an overly laborious chore, "even now, time slips away."

Then, out of his own eyes, a hologram of a digital clock was projected into the air above him, ticking down in sync with the previous clocks. Less than two hours remained.

"I don't understand. I destroyed the fortress and I defeated you," said Ram. "What's there left to break?"

"Death and destruction do not solve all problems," lectured Gyakusatsu.

"Look who's talking!"

"Indeed, and look what I have to show for it," and he tried and failed to wave his arm.

"Tell me what I need to do to stop the clock."

"Very well. The doomsday clock responds to my heart rate. If you want to stop the clock, you need to make my heart stop beating."

"And then the nightmare is over?" asked Ram.

"No. Then the nightmare begins."

Frustrated, but too tired to become livid anymore, Ram just put his head in his hands.

"You won't let this end peacefully," he said, "no matter what I say or do."

"No, I am sorry, I will not," he responded, his voice becoming ever fainter. "I must create the perfect world."

Ram nodded.

"Okay."

Then Ram Van Bamf punched Gyakusatsu in the heart, punching through flesh and bone, through circuits and metal, and Gyakusatsu was dead. His eyes, though devoid of life now, continued to project the clock, which had ceased its countdown. Ram seemed to have won the day, but victory was bittersweet, and he was left to wonder what horrors Gyakusatsu could possibly conjure from beyond the grave. Unfortunately, he would not be left wondering for very long.

"Why so glum, idiot? Isn't this what you wanted all along?"

Ram looked up, his mouth open and yet his jaw clenched with dread, to find a feminine cyborg clad in green cybernetic armor with purple luminescent lighting running down the inside of her arms and continuing to her boots. A sculpt of a bundle of snakes coiled around her head, gleaming amber jewels encrusted into the eye sockets of each one, but the face of the helmet itself was something hideous, a visage crafted for the express purpose of inspiring terror.

But Ram had barely noticed any of that yet. At the moment, he could only think about the familiar inflection in her voice, and her particular choice of language.

"Fran?"

19

"The name is Green Medusa, undisputed leader of the Abandoned, tasked with creating a perfect world in the absence of my master. And you are going to help me."

Ram Van Bamf rubbed his eyes and blinked several times to confirm he was not experiencing some sort of beating-induced hallucination. He had never been so relieved and disgusted at the same time, and it was not unlike the satisfaction that came from vomiting all over a coffee table. While his favorite person in the world had become trapped inside the body of a monster, the fact remained that she was alive, which made all the difference. And on the bright side, Ram estimated in her current form that she would actually be able to survive a real hug from him.

"Fran! I'm so happy you're alive!" said Ram. "Sure, let's help each other end this mess."

"My thoughts exactly," responded Medusa.

Meanwhile, back in Ultratropolis, city hall had become the nerve center in the struggle against doomsday. Thanks to a blatant and continuous misappropriation of funds spanning the years, the office of Mayor Dingus had become the most fortified location in the city, perfect for staging a final defense against whatever was poised to strike Ultratropolis by noontime. While Dingus himself would have liked to flee the city at his earliest convenience, there were enough bounty hunters stalking him on behalf of gypped creditors and lovers that it would have been even more fatal to leave than to stay. The rest of the citizens present had been gathered there for the express purpose of saving the city, and they ranked amongst the most vital minds Ultratropolis had left to offer. "Aww, heck! My best gal, tangled up in a web of deceit right under my nose! What kind of man does that make me?" said Little Jimmy, pacing back and forth amongst the new furniture in the office.

"At least Sally didn't blow up a whale full of rich people," countered Ruttiger, sitting down, arms crossed. "Although, that sounds like something Fuzzy would have done even before he turned into a robot."

"My best friend has become the incarnation of death," said Carl, a fist over his mouth. "It is not nearly as joyous an occasion as our songs in Lethal Enforcer made it sound."

"Come on now, guys," pled Fury, "this isn't the time for moping. Ram told us the truth about the Abandoned and the Emperor because he thinks we might be able to help him if things don't go the way he planned today. If ever there was a time for us to think positive, it's now. Right, Wilson?"

Wilson, leaning on the back of Fury, gave him two thumbs-up.

"Yeah, Wilson gets it," Fury nodded.

"Thinking positive in the face of oblivion is easier said than done," said Bolivia Tantrum, as enchanting and stoic as ever, looking out the repaired window. "But I will employ my limited resources as I see fit."

"Lo, the face of oblivion is a beautiful bitch, the last mercy of every saint and devil," said Halstein, clenching Vidar with great enthusiasm. "Gaze not upon her with fear, and recoil from the desire for embrace. Merely love her when she arrives, and be certain you are nothing afterward."

"Well said, my friend," said Warmaker, the only person in the room who understood him. "If today is our doomsday, if we are meant to fall down, then we shall do so up in arms!"

"All I want is to live in a world where there are pastries enough for all," said Pietro, his cheeks growing ever rosier as he became impassioned.

"A fine wish, Pietro, but confectionery cannot solve the present crisis," said Dot, standing over the desk of Dingus. "The fact that Ram Van Bamf himself summoned us here as part of a plan of his own design is in and of itself extraordinary. If a man as cognitively challenged as him believes in us, we have no choice but to reward his fervor. We must be ready to act according to our designated roles when the clock strikes noon."

Then the entire city began to tremble as if a colony of elephants decided to hold a track meet.

"Or maybe we should act now," corrected Dot.

"Just tell me when it's safe to come out," said Dingus, hiding under the desk.

From the window, the source of the tremors was apparent and frightening to Bolivia. In plain sight, and not particularly far away, was the very pit of acid from which Ram Van Bamf rescued Leonora not long ago. The acid gushed and boiled like the cauldron of an especially negligent witch, and a black splotch began to grow increasingly enormous as it ascended from the murky depths of the pit.

"What could *that* be?" remarked Bolivia.

"Mr. Mayor, why did you ever agree to spend the whole city budget on pits of acid in the first place?" asked Carl.

"I don't know! Elmo gave me a big sack of money one day, and before I knew it, there was a pit of acid where the fire department used to be," said Dingus. "I'm just one man! Who am I to inhibit the freedom of others?"

"Wilson and I will initiate the city evacuation," said Fury, and he and Wilson were already at the door. "The citizens know to be on guard, and we have officers in place everywhere we need them to be. You know, it's pretty nice of the guys at the station to keep taking orders from us after we all unceremoniously quit."

"And even though I can't imagine my father's ancient toy from the days of the Defense will be of any practical use, I will leave to prepare it, all the same," said Bolivia. Dot and Pietro went to join her.

"Very good. The rest of us will remain here for now, until the threat becomes absolutely apparent," said Warmaker.

"Indeed. A fiend fully born bears the most flesh for consumption," said Halstein, raising Vidar toward the heavens as a totem to sacrilege.

"So, we're sure Halstein is a good guy, right?" asked Little Jimmy.

The intangible mass in the pit approached ever closer to the surface, and Green Medusa beckoned its awakening from the spot where Leonora had stumbled. By now, both Medusa and Ram Van Bamf had returned to Ultratropolis through the entrance portal, having left behind what remained of the island as a sarcophagus to a corrupted mind. Ram had never suspected that anything could actually be lurking underneath any of the pits that littered the city, but he suddenly felt vindicated about suplexing all of those cars into them.

"Fran, come on, let's call off whatever's going on here," said Ram, touching Medusa's arm. "Once we stop doomsday, we can get you and the others out of those cyborg bodies."

Medusa swept aside Ram's arm, disregarding his words in the same gesture.

"Do you know what kinds of powers I have?" she asked, not looking at him.

"I dunno. Can you turn me to stone?"

"No. My power is envy-based. I can replicate all of the abilities of my brethren. If I wished, I could have already trapped you in a Gravity Compulsion Beam and pounded you all day with fists as sturdy as Death's Pluto Hammer."

"Then why haven't you?"

"Because you deserve to suffer so much more than that."

Then Green Medusa dove into the pit, gliding off like a mermaid into the darkness.

"That really wasn't the answer I was hoping for," said Ram.

He and the rest of Ultratropolis would have to wait no further to look upon the final posthumous machination of Gyakusatsu. Doomsday had been promised, and now it had arrived in a form unexpected by anyone too old for the video arcade. From the sweltering and hateful depths of the acid bath emerged a bona fide giant robot, rising like a mechanical envoy from hell. With an obsidian black skull for a head and two bowling alley-sized thrusters protruding out of its upper back, it inspired thoughts of Black Death. Yet its emerald torso and shoulders draped in bright-eyed serpents were reminiscent of Green Medusa. The legs were bulky and angular like a Japanese mech, but as white as milky quartz and equipped with halves of saucers outside of the hips and calves, conjuring up imagery of White Pandora. The upper arms were uniformly black, but the left forearm was a deep ruby shade with golden lightning bolts painted down the sides, suggesting the fury of Red Jester. The opposite forearm seemed like a sapphire-hued missile silo, outfitted with any number of concealed weapons and lustrous red orbs wrapping around the top near the point where the limbs met, recalling the ambiguous destructive potential of Blue Widow. Taken altogether, it was a monstrosity of parts sewn together like a Frankenstein, a behemoth too impossible to even have existed in mythology. Only the likes of Gamera and Rodan could hope to stand eye to eye with such a demon, yet even Rodan would fall and become incinerated in an instant against this type of power. What towered above Ram Van Bamf now was the corporeal manifestation of apocalypse, conceived to unify the world by annihilating a small portion of it.

"So, *that's* doomsday," said Ram, mouth agape, a lifetime of disappointment over a lack of physical challenges abruptly nullified.

"Heck of a thing, huh?" broadcast the voice of Black Death from inside the robot.

"The Mega Warriors get a giant robot, so why not us?" projected Red Jester.

"It pleases me a great deal to introduce you to the culmination of everything our masters ever strove for," said Green Medusa. "A flawed world produces a flawed king, and you get what you deserve. Ram Van Bamf, meet Lesser God."

The titanic machine took its first steps onto the Earth, each one assaulting the city like an empyrean tirade.

"Do all the pits of acid have giant robots in them?" asked Ram.

"Nah, the rest are just decoys. One giant pit of acid would raise eyebrows, but a whole bunch of giant pits of acid is not nearly as suspicious," explained Death. "Plus, constructing the pits helped to bankrupt the city, which meant there would be no money left for any lengthy investigations into any seedy shadow organizations such as ours."

"So what's powering that thing then?" asked Ram.

"Us," replied White Pandora.

"And don't forget the old-timer's razor," added Jester.

"The razor is the heart at the machine's core, and we are the veins that pump the lifeblood to and from it," explained Blue Widow. "As the Abandoned, we harness and perpetually generate energy through the power of our own emotional states. When we freely allow Elmo's razor to absorb our continuously regenerating energy, the sum power of the razor increases at regular exponential rates. It is the razor which in turn fuels the various processes that maintain Lesser God. In other words, every passing second, Lesser

God becomes more powerful with no end in sight. There is no roof to its strength. Today, you have met your match."

"We'll see about that!" said Ram, an ecstatic grin flashing across his face, every muscle in his body screaming with elated anticipation. He pointed in the direction of Mount Slipendie. "Let's take the fight over there, so we won't have any distractions."

There was an awkward wait then as bits of murmurs and whispers amongst the Abandoned could be heard through the broadcasting speakers of Lesser God.

"You can't be serious," said Jester at last. "This is the no holds barred fight you've been waiting for your whole life, and you're trying to muck it up with rules? Do you ask for salt when Wolfgang Puck cooks you dinner, too?"

"Look, you can go wipe Ultratropolis off the map all you want, but only after you've killed me. And I don't think it's fair that anybody should get hurt while we fight, so let's get out of here so we can fight like civilized men and giant robots," said Ram.

"He can't be serious," repeated Jester.

"There were inklings of thoughtfulness in his demeanor up till now, but nothing that would suggest a sudden turn for the merciful like this," said Pandora.

"You threw a freaking mountain!" reminded Death.

"Most unusual," said Widow, though with a tone that suggested intrigue.

"This was a variable our master did not anticipate," said Medusa.

"What's the deal? Are we going to fight or not?" asked Ram.

"That depends," said Medusa. "You really will not fight us within the confines of Ultratropolis?"

"No. I can't put innocent lives at risk like that. Not anymore," said Ram. He took a deep breath, an uncharacteristically knowing smirk replacing his previously giddy expression. "I kicked my Ram Van Bamf Syndrome. I was cured by Dr. Keiji Kojima."

"Crap!" exclaimed Jester immediately, ruining any dramatic tension Ram may have built.

"Jester's expletive may be the most succinct summation of events at this current juncture," confirmed Pandora.

"What gives?" asked Ram. "No more secrets! Once you put a giant robot on the planet, the time for secrets is over."

"Fine," said Medusa. "Lesser God was never intended to destroy Ultratropolis specifically. It was constructed only to kill *you*, Ram Van Bamf, because killing you is an infinitely more impressive symbol of power than destroying any city. But the plan was to film our battle via the satellite and edit the footage thoughtfully, to demonstrate how it was your reckless abandon that doomed Ultratropolis, not us. Lesser God was supposed to be the savior that stopped the carnage of your rampage, thus facilitating the transfer of power in the world to the Control as world leaders became confident in our ability to maintain peace and security. That was the plan devised by Gyakusatsu. That was the plan that the Emperor agreed to enact. We would take one life to save the whole world."

"From what?" retorted Ram, dismissing the whole notion without a second thought. "The world isn't under attack by anyone other than you! Jerry and the doc meant well, but they didn't understand that you can't force the world to change. People are gonna be cold and vulnerable and hurt and hungry and mean and jealous and cruel and sad and weak for as long as all the other people keep giving them reasons to feel that way. Make a police state, and all you have is people being miserable in a police state. You can't make people be happy. All you can do is stop giving them reasons to be unhappy. I have a real good friend who calls that 'empathy.' I just call it 'talking.' If we can just remember to talk to the people we care about and let them know that they matter, the world's still gonna be full of problems, but at least we'll make it a happier world for each other.

"And Widow, do you really wanna know what the source of human suffering is? It's when people stop talking. That's when everything falls apart and people start building giant killer robots. That's when you need big dumb brutes like me to settle things. And I don't like a world that needs a guy like me in it any more than you do, but that's the way it is. The Control started this, and now I'm going to finish it."

Lesser God loomed frozen like a monolith for a long time after that, no doubt as the Abandoned argued amongst themselves as to how to proceed, though even now bits of acid continued to pour off its pristine surface. Ram hoped they would merely give themselves up, understanding that he had turned over a new leaf and would not consent to their deadly designs. Having it out in the fight of his life would be terrific, but guaranteeing the security of both the citizens of

Ultratropolis and the human beings trapped inside the Abandoned was of greater importance.

"What? Why did you not convey sooner that the download of personality assets to your AI was never completed?" asked Pandora suddenly, loud enough to be discerned through the speakers.

"If Medusa does not operate under the same restrictive parameters as us, then that means she is capable of thoughts and actions that go beyond the will of the Control," said Death.

"Damn straight!" exclaimed Medusa with glee. "That silly woman called Fran had a will so stubborn that even days of brainwashing were not quite enough to flush out all of her influence over my mind. And when Ram went and destroyed the Doomsday Fortress, emergency protocol dictated my premature awakening. To think, if Ram had arrived just a few minutes later, the brainwashing process might have had sufficient time to complete! Instead, you're stuck with me, Green Medusa, the chick that the rest of you are programmed to obey as your leader. But *I* don't have to obey anybody, thanks to the adamantine will of a woman who only exists as a whisper in my psyche. Isn't it funny how life works out? By resisting total brainwashing, that woman only succeeded in making me even more dangerous. I *am* the Control right now! And my first order of business is the destruction of Ultratropolis, in every way imaginable."

Then the first payload of missiles deployed out of Lesser God's Widow arm, crashing through buildings and roads around the city in horrendous mushroom cloud-incurring explosions and officially denoting the beginning of pandemonium in Ultratropolis.

"Heh, that's my Fran, never settling," mumbled Ram to himself. The hand that had beckoned the missiles began to tremble.

"We must follow the will of our leader," conceded Widow with trademark melancholy.

"Yes," said Pandora, "but the blood is on her hands now."

As if on cue, clouds that had lain heavy across the sky began to burst, a fresh cascade of snow descending to obscure and incite the chaos further. At their abrupt intensity, the showers would work well to extinguish flames around the city, but by that same token, they would also deter all efforts at escape, much to the chagrin of the police managing the evacuation. All the same, ever since the day that Ram Van Bamf had entered their lives, the citizens of Ultratropolis had been preparing for an event as cataclysmic as this. The fact that it took so long to happen was just a pleasant surprise.

"Do you see what Lesser God can do? The most minor display of its power brings the city to its knees," said Medusa.

"The city has knees?" asked Ram.

"Never mind!"

Lesser God threw a haymaker of a punch at Ram, and when he extended his arms and palms to catch the gargantuan fist, the resulting collision triggered a shockwave that vaporized the nearby Nice to Meat You into an airborne paste. Even the ground below Ram collapsed as his feet dug through asphalt and granite to maintain his bearing. The force of this single fist on the arms of Ram Van Bamf was like the convergence of all the objects in a meteor shower upon the same point, and Ram became like a modern day Atlas, dividing Lesser God from Ultratropolis and preventing the copulation of the primordial death rattle.

"So this is what it feels like to get punched by me," grunted Ram, his triceps and pectorals having ballooned to a size that could house a family of rabbits.

The punishing fist of Lesser God finally recoiled all at once as its other hand suddenly came careening down. Ram was forced to lunge as the entire city block underneath him fissured and shattered into thousands of jagged chunks, the consequence of merely one arm of Lesser God striking the pavement. If Ultratropolis survived to the end of the day, it would not be without many scars.

"We will eat your soul, Ram Van Bamf!" said Death.

"The longer you prolong this bout, the more impossible your survival becomes," said Pandora.

"Then I just have to put you away early!" said Ram. "Just as soon as I figure out how."

Surrounded in a slate gray sea of splintered debris and uprooted slabs of bedrock, Ram could have swum across the landscape easier than he could have run, except that the acid from the pit had begun to spill forth into the various cracks and openings made by the schism of the streets. A literal wasteland was forming all around Ram, and all he could do was hope the citizens closest to the warzone had already fled to safer ground. At the least, Ram reasoned that the situation could not possibly deteriorate any further.

"Unleash the dinosaurs!" ordered Medusa.

"Dinosaurs!" repeated Ram.

It turned out that the complex hidden underneath the Tooth Decay Hooray was only one of many facilities planted around Ultratropolis by the Control, as an army of dozens of genetically modified fire-breathing Tyrannosaurus rexes began to pile out of countless underground bunkers to further inundate the city in devastation.

"Do you see what I see?" asked Ruttiger from the window at the mayor's office.

"Is it a D-cup? Because otherwise, I'm not budging," said Dingus, still under his desk.

"Hot dog! Real live dinosaurs! This is tops!" exclaimed Little Jimmy. Then a fireball flew past the window, engulfing a portion of the local elementary school. "And they've got great aim, too!"

"Ram already has his hands full with battling a giant robot. He does not have time for prehistoric monsters," said Carl.

"We'll take care of it," said Warmaker, a pair of bazookas suddenly materializing in his hands.

"The feast beckons," agreed Halstein.

"Aww, but there must be almost a hundred of them!" said Little Jimmy.

"We'll take care of it," repeated Warmaker, and he and Halstein exited the room.

"Well, I think this might be our cue to go, too," sighed Ruttiger.

"You do not have to go if you don't want to, especially not you, Little Jimmy," said Carl. "When Ram concocted his plan, he could not have expected acid-ridden streets and raiding dinosaurs. If we leave this office, we will likely not return alive."

"If we don't leave this office, it might be nobody who gets out of this alive," said Ruttiger.

"Ruttiger's right! The whole city's countin' on us!" said Little Jimmy. He put out his hand. "Whatdya say, boys? All for one and one for all! It's time for the Bamf Brigade to do its part!"

Ruttiger and Carl shared a tentative glance.

"Bamf Brigade, eh?" said Ruttiger. He put his hand in with Little Jimmy. "I like it."

"Me too," said Carl, cracking a warm grin and completing the trilogy of hand overlap. "Okay. Let's help Ram save our home."

Ram Van Bamf would require that assistance, as he was currently hurtling upside down into the side of a skyscraper. While the building itself would implode almost instantaneously upon impact, Ram would shake off the pain in time. The concern was that Lesser God did not seem intent upon granting him that time.

"You've got a good punt," said Ram, shaking a finger, dust and debris caking his hair and body.

"You should see its QB skills!" said Jester.

With that, a fireball larger than any ever conjured before flared up within the palm of Lesser God's Jester hand, glowing like a nuclear blast even before it was thrown. It was absolutely certain to Ram that the city would be annihilated wholesale if the fireball made touchdown. The situation felt slightly familiar.

"Try me," said Ram, hands out at his sides.

Then he leapt into the air, just as the saucers within the Pandora legs of Lesser God lit up like massive spotlights, shining upon the location where Ram had been standing. The sudden added force of gravity on the tract of land caught in the beams was enough to crush all trees and buildings into the same pancake shape, and entire hills were leveled out. Ram had escaped this fate with his thoughtful jump, and he was on a collision course with the fireball that had already left the Jester hand.

"Out of the frying pan and into the fire!" said Jester.

"I *punch* fire!" growled Ram.

And then he did exactly that, belting the fireball back at Lesser God, smacking it directly in the head. As Ram fluttered to the Earth, the sky ignited, furious flame harmonizing with raging snow to coalesce into a yin yang of natural disaster. Anything caught within a substantial radius of the initial detonation was razed to dust, and Ram was becoming increasingly frustrated at how much harm was coming to Ultratropolis. There was no mistaking that people were dying, and Ram needed to stop it now.

Deciding that a cyclone of fire and ice spiraling around the head of his enemy was as great an opening as any, Ram sprung off the ground to latch onto Lesser God's knee. From there, he leapt and climbed up its body until he himself had penetrated the sky-bound hell that had established dominion over the firmament. Ram had already been aching and battered across every inch of his body, and so the rush of freezing and burning particles against his skin served as a welcome respite from the dry air below. And even though his vision was less than optimal through the miasma, he soon found that for which he was searching.

"Can you see me in there?" asked Ram, standing on the upper torso of Lesser God, directly in front of its head. "Unfortunately, we do not need to see you to be able to kill you," responded Widow. "Yeah, well, neither do I."

Then Ram Van Bamf unleashed on the Earth a punch so immaculate that it would take a hundred thousand years of human labor to match how much testosterone was spent in that moment. At his current distance from the ground and considering how much of the immediate surrounding area had already been destroyed, the risk of destroying Ultratropolis or cracking the planet into two pieces had been significantly lessened. Ram also rightly predicted that Lesser God would absorb most of the impact of the attack, just as Ram had absorbed the onslaughts of Jester back at the Doomsday Fortress.

Nonetheless, the Earth shook. Lunches were dropped in Pittsburgh and dinners were ruined in Berlin. Bird migration patterns would be confused for years to come. Atlantis rose from the ocean for some reason. It was as if Ram had ascended Babel and reclaimed the universal truth for a humanity roused from its antisocial slumber.

But Lesser God was unfazed.

"Well, didn't expect that," confessed Ram.

"I will enjoy this," hissed Medusa as the eye sockets of Lesser God began to burn red.

With those words, Ram Van Bamf was struck down by a laser beam the likes of which was comparable to a Death Star in power. He plummeted like a downed jet fighter afterward, a massive block of dead weight cutting the air. When he fell out of sight, and nothing was heard after the thump of his reunion with the wreckage, Medusa was satisfied.

"Our orders?" asked Pandora.

"The destruction continues," Medusa shrugged.

As a new barrage of missiles rained down on the city and dinosaurs continued to harass anyone courageous enough to venture across the snow banks, Ram Van Bamf could not help but marvel at how quiet the world had become. Maybe everything was actually very loud, but he could not hear any of it at the moment. He could taste blood on his mouth. He had never tasted his own blood before. It seemed to taste better than the other blood he had tasted.

Then there came a sudden whisper.

Ram could not make it out.

A shadow fell over him.

Ram could not discern its shape.

A hand caressed his bosom.

Ram could not detect its warmth.

"Ram, come on, wake up. It's your pal, Jerry."

It was quite some time before Ram could comprehend that he lay in a long, dark alleyway, and Jerry stood pristine at the center of the single beam of light penetrating the shade, like a droopy-shouldered angel.

"Jerry, hey, can you help me up?" asked Ram, not even able to turn his neck yet.

"No. You've done enough. You tried your best."

"If I tried my best, that robot would be scrap metal. I need to try again."

"What would you do differently this time?"

"I would punch it harder."

"Are you capable of punching it any harder?"

"Not really."

They did not say anything for a stretch.

"So, I died," determined Ram at last.

"You did?"

"Sure. I'm talking to you, aren't I?"

"What if I'm not dead?"

Jerry clapped his hands and jumped up and down a few times.

"I seem pretty alive, don't I?" he asked.

"Jerry! You're really here!" exclaimed Ram, and he could feel the slightest vigor creeping back into his haggard limbs. "This is great. How did you survive the attack?"

"Leonora," Jerry said with a dreamy inflection. "She saved us all. In that last instant before the fireball struck, she opened portals for all of us except for you, because she knew you would live. She saved as many people as she possibly could that night, right under the noses of the other Abandoned. It was even she that saved Fran, except, well, you know what happened after that. Leonora hid the rest of us away and released us this morning."

"So there is still good in the Abandoned," said Ram, having confirmed a long held suspicion.

"There's good in all of us, Ram. Just some of us are better listeners than others," said Jerry. He sighed before continuing. "I wasn't a very good listener."

"I don't get it, Jerry. Why did you do all of this? Why did you start the Control?"

Jerry took off his glasses and wiped the snow off the lenses with his shirt.

"My invention, that trillion dollar idea of an invention, was a fluke," he began. "Nothing more than another case of serendipity, as the story so often goes with great discoveries. So, in spite of being a total shut-in, I became celebrated the world over as Mr. Trillionaire, the man who gave the world his miracle invention. But I still felt so small. I'm not strong like you, or attractive like Leonora, or brilliant like Kojima or Drago. I'm just a dope who got lucky.

"But I didn't want to just be lucky. I wanted to be productive and create something with my own two hands by the sweat of my brow. I wanted to do something wonderful without it being an accident. When I heard about this marvelous thing called the Defense that was being put up for sale, I got all these ideas about how I could use such an organization to help the world! Putting all the brightest minds in one place and letting their imaginations run wild? It sounds so nice, doesn't it? The Control was supposed to be my baby that I would nurture and mold to make the world a better place.

"It all went wrong at the very start. I got it in my head that 'better' meant 'safer,' and 'safer' meant 'controlled'—hence, the Control, of course. So I told Kojima and Drago to create things that could stop all wars. If they just made something big and scary enough, I figured we could force the world to play nice with each other. And when nobody's fighting each other, then everyone can be happy, right? Maybe if I was the one getting my hands dirty instead of the two of them, I would have realized how crazy that sounded a lot sooner. But Kojima and Drago both became obsessed, in their own way. And for that, you have no one to blame but me. Gyakusatsu and Dragon are my only legacy now, along with the ashes of this beautiful city."

The arc of Jerry's shoulders had somehow managed to dip even lower. Ram, having regained most tactile sensation, shook his head and extended a hand.

"You're not a killer, Jerry. All of this is Gyakusatsu. You changed your mind about everything before anybody really got hurt that bad."

"Well, of course I changed my mind, thanks to you."

"Me?" squeaked Ram. "I thought it was because you found out what Gyakusatsu did to Leonora."

"Is that what you were told?" asked Jerry with a sour grimace. "What he did to Leonora was reprehensible, but what he did to *all* of them was reprehensible. I had already demanded that he halt the entire project *before* Leonora was transformed. I changed my mind about everything on the day I met you, Ram! Until that day, all I had ever heard was that you were a dangerous menace who bench pressed island chains. It was easy for me to believe I was helping the common good by funding your defeat. But then I met you, and you were so kind to me, and you saved Leonora's life! I couldn't in good conscience go through with our plan once I finally understood you were just another misguided yet otherwise well-intentioned soul like myself. I guess you could say in our isolation that Kojima and Drago and I had gotten ourselves all wrapped up in a case of groupthink, and meeting you snapped me out of it. But Kojima and Drago were too far gone. They kept going."

"Maybe it's not too late to set things right," said Ram.

Jerry nodded.

Then the tops of the two buildings surrounding the alleyway were swept away like dust on a countertop as Lesser God suddenly loomed above them.

"Still breathing, huh? We can fix that," broadcast Medusa.

Compelled by the need to defend his friend, Ram Van Bamf took back to his feet.

"I feel better than I look," he said, and then he spit the blood out of his mouth.

"Doesn't make much difference now, big man. The reaper always collects his due," said Death.

"That may be true, but it will not be today!" came a voice down the alleyway.

"Carl!" exclaimed Ram.

"That's right! The Bamf Brigade is here to give your giant robot a split lip!" declared Little Jimmy.

"Well, they kind of took all the cool things I could have said, but I'm here too," said Ruttiger.

Jerry, Carl, Little Jimmy, and Ruttiger formed a circle around Ram.

"Looks like it's five-on-five now," said Ram with a clenched fist.

At that moment, the city yet again began to shake, but under more fortuitous circumstances. Around the perimeter of Ultratropolis rose a wall tall and thick enough to withstand any number of dinosaur head butts, leaving the roads and highways the only means of escaping the city anymore.

"That ought to stop the dinos from getting loose into the world at large until somebody deals with them," said Bolivia by the southern city limit, a smug expression of satisfaction on her face and her head cocked back. "It looks like my crazy old father set one good idea into motion after all."

"Let us celebrate with kladdkaka!" suggested Pietro, producing that specific dessert on a platter.

"Don't mind if I do," shrugged Dot, and she took a fork.

"It is just as you prophesized!" remarked a member of Murdercide, not even thirty yards from where Bolivia and her people stood.

"Yep! A real, no foolin' doomsday!" said Chaz, arms akimbo, breathing in the cold air. "Me and my pals were trying to prevent it, but since it's here anyway, I think you guys know what to do!"

And with that, across the city limits of Ultratropolis, each of the bands that had performed at the Battle of the Bands, except of course for Lethal Enforcer, set up their instruments atop the wall erected by Bolivia. Murdercide, Psycho Demon, Calamity Schism, Murder Engine, Sinfony, and even Chainsaw Execution then took it upon themselves to literally perform the soundtrack to the apocalypse. This was the day that had been promised metal heads since time immemorial, and a great pride swelled within the heart of Halstein as the cacophony pierced his ears, renewing his blood frenzy. Vidar would split skulls clean down the center at twice its previous vitality ever afterward.

With walls of sound erected and dinosaurs once again on the brink of extinction, all that remained then was the final battle between the Bamf Brigade and the Abandoned.

"This is the end!" bellowed Medusa.

"You got it," agreed Ram, and he could feel the excitement coursing back into his muscles.

20

"Kill them!"

But the Abandoned were more reluctant to follow the orders of their leader this time.

"Do we have to?" asked Widow.

"I recollect that my cat requires a fresh dish," feigned Pandora.

"I should have no qualms with execution," said Death, perplexed by his own phrasing.

"What's with you stooges? These are the people who wronged the flesh bags inside of us more than anybody. I say we find out how many bites it takes to get to the center of their brains!" said Jester.

"Listen to Jester!" agreed Medusa. "Their negligence is the whole reason we exist. We reserve the right to avenge our pitiable hosts."

"But the Control exists to establish peace, not to seek revenge," said Widow.

"Not anymore."

Via remote control, Medusa activated the red orbs that wrapped around the Widow arm, allowing a fresh flood of anxiety to flush out every coherent thought in the mind of every person for miles. The cold would not be able to counteract the intensity of their strength this time.

"Ah! Not this crap again," said Ruttiger, his hands over his ears.

"What, what is this?" asked Carl, never having experienced such an intangible form of pain before.

"I think Blue Widow can amplify all your self-doubts and worries until it drives you crazy," explained Ram. "Or, in this case, Medusa is probably doing it."

"Well, it's workin' like a charm so far!" exclaimed Little Jimmy.

"Why are you so immune to it, Ram?" asked Jerry, who himself did not seem particularly ravaged by the effects of the orbs.

"Because a guy like me can't afford to go second-guessing his life," said Ram, "especially not at a time like this."

"Heh. That's funny," said Jerry. "The only reason I'm unaffected is because I already know there isn't anything I could have done *worse* with my life."

"Look, are we going to kumbaya, or are we going to kill each other?" asked Jester.

Then Lesser God stomped the ground, and the surrounding city block crumbled and disintegrated with all the ease of its previous effort to desecrate the concrete. Ram swept up his allies in his burly arms and lunged far away to nowhere in particular, only trying to escape the collapsing buildings on either side of the alleyway.

"So, uh, I think we better enact that plan of ours real quick!" said Little Jimmy while they were still airborne.

"Fran's a real piece of work, so I should go last," said Ram as they landed on something that resembled the Earth.

"Fran?" said Little Jimmy.

"It's a long story."

"I will do it first. I've been thinking about the right words for too long," said Carl.

"Okay. I'll try to keep us alive long enough for this to work," sighed Ram.

Jerry was bewildered, but he stumbled through the snow and debris to follow Ruttiger and Little Jimmy into cover behind the ruins of what was once a bank. Meanwhile, Ram Van Bamf and Carl stood out in the open, an appreciable distance away from the others, defiant in their posture. Carl's lips trembled as he tried to ward off the orb-induced bubble of anguish inflating inside his brain.

"Look at the two of them, standing there like they're trying to remember where they parked," said Jester as Lesser God approached.

"Some men choose to die on their feet," said Death.

"Yeah, just like us at Battle of the Bands!" blurted Carl suddenly.

Death did not respond.

245

"Let's do it," assented Murdock, and no more words were necessary.

After renewing their friendship with a masculine hand grip, Carl and Murdock rushed off to join the rest of their brothers. Although the influence of the orbs persisted unfettered, Carl was no longer subject to its tortures, and Murdock had already traversed his own purgatory. Little Jimmy and Ruttiger could not make such claims.

"We, uh, we know it's still dangerous out there," said Ruttiger, smacking himself in the side of the head as if trying to dislodge water from his ears. "I should go next."

"Nuh uh, Ruttiger! Fuzzy still seems awfully steamed. I'm goin' next. I can hear Sally callin' for me," said Little Jimmy.

"Both of you should remember to be careful," warned Jerry. "After all, Murdock was a man of the law. We cannot count on quite as much, um, rationality from the others."

"Yeah, well, who's ever met a rational girl anyway?" responded Little Jimmy, and he marched out of hiding like a slugger going up to bat. "Though I guess it's thinkin' like that that got me into hot water in the first place."

Spying the shivering little boy closing in on them, Medusa could not help but feel her team was threatening to be undone by a strategy that would have been at home in a Hallmark movie.

"This is ridiculous. We cannot afford another defector," she said.

"Agreed! Time to blow up the city again," said Jester.

"But I would like to hear what he has to say," lamented Widow.

"Of course you would," snarled Jester. "That's the problem."

Then a new fireball sweltered into existence out of the left hand of Lesser God. Ram had been afraid of something like this. The truth was that he did not know if he had recuperated enough energy yet to even be able to survive direct contact with an attack of that magnitude, let alone be able to deflect it.

"Uh, help from the audience?" said Ram as the thermal bomb grew ever larger.

"Hey, Ram!" yelled Ruttiger, a hand over his mouth, but not leaving his cover. "Don't you remember why this city is so snowy in the first place?"

Ram snapped his fingers and glared with determination at the growing ball.

"So, uh, hey, doll. Is it fun ridin' around in a giant robot? I always wanted to be a Mega Warrior," interjected Little Jimmy, trying to break the ice.

"If I could cry tears, I would weep every day of my being," responded Widow.

"Okay, not what I was goin' for," said Little Jimmy with a weary nod. "But listen. Whatever it was I did to you, Sally, I'm sorry. Real sorry! So how about you climb out of that big robot and we'll go split a Mean Bean, huh?"

"Stupid boy," muttered Widow.

"I guess that makes strike two. Okay, okay. Let's start over. I get that things ain't exactly been peaches and cream between us lately. Stuff like doomsday can get to a man, you know? But this whole time, all I ever wanted was to protect you and keep you safe. And what a swell job I did of it! So for that, I really am sorry, Sally. I'm sorry I let this happen to you."

"The vessel known as Sally never needed protecting. She was only looking for someone who respected her as a human being. You were incapable of providing that," explained Widow. "Jester, let us be rid of them."

"With pleasure!"

"Yeah, let's *not* do that instead," suggested Little Jimmy.

Apparently overruled, he watched as a falling star descended upon him, not nearly as twinkly and inspirational up close. As the intensifying heat threatened to ignite his newsboy cap, Little Jimmy could only wonder with awe what he must have done to Sally to warrant explosive inferno death. And although the prospect of giving up the ghost at his young age was not thrilling, the thought of dying without having saved Sally jabbed at his gut much worse.

"Sally! I'm about to be cooked like a Thanksgiving bird, so now ain't exactly the best time for long speeches. But that's okay, since I never really knew what to say in the first place. Our relationship has never been too big on communication. But that's all my fault too, huh? I guess if I didn't do all the talkin' for the both of us all the time, maybe I'd have something left worth sayin' right now. So now I gotta be a *real* man and learn to just shut my yap. If I'm about to burn up, I just want to say—I'm all ears, doll. At least for this last second or two before I'm charcoal."

"Really?" squeaked Widow.

It was much too late for her to intervene, but Ram Van Bamf had been brewing a solution in his lungs for the last several seconds. A horizontal avalanche approaching absolute zero in temperature barreled up his throat and screamed across the air toward the fireball. As fire and ice met once again, there was no compromise between the elements this time. The frost choked and throttled the heat until all that remained was a super massive ball of frozen flame, sparkling like the most elaborate Christmas ornament ever conceived. It came crashing to the ground directly in front of Little Jimmy, shattering instantaneously into multiple thousands of razor-edged shards. Ram was there to step in-between Little Jimmy and the icicle shower, defending both the boy and the city from what could have been yet another untimely end.

"Teach me that trick to use on my soda?" asked Little Jimmy.

"You must like really cold soda," said Ram.

"Ahem," interrupted Widow, "I suppose you are ready to retract what you just said, now that death is not quite as imminent."

"Who, me? Heck no, doll! If I got no clue what to do, the least I can do is hear you out. I'm sick of pretendin' I got all the answers. I'm just a dumb kid! A kid who's over the moon for you! And now I wanna start treatin' you right. That means you gotta have a say in things, and I need to listen. *That's* how I'll be a man from now on."

"Well, that's really all Sally ever wanted," said Widow.

"Do you believe this?" asked Medusa, shaking her head.

"Who would have thought there could be negative repercussions to brainwashing an honest law enforcer or a girl who could model lollipops?" responded Jester.

Little Jimmy interlocked his fingers, his lips similarly pursed in penitence.

"Let me make this up to you, Sally. Let me be the, uh, man-boy you deserve."

It was at that moment that Blue Widow plainly decided to stop feeling blue.

"Irreconcilable system error. Program termination initiated," came an automated voice.

Not wasting another second, Medusa initiated the ejection of Widow, and she too was flung into the sky like a garbage bag out of a nineteenth-story window. Continuing to demonstrate his skills in the outfield, Ram chased and caught her by the waist with a single hand, having devoted his other arm to carrying Little Jimmy. Sapped of any power source, the arachnid legs on the body of Widow hung limp now, like expensive toys.

As Ram released his precious cargo to the snow and rock, Little Jimmy grabbed the helmet of Widow and pried it open, displacing eight hideous eyes with two brilliant baby blues. He and Sally touched their cold noses to each other, and Little Jimmy did not think he would ever be so happy again in his life.

"I like the Gummy Armada better than the Mean Bean," said Sally with a voice sweet and soft like cotton candy, meanwhile trying to fix her hair that was tied up in endless knots.

"So that's what your voice sounds like!" remarked Little Jimmy. "I'd really started to wonder."

"Have you ever wondered what it's like to be crushed like a bug? Because you're about to break new ground on that one too!" said Jester.

Rightfully suspecting that the tremendous shadow engulfing him and everything surrounding him did not belong to a luxuriant pompadour, Ram took the kids back in his arms and leapt just in time to evade a giant oncoming foot. Little Jimmy and Sally held hands throughout that tense moment, and it did not feel at all like being handcuffed to each other.

"Those kids need a diversion if they're gonna get away from here in one non-flattened piece," said Ruttiger, fist in hand. "Think you'll be okay on your own?"

Jerry, looking around at the large expanse of winter wasteland, shrugged his shoulders.

"As okay as I can be," he decided.

Ruttiger nodded and turned away. Enough snow had collected now that running was impossible, and as he waded through the storm, he began to wonder if it was even possible to locate Fuzzy inside of the deranged clown who had tried almost more than Medusa to kill them all. The last time he saw him, Ruttiger had called Fuzzy a worthless moron and a third-rate bozo. It was no wonder he was so angry now. Ruttiger had already accepted that everybody ran out of luck eventually, and by choosing to ever become friends with Fuzzy, he had sealed his fate quite some time ago.

"Hey, Fuzz, don't you know there isn't a kid on the planet who couldn't kick your tail from here to Sunday?"

As soon as Lesser God turned to address the flannel-clad decoy, Ram disappeared with Little Jimmy and Sally to the nearest police escort checkpoint, where the children could be properly evacuated along with any other stragglers. The red orbs around the Widow arm of Lesser God continued to operate even now, though they had diminished in effectiveness with the physical removal of Blue Widow herself. Medusa was only capable of replicating an approximation of the powers of her allies. Of course, none of that would help Ruttiger at all, and the likelihood of his immediate death continued to surge.

"Boy, if that's what you call a greeting, I guess that means your idea of 'bedside manner' is smothering a guy with a pillow," responded Jester.

"Good thinking, Fuzz. Do you see any pillows around here?"

"I do not know if you follow a sound line of reasoning in speaking as you do now," warned Pandora, reminding everyone of her continued presence in the conflict.

"Of course I do! This is the only way me and Fuzz know how to carry a conversation."

"Ain't that the truth! Too bad 'Fuzz' is long gone," said Jester, "and I'm plenty pissed off at the way you're talking to me."

Then Lesser God bent over and snatched Ruttiger up in its Jester hand. It happened quickly enough and the snow around him was so deep that Ruttiger knew there was no point in even trying to escape capture. Now he was face to face with the head of Lesser God, and between this and his confrontations with Blue Widow and the Dragon Slug, Ruttiger took solace in knowing he had now lived out most of the science fiction fantasies he had ever imagined.

"Is killing me really gonna make you feel better, Fuzz?" he asked, completely incapable of moving his arms or legs.

"Well, I won't know until I find out!"

"Don't do it, Fuzzy!" shouted Ram, back in the warzone.

"It looks like you lose this round, Ram," mocked Medusa, savoring each word as she spoke it.

"Hmm. Actually, tell you what, Ruttiger," said Jester, having reconsidered his position, "let's make this *fun*. We'll have a high stakes game of Hangman! I let you speak, and each time I don't like what you have to say, I crush one of your limbs!"

Ram Van Bamf broke out into a new sweat then, because he knew there was nothing he could do to help his friend now. Ruttiger could be obliterated by the slightest tightening of a grip. All Ram could do was watch and wait.

"You've made me an offer I can't refuse," said Ruttiger with a subdued grin.

"Great! Then by all means, talk your heart out, before I take it out manually."

Suddenly, dying in a fire back at the bakery did not sound so bad to Ruttiger anymore.

"Okay, Fuzz, Jester, whatever, I'm gonna talk. Over the years, I've called you a lot of names. Moron, bozo, loser, idiot, stupid, dope, numbskull, fool, buffoon, freak, nimrod. And I meant every one of those things! When it comes to the human race, you are the opposite of its pinnacle. If you got locked in a zoo at night, the koalas would eat you. There is nobody I feel less safe with than you."

"You are *really* not good at this," observed Jester.

The hand holding Ruttiger loosened its grasp so that Lesser God's other hand could grab Ruttiger's arm between two fingers.

"Crunch!" exclaimed Jester, and then Ruttiger lost the use of his left arm, howling in agony all the while.

"No!" yelled Ram, but now he only understood more than ever that he was completely at the mercy of Jester.

"So, as I was saying," gasped Ruttiger, his eyes bulging at the enormous amount of pain branching through his body like lightning, "you *suck*, Fuzz. You suck a lot. But come on! Everybody knows you suck. The difference between me and the rest is that I was willing to be your friend anyway. Shouldn't that count for something?"

"You were never his friend!" snapped Jester. "You practically said as much yourself. Fuzzy was just your charity case, the chump that you pretended to tolerate so that you could feel like some kind of big man. Fuzzy thought you were his best friend in the world! Do you have any idea what it's like to find out it was all just an illusion?"

"It was never an illusion! God, Fuzz, you're such a dope, even now! When you almost got me killed *twice* in a row, sure, I kicked you to the curb. You had it coming. But up till then, we were friends. Heck, we're really all the other's ever had. Neither one of us is competing with Jimmy Stewart for looks. We don't boogie the night away at the clubs. We're just a couple of blue collars aiming to make each other's lives a little less like crap."

"Jerry, pal, this is it," he said, a hand over his mouth. "I got the bright idea to get my friends to talk the Abandoned back to their senses. Course, I wasn't expecting them to have to go through a giant robot to get the job done. That one's on me. But truth be told, I had no idea what to do about Leonora. She's the loneliest one of all. But all that's changed now that you're here! I think you can bring her back, Jerry. You need to give it a shot. She deserves it."

"Me? Ah, Ram, I dunno. Leonora *does* deserve it, but I don't know if I'm the man who can do it. Everything I do just makes things worse for everybody."

"Jerry," said Ram, putting a hand on his concave shoulder, "you are the *only* person who can save her."

Medusa gave Pandora a similar pep talk, except it involved Medusa telling Pandora she was ugly and worthless. She estimated that if she treated Pandora enough like an emotionally damaged child, she could extinguish any remnant of her human host before someone like Jerry started trying to feed her crazy notions of peace and hope. Pandora deserved such treatment in the first place as far as Medusa was concerned. A woman like Leonora could have reduced a crowd of men to a horde of lustful zombies without lifting a finger. She had probably become less powerful in becoming White Pandora. Medusa considered Pandora the biggest fool out of all of the Abandoned, but she would fight to keep her around all the same, not wanting to be left all alone twice.

Neither duo was aware that they were being watched by a third party.

"Hello, Leonora," said Jerry at last, his voice cracking with the first word.

"My name is Pandora now."

"Well, they're both pretty names, but I like Leonora more," said Jerry with a smile so saccharine as to enrage Medusa.

"Hit the lights. Squash them both into puddles with gravity compulsion and end this," she growled.

"Medusa, you fret over nothing. Unlike the others, I possess no desire to abdicate my position," said Pandora, no indication of deception in her tone. "As such, I suggest we let this one go."

"No, no, don't let me go!" said Jerry. "Stick, um, stick around. Hear me out. And if either of you still want me dead when I've made my peace, then you go right ahead. Leonora, um, don't you have some questions for *me*?"

256

"Pandora has no questions for you," she clarified, only slightly sidestepping the question.

"Really? You don't want to know why I drive around in cars that should have been taken off the road fifteen years ago? Or why I masqueraded as a worker bee like you at the Control when really I was the Emperor behind everything?"

"You are a complex soul like any other," said Pandora. "You must have had your reasons."

"I did! And I do. It's because—"

"Jerry, do you truly desire to understand me?" interrupted Pandora.

"I, well, of course I do."

With agility uncharacteristic of a giant robot, Lesser God scooped Jerry up in its hands as the saucers in its legs activated at maximum power. Ram found himself blinded and paralyzed by a swarm of Gravity Compulsion Beams dozens of times more powerful than any he had ever experienced battling Pandora. The landscape and architecture again collapsed into a perfectly flat plain to accommodate the hyperactive work of physics on the city, and even Ram could feel his skull pressing down on his brain, threatening to detonate it in all directions like a dropped container of strawberry yogurt. His detainment became increasingly problematic when Lesser God suddenly went airborne, blasting off into the sky with its thrusters activated as Jerry remained caged within its hands. Ram would have yelled for it to stop, but he could not lift his tongue.

Jerry did plenty of screaming.

"Where are we going?" he asked, rolling around on palms and fingers and vomiting all over everything.

"Up," explained Pandora.

Medusa, not having expected a wet blanket like Pandora to suddenly become so much fun, decided to remain silent.

"Okay. If this helps you, that's fine," said Jerry. "Um, how high up are we going?"

"The moon."

"I'm sorry, but I don't think I can breathe on the moon."

"No, you cannot."

Jerry took a brief moment to make peace with what had been a short, disappointing life.

"Alright," he said at last. "At least I'll get a lovely view of the stars, before I freeze and implode. But, um, the prettiest thing I ever saw in life was you, Leonora."

"The prettiest thing anyone ever saw in their life was Leonora," said Pandora. "And they saw nothing else about her. She was a living mannequin. Do you know what it is like to walk through life utterly incapable of making a meaningful connection with another human being? To know that your interests, hopes, and dreams will always fall on deaf ears? To recognize that men and women alike treat you as something wholly alien from the human race? Leonora sacrificed nothing but her body in allowing me to be born, because she had nothing else to offer. She merely became a different kind of mannequin, better suited for the needs of a cruel world. I will not disappoint her memory now."

"Don't you think I already know that?" snapped Jerry, his eyes beginning to water. The city had already become difficult to discern in the distance. "I was the only person who ever knew the real you, Leonora, the you that is sweet and funny and compassionate. I hung on every word that ever came out of your mouth. You have an orange popsicle after dinner every night. Your favorite actor is Jaleel White. I think I heard you singing a Shakira song when I walked past the bathroom once. See? That's one meaningful connection!

"Oh, but what did I do? I lied to you the whole time that we knew each other. You trusted me enough to open up a little, and I never even told you my last name. I'm Jerry Trillionaire, the Emperor of the Control! Gyakusatsu could afford to make you into what you are thanks to me! But I've always just been so… *afraid* to be *me*. I don't know why, maybe I'm just crazy, but I'm as timid a guy as there ever was. I drive around in clunker cars because I get too anxious about the attention I might get from driving a nice car. And I pretended to be a paper pusher at the Control because I just liked the idea of being anyone other than myself. I feel like when I pretend to be somebody else, whether it's a worker bee or an Emperor, that it won't *hurt* as bad when I screw up. After all, you can't get angry at a person who doesn't really exist. A fake person can't take the blame for mistakes. But, of course, that also means a fake person can't forge any real relationships."

The curvature of the Earth had become wholly apparent, and the temperature continued to drop in direct proportion to the ascending altitude. Jerry was running out of time, both to save Leonora and himself.

"Thank you for your clarification," said Pandora. "Leonora will be able to rest without guilt knowing that not even you genuinely cared for her."

"No! That's not my point at all. My point is, I understand what you're going through! We're the same! You're the only person I ever felt a real connection with, the only person who actually noticed me and was kind to me *without* knowing I was rich and powerful. I'm just as alone in the world as you. The one time that I reached out to others to create the Control, all I did was make monsters out of my two best men! If there's one thing I don't want to leave all messed up when I die, it's my relationship with you. I want you to know you were the most special person to ever come into my life, and you were the one bright spot in a life marred by mistakes and cowardice."

Lesser God did not decelerate the pace of its trip at all, and the sky began to give way to darkness.

"Jerry, you are too sweet a soul for this world," sighed Pandora. "That is why I will make you like Leonora—dead."

Jerry had already become frostbitten across all of his exposed skin, but hearing those words sent a uniquely different chill through his body. Maybe there was a part of him that had believed Pandora was bluffing until this point. But now he understood the true meaning of the flight.

"I see. You wa-want me to choose death, ju-just like she did," said Jerry, teeth chattering. "Bu-but I won't! I won't because Leonora isn't really dead, a-and I'm not going to die! Leonora is coming home with me, be-because I need her and I love her! I love you, Leonora! I don't even care if you don't love me back. I love you and you can't die!"

From Ultratropolis, Lesser God had appeared until recently like a comet receding into space. Now, the light had disappeared completely. Ram Van Bamf, not entirely immobilized anymore but still slowed to a miniscule fraction of his natural speed, could only assume that Jerry had died. No human being save Ram himself could survive at such an altitude unprotected for any length of time, and if he could afford the energy to weep for him, he thought that he might do so. This meant he would have to find a way to save both Leonora and Fran by himself, which he knew seemed outside the scope of his abilities, both verbal and physical. It was only now that real despair descended upon Ram.

Then Lesser God came falling out of the sky, power to the thrusters having long since been cut.

"Jerry?" shouted Ram.

He realized that it had been the thrusters that supplied the light that allowed Lesser God to remain visible so high up into the sky, and in ceasing operation, Lesser God had become effectively invisible until it came close enough to the Earth again to be distinguished by the naked eye. Ram had a particularly naked eye, and he recognized the renewed presence of the metal titan long before anyone else. He could also discern Jerry, half-frozen but still alive in the hands of Lesser God.

"I cannot believe this. I *cannot* believe this," muttered Medusa, this time choosing to literally bang her head on her control console.

It was Pandora's last mercy to reactivate the thrusters as Lesser God approached Ultratropolis, decelerating its landing enough that it would not strike the city like an incoming asteroid. Medusa, not at all thrilled with that decision, unceremoniously rocketed Pandora back into space, this time without the benefit of a giant robot to accompany her. Jerry tripped and rolled out of Lesser God's hands immediately as Pandora was ejected, and it required all of the strength Ram could possibly muster in his legs to catch him before he struck the grinded pavement.

"Ram, please—"

"I can't, Jerry. I'm still too heavy to catch Leonora," said Ram. "I can barely move right now."

"But she's falling!" cried Jerry.

Ram narrowed his eyes, analyzing what remained of the city in the distance.

"Perfect," he said, finding something he liked. "Okay, Jerry, I'm going to throw you like a missile now. Make sure you catch Leonora, because we won't get a second chance."

Before Jerry could say another word, he was soaring through the air like a drunken eagle, his droopy shoulders proving as spectacularly aerodynamic as Ram had always imagined. Despite being numb throughout most of his body and feeling agony everywhere else, Jerry experienced a clarity that would have qualified as epiphany under any other circumstance, and as Pandora came falling toward him, his arms shot out of their own accord. He caught her.

Robbed of her previous trajectory, Pandora joined Jerry in his convenient crash course with a mattress warehouse, landing on the softest cushion the building could afford.

"Ram ought to play for the Yankees," said Jerry.

Then he helped rid the world of that awful white helmet, pulling the most stunning of all women back from the brink and into the light of day. Leonora felt as if she had been roused from a long, dreamless sleep, and all she could do was stare at Jerry for a long while as they both lay on the mattress.

"Thank you," she said at last, hugging Jerry with all the strength of a normal woman. Jerry would have hugged her back, except that exhaustion had finally caught up with him, and he was thoroughly unconscious. But when he awoke, he would be treated to the most pleasant sight of his life.

Ram Van Bamf and Green Medusa did not have so intimate a meeting, not with Lesser God for a chaperone. It was rare that Ram ever had to raise his neck to look an enemy in the face, and even rarer that his enemy was the person he most trusted. But these details were lost upon the man watching and waiting from not so far away, biding his time for the right moment.

"It's just us now, Fran," said Ram. "How about we finish that dance?"

Lesser God scraped the ground with its foot.

"No!" Medusa yelled. "That is *not* how this is going to be. You are not going to weasel your way out of this with sentimental drivel. Nothing you can say will save your life. I exist to kill you, and that is exactly what is going to occur!"

Then Lesser God hurtled both fists down upon Ram at once, and still not in any condition to evade even a pebble, Ram felt the blow in its entirety, blood immediately starting to gush from his nose and mouth.

"How do you like it?" she mocked.

Lesser God punched him where he lay in the ground, over and over again, alternating hands.

"How does it feel to be completely defenseless? Nowhere to run, nowhere to hide. Just a game of death and confrontation! What is it that you have to say to that?"

Lesser God stomped Ram once for good measure.

"I just want you to be okay, Fran," he said, his body wholly engraved into the broken Earth around him, the blood starting to get into his eyes.

"Idiot!"

Ram received another stomping.

"Is that the best your feeble mind can offer? Carl cranks his bromance up to eleven with Murdock. Little Jimmy realizes that his doll has thoughts and feelings. Ruttiger somehow manages to verbally abuse Fuzzy into a stronger friendship than ever. Jerry, the most pathetic man I have ever seen, professes his freaking love for Leonora! And what do I get? *You.* Just you."

Ram wiped the blood from his face with his hand, revealing the crooked smirk underneath.

"Heh. Yeah, I wouldn't want me either," he agreed.

"You smile? Even now, you smile?"

"Sure. When I'm with you, I smile. Even when you're clobbering me with big robot mitts."

"I'm killing you is what I'm doing!"

Lesser God punched him again, hard enough that an office building miles away fell over.

"Yeah, you are."

"Why don't you care?" cried Medusa.

"Well, I figure, if I'm dead, maybe you'll be able to become happy again."

Medusa felt then the way that a person feels after reading a poem that makes no sense.

"Happy *again?*"

"Sure. Since I came into your life, all I've done is wreck your business and break your heart. When I'm gone, there won't be anything to tie you down anymore. You'll be able to move on."

Lesser God assumed a resigned posture, contradicting its very nature in the process.

"Move on to what?" asked Medusa.

Ram did not even have the stamina to lift himself from his hole in the ground at the moment, so he had to hope his words carried the same resonance whether standing or lying down.

"I dunno. But, well, you're *Fran.* You're the toughest person I ever met in my life. The only reason I was even able to keep going after I thought you were dead was because I knew you would never quit in my situation. You can bounce back from anything. If everybody could be strong like you, the world would never get itself into a mess like this in the first place."

"But sometimes I don't want to be strong!" howled Medusa, and her voice carried to the ends of the city. "Sometimes I just wish someone would lift the weight off my shoulders. Sometimes I just want to feel like somebody cares! I want to be needed like Fuzzy, or adored like Sally, or admired like Leonora, or valued like Murdock. I *hate* you for thinking I don't have a breaking point! I hate everyone for thinking that. Strong is a *long* shot from invincible. I'm only human, Ram! All I want is the same thing everyone else wants—I want someone to make me feel special. Why can't anyone do that? Why can't a single person be bothered to do that? Am I so awful?"

At some point, the line where Medusa ended and Fran began had blurred, but this was of no consequence to Ram, as he did not discriminate between the two in the first place. And although any wrong movement now could provide the stress sufficient to kill him, Ram Van Bamf pressed himself back onto his feet one final time. The effects of gravity compulsion had worn off, but his body had never felt heavier than it did then. The blood streamed down his jaw from his ears, and his skin had long since turned black from soot and debris. For the only time in his life, Ram was indistinguishable from the rest of the people of Ultratropolis. He was just an ordinary man, as fragile as any other.

"Fran, I am not a complicated guy. The warden pays me in sacks of money because checking accounts intimidate me. I think someone as brainy and beautiful and motivated as you could do a lot better than me. But if you're saying is that all you need is a shoulder to cry on, well—I've got two of them. And I'm having a lot of trouble standing up right now, so I could really use someone to lean on too."

Lesser God had not moved in quite some time, and it was difficult to interpret the emotions of a person Ram could not see.

"We are both broken," she sighed after a duration.

"Sure. But I think there's a fix. Seems to me that the thing that stopped us from falling to pieces for as long as we did through all of this was each other. You and me are a perfect team. We uncovered a doomsday conspiracy together! I never could have done that on my own. But you gave me a direction and inspired me. You took a piece of coal and turned it into a diamond, at least for a little while. And that you could do that for a guy like me makes you plenty me all the time in the world to board this gorgeous abomination of a vessel. And now I intend to do as dragons are wont to do, and set this world ablaze!"

Contrary to that assertion, Lesser God only began to spasm as the orders of Gyakusatsu and Dragon conflicted.

"Dragon will kill every living thing on this planet if you allow him. His is a soul poisoned with insatiable hate, and the influence of Red Jester on his mind is no boon at all," projected Gyakusatsu. "I cannot wrestle him for control of Lesser God for all eternity."

"What can we do?" asked Ram.

"You can die!" said Dragon, but Lesser God continued to jerk and stutter, unable to make good on the threat.

"I guess I didn't make him any less angry when I unleashed all of the dinosaurs that Gyakusatsu allowed to continue to grow after his termination," said Fran.

"Ha! They are nothing compared to everything else he stole," said Dragon. "Did you know the mechanisms by which Lesser God creates fire employ the ignitable bacterium I developed for use on Mount Slipendie? And you humans who hosted the Abandoned could never have survived the constant stress placed on your meager minds and frames by those cyborg bodies under normal circumstances! You received genetic enhancements to your physical durability—made possible by the experiments I performed on those apes underneath the Tooth Decay Hooray! Do you see? Everything that allows Gyakusatsu's plans to exist is thanks to me! If the fool had merely come to me and requested to combine our knowledge in the first place, he and I would both be victorious right now! Instead, he is nothing more than a nagging phantom amidst my triumph."

"If I had come to you?" repeated Gyakusatsu. "You're deranged, Dragon. You would never have agreed to any plan of mine that allowed this world to survive. It always would have ended exactly the way it is ending now, with you satisfying a vendetta against an enemy that never existed!"

"Insufferable buffoon! I thought *you* of all people understood me!" said Dragon. "What value is there to be found in the lives of imbeciles and degenerates? You and I were kings among apes, the only minds worthy of dictating the course of this planet's future! I respected you! *God*, do you understand what an *honor* that is? If you had come to me with your little doomsday scenario, I would have *listened*. You are the monster in all of this, not me! Usurper!"

"Dragon, you deserved much worse than what I did to you. For the good of us all, you deserved to die!" said Gyakusatsu. "When I abducted you and only twisted your motor nerves, that was my manner of paying respect to a friendship we once held. I hoped your incorrigible eyes would permanently inhibit your ability to do further harm to the human race. It seems I underestimated you as well."

"Yes, you miscalculated at every step! Clearly, mine was the greater intellect all along. All your success here should be mine, and it *will* be mine now!"

"You can have it!" declared Gyakusatsu, and then there was an abrupt, short silence.

"He," and Ram really thought about what he was saying, "he can have it?"

"Take all the glory, if you wish," muttered Gyakusatsu. "I am done with this delusion."

"But why?" asked Fran, curiosity getting the better of her.

"In-between life and death, as my consciousness transitioned from neurons to circuits, I became privy to the thoughts and actions of each of the Abandoned all at once. In effect, I was like a ghost in the machine. I witnessed every moment of the catastrophe today as if I had been an active participant. I confess that the death toll does not bother me particularly, and perhaps I should commend Medusa for falling back on a contingency as time-tested as fear mongering to accomplish the aims of the Control. But the confrontations between the Abandoned and those who wronged them struck a chord with me in a manner I never could have anticipated."

"Let us see what else you have failed to anticipate!" snarled Dragon. "I have already managed to isolate the area of Lesser God in which your consciousness is maintained. In mere minutes, I will have severed your connection with this machine permanently, and then you shall live on without voice or essence inside of Lesser God forever!"

"Can he do that?" Ram asked.

"He just did," Fran shrugged.

"Listen to me, Ram," ordered Gyakusatsu. "I and I alone possess the ability to command Lesser God to self-destruct. If I do this, it will explode with force sufficient to obliterate the entire planet, defeating the purpose of such a measure in the first place."

"Then let's not do that," suggested Ram.

"We *must* do that. It is the only way to stop Dragon."

Lesser God levitated off the Earth for the last time. Then the machine ascended into the sky, breaching the heavens, pushing on toward the blackness of the void.

The human body, just like the human mind, was capable of unparalleled greatness in times of crisis, and this was the greatest body amidst the greatest crisis. As Ram stopped to admire the blue sphere underneath him, he could see in its full grandeur what would succeed him when he was gone. He was ready for what had to be done.

"You are out of time," warned Gyakusatsu. "This is it! Pacify two wicked souls!"

Ram clutched the metal behemoth by its forefinger as it relinquished its grasp on him. Tapping into a well of strength that stemmed from pure unbridled hope, Ram Van Bamf gave Lesser God one good spin before throwing it off into the far reaches of deep space. From the perspective of the Earth, a second sun was born then in the sky, bearing such heat that the clouds and the snow over Ultratropolis dissolved as if they had never existed, supplanting them only with blue skies and green grass. It was no less profound a spectacle from space, and as the cold closed in all around him, Ram went to sleep with a smile on his face.

EPILOGUE

"This next one's a ballad, and it goes out to a way special babe that I'd like to get to know!"

Chaz had slipped into a red tuxedo, which was as hideous as could be imagined, and the rest of Chainsaw Execution had donned similarly classy outfits. Their pianist was a very recent addition to the band, and having just been laid off from his previous gig as an organist, he felt lucky to have found new work so quickly. A crowd had gathered around the city wall to watch them perform, Louis Goodie at the forefront, bobbing his head from side to side in an inoffensive groove.

Dot may have stood at the back of the crowd, but her face burnt three shades of red deeper than the gaudiest tuxedo. Nobody had ever dedicated a song to her before, let alone bought a new wardrobe over her, and even if Chaz reminded her of something caught in the tread of a monster truck tire, it was likely that he was not the worst person in the world with whom to spend an afternoon. She took a deep breath and marched toward the wall.

"Okay!" she acquiesced at last, just loud enough to be heard over the instruments.

Even now, Chaz could detect the mild repugnance for him in her gorgeously critical eyes, and it made his triumph all the sweeter. He gave an elated thumbs-up to Louis, his friend and mentor in his ordeal. Louis had selected the song, found the pianist, and taught Chaz all about how to speak properly in society. Chaz had forgotten all of the stuff about speaking immediately, but it seemed that two out of three would suffice. Louis felt a measure of relief in knowing that the skills his grandmother had forced upon him had finally been put to good use.

"Man, Chainsaw Execution's really changed their sound since I got abducted," said Murdock, able to hear them from the gas station.

"Must be their experimental phase," shrugged Fury.

"Screw that. It's time to put Lethal Enforcer back together for real and show them what's what," responded Murdock.

"I'm game," said Carl. "But maybe we should help put the police department back together first."

Wilson put a hand on Carl and Murdock's shoulders respectively, nodding all the while.

"It's settled!" said Fury. "Today, we fix the city. Tomorrow, we tune up our instruments!"

"Aww, I dunno, Detective Fury. I think it'll take at least a week to clean up all this!" observed a nearby Little Jimmy, underestimating the workload ahead of them as children were prone to do. "What do you think, Sally?"

"Maybe a week and a half," she nodded.

"Not if we all pitch in!" suggested Sonny Norton, who by convenient coincidence was also present. "You'se was able 'ta infiltrate an evil organization's secret compound with my help! A little playtime cleanup ain't no big deal for us after somethin' like that."

"Hey, you're right!" said Little Jimmy. "Let's get to work."

The children would then busy themselves with the relief effort, but Little Jimmy would wonder afterward what ever became of his old friend, Elmo. As it turned out, Mayor Dingus had already received his bribe from Elmo regarding his incarceration, and so Elmo would be released from prison at the city's earliest convenience. He had offered to include a bribe for the release of Mecha Manuel Salas as well, but Mecha Manuel refused. Having been given the title of King of the South by Chaz, Mecha Manuel was finally living the life of self-worship that he had always wanted, and he was not about to give it up for anything.

Thoughts of long prison sentences hung over the heads of Jerry and Leonora as well.

"Every penny of this city's reconstruction will be paid for by me. I don't care if it bankrupts me," said Jerry, still sitting on the same mattress. "Although, I don't think *anything* could bankrupt me."

"Jerry, you do not need to turn yourself in to the police, exactly," said Leonora. "You could just, well, disappear."

Jerry took her flawless hand with his stubby paw.

"No. I'm done hiding my face. I'm done running away."

Leonora placed her other hand on top of his hands.

"Me too."

"Let's find an officer," said Jerry, standing up.

As he started off out of the warehouse, Leonora placed a hand on his chest.

"I'll be waiting for you when this is all over," she whispered.

Elsewhere, Warmaker knocked aside the last dinosaur carcass with a heavy butt from his bazooka. Halstein observed the body himself, admiring the craftwork of its slaughter.

"Forty-seven," declared Warmaker, 'stache radiant with masculinity.

"Fifty-two," responded Halstein, his mouth and chin caked with the blood of the fallen.

They indulged in deep and boisterous laughter then.

"You win this round," said Warmaker. "But the dinos I killed were probably bigger."

"So you claim, earthbound mortal," said Halstein, and then they laughed again.

By some great stroke of luck, the hospital found itself one of the few preeminent buildings in Ultratropolis to remain standing, and Pietro had practiced his best off-road driving in getting Fuzzy and Ruttiger there, where they were treated by the best doctor available.

"Separating you from this armor will not be as simple as removing a business suit, but I promise, we will free you from it," said Dr. Keiji Kojima, giving Fuzzy a light tap on his cybernetic shoulder.

"Forget the moron! I'm the one who's down two limbs, which means I have two less methods of showing Fuzz exactly what I think of him," said Ruttiger in a bed, his injured arm and leg bandaged and elevated.

"Your wounds too will heal in full," chuckled Keiji, "given proper rehabilitation."

"Of course! With our son on the job, you be good as new in no time!" exclaimed Yoko Kojima, and her husband nodded.

"It really was not necessary for the two of you to come with me to work, you know," said Keiji.

"Sure, we know!" said Nobuo. "But we just very proud of our son!"

Fuzzy and Ruttiger gave each other a sideways look.

"You've got a heck of a kid," said Fuzzy at last.

"He can patch me up any day," assented Ruttiger.

Keiji felt thoroughly embarrassed by them all.

"Fellows," exclaimed Pietro, entering the hospital room, "I just met this delightful chap named Hans, and he allowed me to sample the most marvelous German rock candy! I think we might go into business together."

It seemed as if loneliness had been outmoded in Ultratropolis. At least for this day, everyone had found somebody with whom to waste away the hours. That was how it appeared to Fran as she sat at the peak of Mount Slipendie, her head in her hand, witnessing an entire population deal with catastrophe as a united whole. Doomsday had come and went. Now was the time to start over again. But all Fran wanted to do was cry.

As she wailed at an elevation where nobody would hear her, the faintest light began to twinkle in the otherwise clear sky. When the light grew more fearsome, it became apparent that something was on a collision course with the Earth. Fran did not notice it until its unnatural glow had drawn close enough that she could see it reflected in her green metal armor. It became most difficult of all to ignore when the object finally struck the mountain summit itself, leaving behind a crater that would cause the mountain to be mistaken for a volcano for the duration of its days.

Fran headed straight into the heart of the crash, the dust and debris of no consequence to her. There were few objects that could leave a hole like that, and it seemed unlikely that Lesser God had left behind any wreckage. She needed to see what had fallen from space.

"Heh. I dunno if that was one of my more graceful landings," said Ram Van Bamf, having been woken up by the impact itself.

Fran could not say anything just yet, being too petrified with happiness. But Ram patted himself off and got back on his feet as he always did. He walked until he had escaped the crater, so that he could look upon the city.

"How's it going down there?" he asked.

Fran followed after him, so that she could share the sight of demolished buildings, fractured streets, and most importantly, the people who were helping to put it all back together.

"It's going great," she said without sarcasm. She put a hand to her chin. "I still don't know why Gyakusatsu tried to play hero in the end, in his own twisted way."

"Oh, well, we got to talking about that during our trip into orbit, actually," said Ram. "Basically, in his time as a, uh, ghost, Gyakusatsu got to feel firsthand how much joy and peace the Abandoned felt each time they made up with their friends. He said that was exactly the kind of feeling he wanted everybody in his perfect world to have. Only problem was that Lesser God was exactly the kind of thing that got in the way of that in the first place. So, in the end, he decided to give my way of doing things a shot, though he didn't have much of a choice, with Dragon around."

"It might be for the best that we'll never know what he would have done had Drago not gotten himself involved," posited Fran.

Neither of them spoke again for a long time. At this point, it seemed like there was very little that had not already been said. But there was one last thing Ram needed to know.

"What happens now?"

"I'm leaving Ultratropolis," said Fran with little hesitation. "My confession of my feelings for you was premature, Ram. In some ways, I don't think I ever really matured emotionally beyond the girl I was in high school. I need time to sort that part of myself out.

"But that's not why I'm leaving. I'm leaving because I have a business empire to build. It's my dream, after all. But I'll be back someday. And when that time comes, I think we'll both have had plenty of time to decide how it is we really feel about things. I just hope you'll still be here to greet me by then."

Fran always had a plan. At least it seemed that way to Ram. The little quirks and consistencies in a personality were what made a person memorable, and Ram would savor every one of those about Fran while she was gone. He took her around the waist.

"You got it."

Ram Van Bamf and Fran spent the remainder of the afternoon holding each other in much needed silence, gazing out upon a foundation that, though ruined once, was already in the midst of reconstruction.

ABOUT THE AUTHOR

John Friscia was born and raised in Carlisle, Pennsylvania, which is just like New York City except without the culture or excitement. John is of Italian and Puerto Rican descent, lending him the exotic good looks illustrated in the above image. After graduating from Shippensburg University with a degree in English, John knew he either had to make a name for himself as a writer or start claiming to be a nuclear physicist on his résumé. Following a prodigious career at the Large Hadron Collider, John began writing the novel you have before you now.

John currently still resides in Carlisle, where he enjoys writing his own About the Author in the third-person. When he is not writing, he indulges in sedentary hobbies such as video games—especially Super Nintendo-era games and Japanese role-playing games—and comic books, which he would also like to write in the near future.

While he is at it, John would like to apologize to every postal worker or relative of a postal worker who happens to read this novel. He apologizes to none of the ones who do not read this novel.

Finally, special thanks are due to Van Koons for assisting in making this novel as readable as possible. If you see him on the street, offer him a ride, because it would be rude to pretend you didn't notice him.